THE
NEW
AGE

Also by Chris d'Lacey

The Erth Dragons

The Wearle

Dark Wyng

The UNICORNE Files

A Dark Inheritance

Alexander's Army

A Crown of Dragons

The Last Dragon Chronicles

The Fire Within

Icefire

Fire Star

The Fire Eternal

Dark Fire

Fire World

The Fire Ascending

Rain & Fire (with Jay d'Lacey)

LACEY

THE ERTH DRAGONS

THE NEW AGE

BOOK THREE

SCHOLASTIC PRESS
New York

First published in 2018 in the United Kingdom by Orchard Books.
Orchard Books is a division of Hachette Children's Books,
a Hachette Livre UK company.

Library of Congress Cataloging-in-Publication Data

Names: D'Lacey, Chris, author. | D'Lacey, Chris. Erth dragons; bk. 3.
Title: The new age / Chris d'Lacey.
Description: First American edition. | New York: Scholastic Press, 2019. | Series: The Erth dragons; Book 3 | "First published in 2018 in the United Kingdom by Orchard Books, a division of Hachette Children's Books." | Summary: The coming of the dragons has upset the balance on Erth, and now other creatures, the wild Gibbus, and the Wyvern, are being drawn into the conflict between dragons and humans; while the dragons Gabrial and Grendel guard the young dragonets in their care, and the human boy, Ren, struggles to control his new powers, the world seems to be coming apart around them—and the firebirds are manipulating the threads of destiny.
Identifiers: LCCN 2018033251 | ISBN 9781338291926
Subjects: LCSH: Dragons—Juvenile fiction. | Magic—Juvenile fiction. | Human-animal relationships—Juvenile fiction. | Interpersonal conflict—Juvenile fiction. | Adventure stories. | CYAC: Fantasy. | Dragons—Fiction. | Magic—Fiction. | Adventure and adventurers—Fiction. | LCGFT: Action and adventure fiction. | Fantasy fiction.
Classification: LCC PZ7.D6475 Ne 2019 | DDC 813.6 [Fic] —dc23
LC record available at https://lccn.loc.gov/2018033251

10 9 8 7 6 5 4 3 2 1 19 20 21 22 23

Printed in the U.S.A. 23

First American edition, February 2019
Book design by Shivana Sookdeo

For Niki Rogers and Jen Morgan

May you always believe

List of Characters

Dragons

Gabrial • a young, impulsive blue dragon. Despite his good intent to serve the Wearle well, Gabrial is often drawn into dangerous conflicts and arguments with his superiors. Guardian to the wearlings Gariffred and Gayl.

Galarhade • Prime of the second Wearle to visit Erth. Died at the age of 239.

Gallen • ex-commander of the feared wyng of fighting dragons known as the Veng. Met an untimely end during the goyle wars.

Gannet • a good-natured green roamer.

(Per) Gantiss • mentor to many young dragons, including the intelligent blue Goodle.

Gariffred • a male wearling born to Grystina. His name is controversial because it means "flame of truth," implying he is closer to Godith than other dragons.

Garodor • a highly intelligent member of the De:allus class, sent to Erth to research and assess the situation after the devastating battles with the goyles.

Garon • Gabrial's father, who went missing, presumed dead, during the first goyle war.

GARRET • a talented dragon whose principal role is to construct maps of any territories the Wearle wishes to colonize.

GARRISON • a seasoned roamer, promoted to second-in-command of the Wearle after the shocking death of Gallen.

GAYL • Grystina's female wearling and Gariffred's sibling.

GIVNAY • spiritual leader turned traitor. His lust for power and his brooding resentment of Grystina's nobility ultimately contributed to his gruesome end.

GOODLE • a studious blue dragon with ambitions to be a healer.

GORENFUSSENTAL THE TWENTY-THIRD • the fusty curator of the mysterious Kashic Archive, a role his family has undertaken for as long as records have been kept.

GORME • a young roamer ridiculed for becoming lost in the boundless Kashic Archive.

GOSSANA • an aging and fearsome matrial, originally sent to Erth to oversee Grystina's laying cycle. Promoted to Elder status after the deaths of Givnay and Galarhade.

GREFFAN • leader of the first Wearle to visit Erth.

GRENDEL • a young, intelligent female with touches of

gold in her purple coloring. She bravely fosters Grystina's wearlings and is the emerging queen of the entire Erth colony.

GRENDISAR • a historical De:allus whose theories about the legend of Graven once caused much controversy among the superior ranks of dragons on Ki:mera.

GRINWALD • an aged dragon of the De:allus class.

(PER) GROGAN • aged mentor to Gabrial and a tragic victim of Givnay's deceits.

GRUDER • a good-natured green sweeper with a kind but nervous disposition.

GRYMRIC • herbalist, potion maker, and practitioner of the healing arts. His role is to gather Erth's flora and assess the benefits of what he finds.

GRYNT • a tough, no-nonsense Elder who assumes command of the Wearle following the death of Prime Galarhade. His shaky leadership decisions often cause him to clash with his advisors, particularly De:allus Garodor.

GRYSTINA • a highborn female who comes to Erth of her own volition, apparently to maintain the Wearle's breeding program. Her suspicions about Givnay's motives eventually led her into tragedy.

GUS • a gentle giant of a roamer. His one desire is to serve his Wearle faithfully and well.

THE HOM (THE KAAL TRIBE)

REN WHITEHAIR • a boy of twelve winters who is obsessed with dragons, a passion that ultimately takes him right into the heart of the Wearle—and beyond.

NED WHITEHAIR • Ren's father. A brave but slightly reckless man, who clashed, mortally, with his own tribe about their plans to win back the Kaal's mountain territories.

MELL WHITEHAIR • Ren's mother. A brave, free-spirited soul who is never afraid to do what's best for her family and her tribe.

PINE ONETOOTH • an orphan girl who "wafts around the settlement like a leaf on the breeze." Pine's life is changed forever when she is bitten on the hand by the wearmyss Gayl.

ROLAN WOODKNOT • a young man, not much older than Ren. He is catapulted into a dangerous quest to raise an enemy against the dragons, only to be captured by the Wearle.

WAYLEN TREADER • a farmer, one of many men lost in the conflict with the dragons.

THE TREEMEN (OR TREE PEOPLE)

LEIF • a free-spirited treegirl who volunteers for a quest to make an alliance with the Kaal, a journey that will lead her into terrible danger.

ODUM • a simple treeman who aids Leif on her journey to the Kaal.

THE WYVERN

L'WEN-GAR • a female Wyvern who becomes the voice of her community when visitors unexpectedly arrive from the Wearle on Erth.

THE GIBBUS

A warrior tribe from the Wild Lands, unnamed.

THE FIREBIRDS

AZKIAR • a grumpy male firebird who is never keen to leave his comfortable shelf on the upper floors of the Librarium.

AURIELLE • a female firebird who normally is the one to alert Azkiar to the fact that they have work to do . . .

ALSO

AGATHA WHITE • a distant relative of Mell Whitehair, charged with the responsibility of passing on the legacy of dragons to the rest of humankind.

DR. WHITAKER • a doctor who visits Agatha when she is elderly and in a retirement home.

EMILY • an employee at Agatha's retirement home.

GODITH • a female deity who, according to dragon legend, created the world from a single breath of flame and afterward made dragons in Her i:mage.

GRAVEN AND G'RESTYN • the two fabled sons of Godith, who allegedly fell out in a spat of jealousy, which ended with G'restyn dying in his brother's flames and

Graven's third heart being ripped from his chest by his grieving mother. Superstitious dragons have always believed that Graven will rise again one day and take his revenge on all dragonkind.

WIND • Ren's strangely magical horse, inherited from his father, Ned.

PROLOGUE

I: WHAT AURIELLE CHASED

Floor 47 of the Great Librarium
Time period: Undefined

Wind. It always worried Aurielle whenever there was *wind* around the Librarium. Sunshine, she loved. All firebirds did. It brought out the best of their brightly colored plumage. She didn't mind the rain when it came, either. Rain made the daisies grow and brought a welcome freshness to the air. It also left pools on the great stone sills in which she could dip her fluffy cream feathers to wash out the dust from the books. There were a *lot* of books in a building as tall and lean as this, and an awful lot of dust.

But wind. Wind moved things around. It played with the dust motes and made the aged bookshelves creak. It also made the daisies bend, making it harder to spot irregular patterns evolving in the timelines. A junior firebird's most important duty was to monitor glitches in the space-time continuum. Wind could be a serious nuisance.

Raising her long hooked beak, Aurielle glanced at the sky for a moment. The clouds were puffy and mostly still, sitting happy in the blue infinity. Yet there was a definite ripple in her ear tufts. And ripples in ear tufts could not be ignored. She drummed her claws and hopped a little closer to the edge of the sill so she could see the daisy fields better. Time was running smoothly all over the universe, except for a *tiny* wiggle in the sector belonging to the dragon world, Ki:mera. That made her heart pump a little bit faster. Dragons were the only creatures other than firebirds who were allowed to phase across the verges of space. Whenever dragons got involved in timeline disruptions, there was always . . . well, there was always trouble.

She sat back and pondered a little. Should she go and wake Azkiar from his nest of twigs on Floor 108? He wouldn't be happy to be woken, but then, he never was. Sometimes she wondered if the only true benefit of rising up the Librarium floors was that you simply got to sleep more often and were allowed to be grumpier when you woke. All the same, if an Event was forming, especially one that might involve dragons, a senior firebird ought to be told.

She stood up and spread her wings. At the very same moment, a *gust* struck. A strong current of wind that whined as it wrapped itself around the Librarium. She heard a thud and looked back into the room. Zooks! A row of books had tipped to one side. The tiny spiracles in Aurielle's neck nearly popped. As she turned for another look at the daisy fields, an object flapped past her. It was thin and papery and fluttery and *free*.

A single page had escaped from a book.

There was no time to gasp (though the Librarium kindly allowed her some); she had to catch that page and check its contents. Oh, it led her on a merry flight! Room after Room. Floor after Floor. This shelf. That shelf. So much dust! Up, up, up she went, paying no attention to how high she was flying. Until, of all the places the page might land, it skipped through a window on Floor 108 and draped itself over Azkiar's nest.

Aurielle skidded to a halt. Oops.

Azkiar rose up very slowly, stretching his bright red wings. He dragged the page off his beak. He did not look happy.

"What?" he said, catching sight of Aurielle. Azkiar was a bird of very few words. There was an infinite supply of words all around him. Why add excessively to the count?

"There was a gust!" she panted, flapping her wings in a circular motion. "I need to see which book that page came from!"

Azkiar sighed and cast his eye over it.

As was his way with words, the senior firebird had very few changes of expression. Aurielle thought she had seen them all. She was wrong. She had never seen him pale before. And that wasn't easy for a bird with deep red plumage.

"Graven," he muttered.

Aurielle gulped. Her tail feathers began to quiver. Graven? The fallen son of the dragon deity, Godith? Long, long ago he'd been banished (in part) to a planet called Erth for accidentally killing his brother, G'restyn.

"This can only mean his heart has been found," said Azkiar. "You'd better study this."

He crunched the page between his claws and threw it into the air. It rolled out its header for Aurielle to read:

Chronicle #264986343: The Day of Moons

Underneath the header was a myriad of i:mages.

Azkiar blew on the first and a scene played out.

Aurielle watched it through twice. After the second play, she said, "We're going to need a plan to deal with this, aren't we?" *A very BIG plan*, she thought.

She was wondering how Azkiar meant to go about it, when he settled back into his nest and said, "The page came from a book in your sector. For some reason, the Librarium wants *you* to repair this."

"Me?" she squawked.

"You," he repeated when his ear tufts had recovered. He collapsed the web of i:mages into a sheet and handed the page back. "Get on to it. Immediately. And, Aurielle?"

"Yes?"

"Try not to mess it up . . ."

II: What Aurielle Saw

Chronicle #264986343: The Day of Moons
Recorded on the dragon world, Ki:mera, shortly before the exploration of Erth by the Wearle of Prime Greffan

Matrial Grystina.

Grystina gave a start. It always alarmed her when a dragon came close and spoke to her in thought, not words. Had it been any dragon other than Elder Givnay she might have been tempted to snort a rack of flame. As it happened, Givnay was mute and could therefore be forgiven, though the fact that he had chosen to speak to her at all had come as a mild surprise. Of all the dragons gathered in this viewing place, waiting to see the eclipse of Seren, why did she have to be positioned next to him? Long ago, when Givnay was a wearling, Grystina's grandfather had caused the injury that had crushed Givnay's throat, draining his colors and leaving him without speech or fire. An accident, of course. But the tension between the families had been high ever after. Even now, more than half a century on, they barely acknowledged one another. But Givnay had spoken and she must respond.

"Elder," she said, nodding, not bowing.

In most circumstances, that would have been enough—had De:allus Grinwald, sitting on Grystina's other side, not drawn them into conversation.

"Such a splendid sight," he exclaimed, training his elderly yellow eyes on the pale star at the center of Ki:mera. "See how the shadow approaches, Matrial. It can only be moments now before Crune floats perfectly across Cantorus and Seren is eclipsed."

Grystina did her best to look interested. "I hope it's worth a wait of 247 orbits."

"246.9," he corrected her. "Would you like me to explain why Seren changes color, rather than darkens? It's really rather fascinating."

I find it odd, Givnay butted in, saving Grystina the need to make a choice, *that we mark the exile of Graven with such . . . ceremonial enthusiasm.*

"Oh, come, come. It's hardly that," said Grinwald, clearing a wedge of phlegm from his throat. "I'm surprised at you, Elder. G'ravity moves these moons, not fable. The De:allus do not hold with the myth of Graven."

I disagree, Givnay said. Curtly, Grystina thought. *I've been studying the work of De:allus Grendisar. His maps of the planet Erth are intriguing. He was of the opinion that—*

"Oh, yes. We all know about Grendisar," Grinwald cut in. "His deluded search for Graven is a subject of much amusement at the Academy Scientii. Such a waste of a brilliant mind. I told him once that if Godith had shattered Graven's heart there would have been blood. *Search for the blood!* I advised him. A jest, of course. Matrial, forgive me. I did not intend to tire you with gory talk about dark dragons."

"I'm not offended," she said, "though perhaps I should move to another viewing ledge and let you and the Elder continue your debate without me?"

Grinwald rumbled low down and bowed.

Grystina flexed her wings to leave. But before she could rise, another thought from Givnay passed across her mind. *Would it have crystallized or soaked away?*

"What? What, what?"

The blood, De:allus. Soaked or crystallized? Theoretically, of course.

Grinwald gave a blustery snort. "Well, that's impossible to say. It would depend on"—he twiddled his claws as he fashioned a list—"ground conditions, wind movement, precipitation, sedimentary drag. An entire forest could have grown over the spill by now. And the whole composition of the blood might have changed."

How?

"How? Are you serious?"

Grystina looked at Givnay and saw he *was* serious. Deadly so. It chilled her to see his green eyes narrow. Had she known then what tragedy her next few words would lead to, she might have slipped away as she'd first intended. Instead, she heard the gasp from the dragons around her and looked up at Seren. Crune and Cantorus were in alignment. The eclipse was happening. "Perhaps the blood . . . changes color," she said.

Givnay threw her a questioning look.

She pointed at Seren, her eyes lit with humor.

He turned his head slowly to view the star.

It was glowing a subtle shade of pink . . .

Part One
Leif

1

The Whispering Forest, home to the people known as the Treemen
During the second colonization of Erth by dragons

When the burning of the scaled creature was done, and the rain had finally quenched the flames and stopped the fire ravaging deep into the forest, the Treemen came to look upon the savagery and mourn the loss of life, of wood. Where a gathering of ancient pines had stood, fully green and reaching tall to the sky, there was now nothing more than a filthy stubble of perishing timber. Charred stumps poked out of a forest floor sullied and dead and still daring to flicker. The damp was foul, the calm distressing. Nothing moved except threads of smoke and the scent of dying heartwood. No wild thing scuttled through the smoldering ash. No birds flew across it.

At the center of it all lay the wasted body of the creature, its form sketched out by what still stood of its desiccated bones. No bright green scales protected it now or held back the fumes from its cauterized innards. Not a claw nor a stig nor an eye had survived. And though toughened scraps of the vast wing canopy clung resolutely to the framework of the carcass, it was hard to believe that a thing of such bulk had once soared easily over the forest. The beasts who had come to seal it in flame had done their work well.

Leif, daughter of Leif and Leif before her, had seen the whole drama unfold. On the day before the burning, she had been gathering brown-capped frooms, when a great flock of crows had descended on the trees. Crows were not forest birds, and the trees were soon irked by their grating cries and querulous shuffling. Leif put a hand on the nearest tree to calm it. She called high to the birds, asking why so many were present. The birds replied gruffly that they had been summoned.

Who summons you? Leif had wanted to know.

Being the belligerent sorts they were, the crows told her to mind her business.

They caarked in unison and warned her away.

And so Leif quickly cached her harvest, worried now that danger was approaching. The trees, having woken, were already sending restless ripples throughout their network of aged roots. The forest floor was bristling, the tree bark quivering. Creatures were diving for their holes.

Leif put her ear to the bracken and listened. Among the pattering drops of rain, she heard the tree roots crackling in fear. Something dark had invaded the forest, at the end where the hill flattened out toward the river.

What is this something? Leif asked the forest. Other members of the tribe would be kneeling with their ears to the ground by now. News would fly faster than a needle could fall, but Leif wanted it first from the trees themselves.

The forest breathed its reply. *The darkness has the shape of a child of the Kaal.*

Leif jumped straight up. The Kaal were not welcome in the forest. They took little from it and rarely left scars, but their home was the mountains—at least it had been until the scaled ones had driven them out to the flatlands, beyond a line the creatures had burned in the erth. The Treemen avoided the Kaal wherever possible. Their hunting men were swift to anger, and far too quick with arrows and scorn. They mocked the Treemen's fingers of wood, and laughed at the array of moss and flowers that grew across their erthy backs. But the Kaal had never caused trouble before, not the kind the forest was warning of now.

Leif pricked her ears and listened to the calls bouncing through the trees. A lone voice chipped by many growth rings told of smoke rising near the river, started by one of the flying giants. Leif felt her heartwood moan. Every creature of the forest lived in terror of the beasts she had heard the Kaal call skalers. Nothing bore destruction in its wake like them.

She started to run for the river's end. But barely had she crossed a single twig, when she heard the crows screaming, *Attack! Attack! Aark!*

Into the sky went the flock. Puzzled, Leif changed her mind about running and scrabbled up the nearest pine instead. Faster than a nutterling could open a cone, she was at the top. Despite the rain slanting in from the mountains, the air was wild with waves of heat. To Leif's amazement, a bright green skaler was battling an army of crows. She saw a bird ignite from wing tip to wing tip as it gyred too close to a spurt of flame. Many more expired in the same lick of fire. They were falling all around like fizzing hail, spreading sparks among the branches as they hissed through the treetops. Leif had to leap to another branch as a half-blazed bird came hurtling toward her. She beat out its fire and looked up again. The death toll of crows was steadily mounting, but Leif could see that the birds were winning. One by one, they were landing on the skaler, pecking every part of its wiry body, until there were so many on its back that the green of its scales was fully obscured. The creature wailed and clawed at the sky. Leif thought then it would crash into the forest, but she could never have predicted the way it would happen.

A second skaler bore down on the first. It was blue, this one. Wide of wing. It flashed through the rain clouds quicker than anything Leif had ever seen. She heard the click as its jaws sprang open. A ferocious burst of fire lit the sky, driving a wall of steam at its head. For the crow-covered skaler, there was no escape. Leif squealed in fright as the fire erupted on its broadest side and spread to the farthest points of the body, engulfing the helpless creature in flame.

Down came the crow-covered beast, streaming incinerated feathers in its wake. The smell was horrendous, tarred and thick, cloying enough to choke the life out of any delicate, air-breathing flora. Leif dived for the safety of the lower branches, knowing that the impact would feel like thunder cracking in her breast. *Ba-whump!* The forest reeled beneath the huge entanglement of weight. Leif was flung sideways, almost punctured by a severed branch. She caught her breath and held on tightly, fearful of the small fires springing up around her. She could hear the lament of the injured trees but guessed the shock wasn't done with yet. The smitten trunks, though sturdy and strong, were struggling to hold the body aloft. The beast was going to fall.

Sure enough, as the forest steadied and the skies above cleared, the creature began to slide. Some of its less-scaled underparts had been speared in the impact and would never see the ground again. But the heavy tail had already found a downward course and was slowly dragging the rest along with it. Branches snapped like brittle leaves as the body gathered momentum and dropped in a hump to the forest floor, dead.

For one day, that was how it remained: a stinking mound of alien fauna, a swelling that was going to take years to seed and overgrow.

That was the first time any Tree People spoke of vengeance.

Leif and her tribe had gathered around the corpse, where there was talk of what they might do to fight back. Some voices were saying they should form an alliance with the Kaal and join them in their struggle against the beasts. One voice said they had met a Kaal boy who ran with a skriking skaler at his breast and could send out shoots of fire from his hand. *Aye, his hand*, they insisted. They pointed to Odum's beard, which had been burned in the conflict, they said. But the old ones ridiculed this, and in the end, it was left to the wise ones to decide there was nothing to be done. The beasts were too powerful to fight. Let the next rings of wood record that the People of the Trees would mark this spot with healing flowers. All present would bend their heads and whisper to the Erth sprites. Pray that this beast would feed the ground, not poison it.

Spears were raised in agreement.

Aye. Let the forest be at peace.

And it was—for less time than the passing of a shadow.

As Leif started to make her way back into the forest, she saw the Kaal child who had caused the trees to quake. A pale-skinned girl with straggly hair. She looked plain enough to Leif, but there was blood all down her tattered robe. Black points marked the centers of her eyes.

Her teeth were very strange.

The trees begged Leif to stay clear of the waif, and Leif was glad she did, though she continued to watch the girl well. Not long after, a boy turned up. The girl drew him into a wide clearing. She called him "Whitehair"; he called her "goyle." They argued, but Leif did not see it all. For one of them summoned up a dreadful phantom, a vapor in the shape of a snarling skaler. Leif was greatly afraid of vapors. She fled in terror and waited for the trees to tell her the rest. To her relief, no trees were harmed this time, despite the fact that some skalers had landed in the clearing and one had used fire against the boy.

And the girl? she asked. *What of her?*

Taken, said the trees.

By the skalers?

By the boy. He left unharmed on the spirit of a whinney.

Unharmed? Leif sank into the bracken, drawing her knees tight up to her chin. *Is he a sprite?* she asked.

The forest did not know.

The next morning, the burning began.

Leif woke to see shadows crossing the tops. Skalers! They had returned in force. Leif thought at first they might be looking for the boy, but they had come instead to burn to ash the skaler the crows had attacked. In doing so, they set a fire so feral it ran like a pool of hot blood through the forest. Leif called on the rain sprites, begging their aid. Other Tree People did the same. The sprites answered as fast as they could, dragging dark clouds across the sky. In time, those clouds did quench the fire and later flaked the forest with snow. But many trees had been razed by then, whittled to black by a cruel and needless act of destruction.

The Treemen gathered again, though some never made it as far as the ruin. Their heartwood sobbed so much that their sap ran free and they fell to the forest floor in grief. Those who survived looked at the hole and swore they would not rest until the skalers were punished.

There must be a way! they cried.

But what use were a few crooked spears against creatures with claws that could tear down bark?

Poison, said some. *We have roots and wild frooms that would kill a strong man. Why not a beast?*

Aye, they said. *Poison.*

But how to deliver it? How to put venom in the mouths of the monsters?

Bait, said a voice. *Slaughter ten snorters and pack them with frooms.*

The tribe agreed. *Aye! Throw the bodies of the snorters over the scorch line and let the beasts feed on them, all they will!*

Now Leif was right at the front of this talk, and she spoke up loud and well. "Snorters have no grievance with skalers. I would liken their deaths to the wasting of the trees. Would the Erth sprites not be angered by this?"

That made for a solemn moment.

The treeman Odum said, "The Kaal do not see sprites. They could set the bait."

There were murmurs of agreement, but Leif shook her head. "If we ask the Kaal to do our work for us, I say we will yet have to answer to the sprites."

But the ugly seed was sown. Louder voices began to water it. *Who shall go?* they cried. *Who will carry this plan to the Kaal?*

A cold wind stirred the ashes of the trees. The silence tickled Leif's throat. "Me," she said quietly. "I will go."

They did not mock her, for this was brave talk. Crossing into Kaal territory was dangerous. Even to step outside the forest for too long was a risk. Leif's people revered the sun, for it warmed the soil and made the trees grow. But too much exposure to the Orb of Plenty could weaken a treeman and cause his skin to crack and dry out.

"I will pray to the sprites," Leif said, unafraid. "I will ask them to show me fair passage—and beg them to forgive me if I do any wrong against the Erth."

But Leif, you are nought but a child, said a voice.

"Aye, and fast across the ground," said she. "Light enough to be lifted by the wind." She raised her voice again. "I am no threat to the Kaal. I will carry no spear, only frooms and words—if that is what the old ones wish."

The old ones rubbed their beards.

They nodded.

You must take them something—to prove our bond, said one.

"What?" said Leif. "What shall I take?" What gift would a murderous Kaal desire?

An old one gestured at the bones of the beast. Odum put down his spear and moved cautiously across the ash. He wrestled something off the corpse.

"Take this," he said.

He held up part of the broken skull of the beast.

The skull of the Veng commander, Gallen.

2

The skull was lighter than Leif had imagined, but long in her hands and awkward to carry. Odum offered to carry it out of the forest, to spare Leif's strength for the long walk down the river, a path that would lead her to the Kaal settlement. Leif accepted Odum's help but had an idea of her own. If she made a strong raft, she could float to the settlement on the river's current. There would be no need to walk.

They praised her quickness of mind and set to it. The raft was made at the water's edge, from thick lily pads and whittled wood. Odum launched it on a spill of reeded water out of the pull of the main current. Leif jumped on with her strange cargo. The raft felt good. It sat evenly in the water and sprang no leaks. Odum threw her a carrying pack made from a mulch of leaves and twigs. She secured it to her back with loops of twine. In the pack was a mass of deadly frooms.

Lastly, he handed her a branch to steer by. "May the sprites protect you," he grunted.

He bade her a nervous farewell.

Leif said in return, "I will be back before the moon sees me gone."

"Find the boy!" Odum called as she pushed against the

mud flats and the raft spun slowly toward the river. He tugged at what was left of his beard.

"He was in my dreams this last night," she replied. "I will try, Odum."

She waved to him once, and was off.

The current was kind, the steering easy. No river rocks came to poke at the raft. Thick clouds shaded the midday sun. A weary but refreshing mizzle fell. Birds flew over in the shape of an arrow, honking as they made their way toward the sea. The wind was light, the going ponderous. But the sky was clear of skaler patrols, the one thing Leif had truly feared.

So in time, she came upon a run of trees that bent their branches into the flattest part of the river. This was the mark she'd been given by Odum. "Look for the willowing trees," he'd said. "Behind them lies the Kaal settlement." It was all the information he'd been able to glean from the twittering birds who lived off Kaal scraps and occasionally came to the forest for shelter.

Leif steered the raft to the shore. Through the gaps in the trees, over a shallow rise in the ground, she could see the mud-stone walls of Kaal dwelling places.

She stepped onto the bank and wedged the raft among

the willow branches. Then she tightened the twine on her pack of frooms and dragged the skull ashore.

For the first time, her heartwood began to creak. There was no way of telling how the Kaal would react to a forest girl carrying the bones of a skaler. Many Kaal had died in skaler fires. They were sure to be wary of any new arrival. And arrows flew faster than Leif could run.

She crept forward, moving from tree to tree with as much stealth as the skull would allow. At the last tree, she made an important decision. She laid the skull down and covered it with leaves. When the time came, if the Kaal proved agreeable, she could bring them to the tree and the gift would be given, the bond made. If they rose up against her instead, she would have a better chance to flee at pace.

She gave her sap a moment to settle, then stepped into the open. As she did, the wind changed and she detected smoke. She knew from her teachings that the Kaal made fires to heat meats upon; she thought it was nothing more than that.

She was wrong.

As she pressed against the rear of the first dwelling place and carefully peered into the central clearing, she noticed burn holes in the thatched roofs opposite. They had been recently lit.

Skalers. That was Leif's first thought. But if skalers had burned these dwellings, there would be nothing left for the rain to save. That meant the fires had been set by hand. But why? Why would the Kaal want to burn their own homes?

She lifted the flap on a window space and peeped inside. What she saw nearly made her crumble to dust. The bodies of at least eight men were lying in a row, already pestered by anything that buzzed. The chest of the nearest man had been opened. A mutt was lapping at the blood.

Leif gasped and dropped the flap.

Too late. The mutt had seen her.

Why it had to bark, she would never really know.

She turned immediately, intending to run.

Blocking her way was a figure that in some ways was more grotesque than the body in the hut. She guessed right away what it was. Until the skalers had invaded their world, there was only one monster the Treemen feared: a warrior tribe from the Wild Lands beyond the Barley Down Hills.

They called themselves the Gibbus.

In form, they were somewhere between the Kaal and the Treemen. They stood erect on two clawed feet, which were as good to them as hands when they swung through trees. Their muscular bodies hunched forward at the shoulders where the Kaal's ran straight. Most of their bodies were covered in hair. They wore no cloth of any kind. Their faces were ugly, their eyes set back. Small eyes. Brown. Deceptively quick. More fearsome than their claws were their prominent teeth, as big as flat stones when they rolled their lips back. The teeth on this one were hidden from Leif.

It was holding the skaler skull to its face.

She turned in terror and ran into the clearing, where she was quickly surrounded by a whole clutch of Gibbus.

"I mean no harm on your kind!" she cried. "My enemies are skalers! I seek help to fight them! I—"

A powerful hand clamped her mouth. One Gibbus tore the pack off her back, ripped it open, and spilled the contents. Two Gibbus went for the frooms, squealing over who should have them. But as fast as the first show of teeth, an awed hush fell upon the camp. The Gibbus with the skull had walked into the clearing. It barked what sounded like a fatal warning. The two Gibbus backed away, leaving the frooms scattered on the ground, but not before one of them had filled its face with the frooms he'd managed to grasp. Leif shuddered as she watched the creature swallow. In less than two days, its gut would shrivel. Without sweet clover, the beast would die.

On the orders of the skulled one, she was dragged away and thrown into one of the shelters. There were Kaal in there, kneeling, their feet and hands bound. All were women and children.

The Gibbus bound Leif too and growled at her. *Silence!*

"I have done no wrong on you!" she wailed.

For that, it struck her with its heavy-boned hand.

"Child, be still," a voice beside her whispered. "They will hurt you sorely if you cry out again."

Leif looked up, hot sap trickling down her cheeks.

The speaker was a woman. She had kind green eyes and waves of red hair. "What is your name?" the woman asked quietly.

"Leif," Leif replied, twig dust dropping from the soft-woven bracken that formed her dark hair.

"What brings you among us, Leif? What foul wind blew so slight a creature this far from her forest home?"

"Skalers," Leif said. Her sap dripped on to the erth.

The woman gritted her teeth and nodded. "Skalers have brought this world to its knees. And now they draw these Gibbus upon us."

Leif shivered. "What do they want?"

"I know not," said the woman. "They have killed our few men, but spared the rest. They came a day ago as we were readying to leave in search of new lands. Their talk is as good as mush to my ears, but I see their eyes turning long to the mountains. They have some ugly purpose there."

"You think they have come to war with the skalers?"

The woman gave a shake of her curls. "Whatever they are planning, it will be of no value to your tribe or mine." She moved nearer to Leif to warm her a little. "Leif. That is a kindly name. It sits well on you."

Leif gave a small nod of thanks. "And you? What do I name you?"

"Mell," said the woman. "My name is Mell Whitehair."

Leif jerked her head up. "Whitehair? You have a boy of that name?"

"I did once," said Mell. "Ren is disappeared, taken by skalers."

"Nay," said Leif. "I spied him in the forest, with a girl of odd teeth."

"Pine?" Mell's eyes came alive. "He was with *Pine*? What else do you know?"

"Only what the forest whispers: He lives and rides free on the spirit of a whinney."

Mell closed her eyes. She let loose a sigh and put her head back. "Bless you, child. You have answered my prayers. Now, now it will come."

"What will come?" said Leif.

Mell opened her eyes. She looked through the hole in the roof of the shelter and smiled as if the stars were shining upon her. "Hope," she said quietly. "Hope."

3

Darkness fell. And with it, some snow. With that came a stabbing cold, though it wasn't the chill outside the shelter causing Leif's delicate teeth to chatter.

The Gibbus who had taken the frooms was dying. Leif could hear its death throes splitting the night. Its whimpering growls were hard on her ears, but the fate she knew must fall on her was worse.

"Leif, why do you weep?"

Mell shuffled up, settling herself with her back against the wall. The Gibbus had moved their prisoners to a different dwelling a short way beyond the main settlement. It had once been the keep of the farmer Waylen Treader. Its roof was sagging but mostly intact. Every now and then, when the clouds would allow, weak strikes of moonlight broke through a window space, throwing some rays across the straw-covered floor. The shadow of a Gibbus guard regularly appeared in them.

"They will hurt me," Leif whispered. "When it dies, they will come." She explained about the frooms—and their deadly purpose. That plan—to poison skalers—was blown away now.

Mell chewed her lip in thought. "Can you speak the Gibbus tongue?"

Leif wriggled her shoulders. "Some words are easier than

others. But I do not think they will listen to my plea—if that is what you were thinking."

Mell shook her head. "I must ask you something. Did you arrive here alone?"

"Aye."

"By what means?"

"I came along the river. By raft."

Mell nodded. "Did you lodge it on the riverbank?"

"Aye. In the shallows, where the trees droop."

Mell nodded again. A determined smile passed across her lips. "How many small ones do you think it will carry?"

Leif looked at the children, huddled up in the shadows. "You have a plan for them?"

"*Shhhh*. Yes. How many?"

Leif counted the heads. "Some, not all."

"Good. Harken well to me now. On my word, I want you to call the guard. Use whatever talk you think it will know. Say you are unwell, in need of healing. You must draw it through the door space, into the shelter."

Leif looked at the bulky shadow. "Why?"

"Our captors are not as wily as they think. This place was once the home of a farmer. He kept tools here. On my word. Be ready."

With that, Mell nodded at a woman in the corner. That woman in turn passed a message to another. Quietly, the second woman moved aside some of the straw with her feet. Leif, whose eyes were used to seeing in shade, could make out a large iron ring in the floor. Her sap quickly rose. A trapdoor!

On a nod from Mell, who was all the while watching for movement from the guard, one of the women, a broad-shouldered lass of about Mell's age, knelt by the door and extended her hands to slip her fingers into the ring.

She clenched her teeth and tugged.

Up came the door. But not high enough. Mell nodded at two other women. Both shuffled around and pushed their legs into the gap, supporting the weight of the door between them.

Now the first woman let go of the ring and put her hands under the door itself. With a mighty effort, she straightened her back. The door surrendered with the slightest of creaks. Another woman managed to stop it with her shoulder before it could knock back against the wall. Gently, she set it there to rest.

Mell shuffled forward. By the time she had reached the hatch, one of the women had dipped into Waylen's cache of tools and lifted out a knife between her feet. She quickly moved the knife into the hands of another, who turned to creep over behind Mell's back. Moments later, Mell's hands were free. *Praise you*, she said to Waylen's spirit. The farmer had always kept his tools sharp.

Mell cut through the ties at her ankles and swiftly cut the twine on the women who'd opened the trap. While they raided the store for any kind of weapon, Mell began releasing others from their binds, including Leif. As she freed the children, she touched her fingers to their trembling lips and bade them shut their eyes and bow their heads.

Mell stood up. She looked at a woman who was handing out tools. The woman threw an object across the gap between them. Mell caught it and twisted her fist around the grip. Leif gulped. It was a hooked blade, a sickle, used for reaping crops.

With all the stealth of a creature of the night, Mell slipped into the shadows close to the door. She closed both hands firmly around the handle of the blade. *Now*, she mouthed at Leif.

Leif's sap was bitter with fear. But the pity she felt in her heartwood for the children spurred her on. This might be their only chance to live.

Putting her hands behind her back to mimic being tied, she gave out an aching moan. The guard didn't move. On a nod from Mell, Leif moaned again. This time, the guard looked into the shelter. It barked a command, clearly wanting silence. "Help me," Leif groaned. The guard barked again. "I have a fever," said Leif.

She rolled onto her side.

The guard filled the doorway, blocking the light. It snapped out two harsh words. The words were rough and set deep in the throat, but Leif understood them as "Come. Show."

"Too weak," she wailed.

She brought froth to her mouth.

The guard snorted and bared its teeth. It looked over its shoulder, perhaps thinking it should call for assistance.

That would have been a wise move.

Instead, it stepped into the shelter alone and bent its head to stare at Leif.

The instant she saw Mell move, Leif turned her face aside. She heard the swish of a blade falling fast through the air. Something warm and moist sprayed across her face. She heard a sickening thump as the Gibbus collapsed. When Mell touched her on the shoulder a moment later, it was all Leif could do not to wail in terror. She was shaking like a sapling in the wind.

"Be swift," Mell whispered closely. She ran her hand down the treegirl's face. "Do not look at the beast, for I tell you plain it cannot look at you. What's done is done. Blood for blood. We must go. To the river. Take my hand, girl. *Come!*"

And they fled, ushering the children first, carrying any who could not run. A light wash of snow had stuck to the ground, making their passage soft and quiet. Leif was worried about the trail they had left and told Mell this when they reached the river.

"There is nought we can do," Mell said. "If they come, they come. It was a risk worth taking."

Leif looked down the bank. The raft was already filled with children. Two women were in the water, guiding the raft out into the river. "What are you planning?" said Leif, a little panic in her voice. "The raft will only hold so many and the mothers will freeze in the water. If the Gibbus come, they will slaughter the innocents left on the shore and—"

"Shhhh," Mell said kindly, "be calm. We will ferry the young to the far side of the river. The Gibbus do not like water. And have no fears for the Kaal. We are mountain people. We wear the cold well."

Despite these words, Leif could see it was going to take at least three crossings to move every child to safety. And so she spoke to the nearest willow and broke off a branch, one with many twigs and leaves. She said to Mell, "I am going back—to sweep the trail."

"No!" Mell took her arm.

"I must," said Leif. "If I sweep the tracks, they may look another way before the river."

"The danger is too great," said Mell.

Leif eased Mell's hand away. "I can run faster than any of them. And though I traveled here by water, I cannot swim."

"We have the raft."

Leif shook her head. "I will not put myself ahead of your young. But nor will I wait when I know I can help them. When I'm done, I will make my escape to the forest. I must warn my people, Mell."

Mell saw the need in this. She put down the sickle and drew Leif to her, holding the girl in close. "I give you my pledge I will see you again. May the spirits of your people bless and protect you."

"And yours," said Leif, her heartwood swelling.

And she turned for the shelters and hurried away.

It was as the raft was taking its final load that Mell heard a sound that chilled her bones. It was high-pitched, a little way off, unmistakably a cry of pain. She was in the water up to her middle, helping to push the raft off the shore. She turned her head to look back. "What was that?"

"Redfurs, scavenging," the nearest woman said. She leaned against the raft. "Hurry, Mell. We are almost away."

"That was no redfur," Mell said quietly. "That was Leif. I must go to her." She lifted her robe and turned back for the shore.

"Mell, stop! If they have caught her, her sap will already be spilled!"

"Then mark me as foolish in your memories," said Mell. She jumped ashore and picked up the sickle and a knife. "The girl has given our tribe a chance. Now I must show the same favor to her."

The woman shivered but gave a slight nod. She made the sign of the Fathers and said no more. By the time she'd slipped fully into the water, Mell was racing back toward the shelters.

They had dragged Leif into the central clearing. The girl was on her knees, held by her hair. As Mell approached, the Gibbus holding Leif pulled back her head to expose her throat. Mell saw the beast's evil claws slip out and knew the girl was moments from death. By then, Mell was closing so fast she had no time to think of the peril. With a savage cry, she burst through the crowd and slammed the heavy sickle into the back of the Gibbus holding Leif. The blade stuck there like a crippled moon. Fluids gurgled in the throat of the beast. It coughed and spat its own blood as it fell.

Mell stood over Leif, switching the knife between both hands and shouting her battle cries at the creatures: "WHICH OF YOU WILL GO TO THE NEXT WORLD WITH ME?!"

For that was the fate she was now resigned to: one more Gibbus on her blade before she died. But one crept forward from behind and wrested the blade from her. Then she was on her knees beside Leif, both their throats exposed.

A heavy-looking Gibbus with flecks of gray hair in its face came forward. The rest of the creatures were beating the ground, screaming for blood and sap and vengeance. Mell gritted her teeth. The sound was deafening. She glanced at Leif. The girl had almost passed out.

The gray Gibbus raised an arm. The noise fell to a dribble of irritated chatter. The gray one spoke at some length. The Gibbus holding Mell shook her hard, clearly not liking what the gray one had ordered. Another one picked up a half-squashed froom and made gestures suggesting they should fill the prisoners' mouths with the poison. But the voice of the gray was law, it seemed. The next Mell knew, she and Leif were being dragged into a shelter again, where they were bound and put under guard once more.

"What did it say?" asked Mell when she could get close enough to Leif to whisper. Outside, the Gibbus were dancing, taking it in turns to wear or hurl abuse at the skaler skull. "Leif, why did they spare us?"

"You should not have returned," Leif croaked.

Mell threw back her hair. "I heard your cry. I could not forsake you. Tell me. What did the gray one say?"

Leif shuddered and put her head on Mell's shoulder. "They are going to lay your men on the hillside."

"Why?"

"To draw a skaler down from the mountains."

Mell took a slow breath. "And then?"

"They plan to take a young one."

"How?"

"I know not."

Mell shook her head, trying to make sense of this. "How does a skaler pupp aid their cause?"

"They do not say," said Leif. "But to keep it, they will have to feed it. Those were the last words of the gray. That is to be our punishment, Mell. We are spared—to be fed, in pieces, to a baby skaler."

Part Two
Renegades

4

Prime Grynt's eyrie on the mountain known as Skyt
Two days after the burning of Gallen

"Find him," Grynt hissed, almost grinding the words into dust, so harsh was the snarl going through his throat. "Find the boy and bring him to me in as many pieces as you care to tear him."

"Prime, with respect—"

"Don't tell me it cannot be done!" The stone walls of the giant eyrie shuddered to the thunder of Grynt's response. The two dragons attending him stepped back a little, obediently bowing their heads. They were De:allus Garodor, the chief advisor to the Prime, and the brave young roamer Gabrial. Gabrial settled his striking blue wings and glanced nervously at Garodor, urging him to speak again.

Garodor was bold and to the point. "Two days ago, Ren stood in the forest in the arc of your flame and not a hair on his head was harmed. How this came about, we don't truly know. But if his boasts about Graven are true, it's little wonder we can't find him. He is now much more than a mere Hom boy. He has the auma of *Godith's son* burning in his chest."

looked out at the silent,
by Grynt's surprising lack
f all dragonkind, had bru-
en, for accidentally taking
'restyn. She had removed
l it here, on this strange
–the boy the dragons were
heart but apparently laid claim to its power as well. This had given credence to the age-old myth that Graven would one day rise again as an evil black dragon, though no one had expected a *Hom* to be involved. That somehow made the prospect much more terrifying.

"*I* would like to ask a question."

A fourth dragon emerged from the back of the cave, speaking in a voice that sent a chill creeping under Gabrial's scales. Her name was Gossana. Like Grynt, she was an Elder, and the highest-ranking female in the colony. Gabrial disliked her intensely. If ever there was a dragon with cruel eyes, it was she. They were like two gashes on her pointed snout, one a common shade of amber, the other continually swimming with red. Both were capable of changing color, a trait Gossana typically employed to instill fear in any dragon she considered beneath her.

Raising the sawfin scales that fanned out across the back of her head, she stared imperiously at Garodor and said, "If the boy is not to be dragged before us like a skewered rabbit, what *does* De:allus Garodor propose?"

Garodor released a plug of gray smoke. "In my opinion, we should release the two Hom we're holding prisoner and the Wearle should stand down from their battle positions."

"What?" said Gabrial. He hadn't been expecting a strategy like that. He looked nervously at Grynt, aware of the heat building in the Prime dragon's nostrils. Grynt had been a fearsome warrior in his youth. His silver breast scales were still fully armored and made an impressive shield to this day. He rarely engaged in battle now, but the idea of retreat would be alien to him. His answer, not surprisingly, was suitably ominous.

"I would rather cut off my tail and feed it to a crow than let that boy or any of his kind undermine my command. Too many good dragons have perished because we were slow to stamp out the Hom threat."

"A questionable threat at best," argued Garodor, a response that made Grynt visibly seethe. "We should not forget Ren sided with us against our enemies and has only ever shown what you would call treachery when he has been unkindly treated. To go to war with him now would be dangerous. The roamers might not have the stomach for it. This business in the forest has caused great anxiety throughout the Wearle. The young dragons circling the sky that day witnessed your failure to kill the boy and heard his warning to you not to oppress his people, the Kaal. All that has done is fuel the rumors that Ren now commands the power of Graven. The roamers are frightened, Grynt. They would be doubly disturbed if they could hear what I'm about to tell you next. There's a sinister undercurrent to this mission. The Wearle who came to Erth before us were ordered to seek out and mine fhosforent in these mountains. Note those words. They were not expected to map and explore. They were *ordered* to dig."

"Your point?" drawled Gossana, picking at a shred of meat between her fangs.

Garodor fixed his gaze on Grynt. "I believe fhosforent to be the blood of Graven."

"What?!" Gossana coughed out loudly, spraying Gabrial with spots of fiery saliva.

"Someone on Ki:mera knew about Graven and where to look for him," Garodor pressed on. "But I can't prove anything by staying here. I therefore request I be allowed to return to Ki:mera without delay, so I might access the Kashic Archive and research the findings I've made. I further suggest that because of the unresolved tension on Erth the more vulnerable members of the Wearle go with me."

"You mean Gayl and Gariffred?" Gabrial stared at Garodor as if the De:allus had suddenly betrayed him.

"The wearlings would be safer on Ki:mera," Garodor admitted.

"But that would mean Grendel, at least, going with them."

"Or a suitable guardian," Gossana said. Talk of the remains of Graven seemed to have made her distinctly uneasy. "Perhaps I could . . . ?"

"No," said Gabrial, ruffling the small scales around his ears. He was speaking to Garodor again, not Gossana. "Gariffred and Gayl were born here. By our laws, this world is theirs to inherit. They are the first true Erth dragons. Besides, if Gariffred is taken, it might anger Ren. It will certainly upset the drake. Their bond is—"

"ENOUGH," snapped Grynt. He trained his powerful gaze on Garodor. "The wearlings are going nowhere. And the Wearle will not stand down. Nor will any prisoners be released. My duty is to hold these mountains and prepare this world for colonization. That is what we are going to do, and no Hom will prevent it. I do not believe that Graven is among us or that the boy is indestructible. And before you remind me that I failed to burn him, perhaps you need to be reminded of his cunning. Yes, he has inherited some dragon auma and with it learned some of our skills. No doubt that includes the ability to i:mage. How can we be certain that it was nothing more than a projection of himself that stood in the forest before me? If so, the boy can burn like any other Hom."

Garodor's yellow eyes dimmed in thought. "I see your logic, but I believe you are wrong. The boy had a point to prove and he did so—impressively."

"He also glamored Grendel," Gabrial said. "It takes real power to do that. What I don't understand is why he delivered the girl, Pine Onetooth, to my cave."

"To spy on us, of course," Gossana said sourly.

"I doubt it," Garodor countered. "I think Pine is there to test our trust: If the girl is mistreated, Ren will surely retaliate."

"She has forged a strong bond with Gayl," said Gabrial. "Ren made the myss bite her hand so that Pine, like Ren, would receive some of our auma."

"Hom: They disgust me," Gossana rumbled. "Surely this just makes the girl a bigger threat? I say we roast them all."

"Again, I urge caution," Garodor growled. "We must be vigilant, certainly, but—"

"Enough of this bickering!" Grynt interrupted, filling the air with his heat. Turning to Garodor, he said, "Go back to Ki:mera and do as you will. I find your theories disruptive and your arguments weak. Your deference to the Hom makes my back teeth grate. Gabrial, your orders are as they were at the beginning of this tiresome conversation. Get the boy out of hiding and bring him to me."

"And how do you propose he does that?" sighed Garodor.

Grynt exhaled a raft of smoke. "As you've already told us, the boy was fool enough to leave not one, but two of his companions behind. We'll start with the girl."

"What do you mean?" asked Gabrial.

"Take her somewhere high and call the boy out. He'll hear you and come to save her from the drop. I'll send the Veng to cover you. They will do the rest."

"And if he doesn't show himself?" Garodor asked.

"Then the birds can pick her off the valley floor," said Grynt, as cold and blunt as the stone he was standing on. "And if that doesn't work, we'll take the man up next. Either way, we win." He flicked his tail toward the cave mouth. "Go."

5

"No."

Before Gabrial could get the whole story out, Grendel was refusing to accept Grynt's orders.

"There's been too much killing," she said, the golden braids glowing on her purple face. "The girl is no threat. You told me yourself: Ren drew all the darkness out of her. She is empty of evil. Look."

Gabrial turned his anxious gaze toward Pine. The girl was sitting calm and cross-legged on a spur of rock at one side of the cave. She was singing quietly. Beside her lay the last of a heap of blue flowers, plucked from the patchy grassland outside and brought to her by Gayl, the female wearling. Pine was weaving them into a chain. Gabrial shook his head in awe. Dragons could think what they liked about the Hom, but there was no denying the Kaal's dexterity. And this off the back of the injury to her hand. Pine had made a remarkable recovery from Gayl's bite. Just like Ren, who'd been similarly wounded by Gariffred, Pine's body had reacted by producing a sheen of scales along her arm. They glinted every time she threaded one flower stalk into the next. Dragon auma in another Hom child. No wonder Grynt was fearful of them.

Gabrial watched as Pine completed her chain, turning it into a ring of flowers that she slipped over Gayl's grateful head. The wearmyss graarked in delight.

"I don't know what to do," Gabrial said in distress, curling the end of his great blue tail. "The Veng will be here as soon as they receive the order. If I defy Grynt, they could strike at me."

"Then they'll be fighting us both," growled Grendel.

"And what then?" Gabrial huffed. "One of us, possibly both of us, killed or maimed in front of the wearlings? How's that going to help? And if Gariffred joins in . . . Where *is* Gariffred?"

"Out. Flying."

"Alone?"

Grendel creaked a shoulder. "You can't ground a wearling for long. You know what it's like when you first find your wings. Don't worry, Gus is with him."

"Gus? What's he doing here? I thought he was supposed to be at Grymric's cave, guarding the male Hom?"

"He came to check on the girl's progress, looking for signs of hope, I think. The man you call Rolan is dying. Grymric's potions aren't enough to heal him."

Gabrial was not entirely surprised. He remembered how badly Rolan had been hurt during the bitter conflict with the goyles. Half the man's chest had been crushed. Not to mention the goyle venom that had taken off an ear and left its poisonous trail inside.

"I sent him out with Gariffred to stop him brooding," said Grendel. "Unless you want to be similarly afflicted, I suggest you ignore Grynt's orders and set Pine free."

"What?"

"I mean it. Let the girl go. Fly her to the forest where we know she can hide. What other choice do you have?"

Gabrial shook his head until his spiracles popped. "I can't *free* her. That's treason."

"Not if I overrule Grynt's command; I am to be the queen of this colony, after all."

Gabrial fanged his lip. He replied softly, not wishing to hurt her pride. "Grynt will never accept you as queen because you're not the wearlings' mother. If I disobey him, it could cause a war within the Wearle. There has to be a better way, Grendel. Ren is the key to this. I must find him. Where is Gariffred, exactly? Which way did he fly?"

"Seaward. He likes to chase the white birds that cluster on the cliffs. Don't draw Gariffred into this. You haven't time to contact Ren through him. Just take the girl and fly her clear. I'll tell the Veng you took her across the mountains. That will give you more time."

Gabrial thought for a moment. "All right, I've got an idea." He swept toward Pine. The girl put down her flowers and stopped singing. "We must leave," Gabrial said in slow dragontongue, careful not to choke her airways with his smoke.

Right away, Gayl began to flap her wings, aware that her "friend" was about to be removed. Pine, for her part, seemed less concerned. She widened her mouth, exposing the single upper "fang" that had earned her the derisory surname. She nodded faintly, twisting her damaged hand as though she knew it was the key that would unlock her destiny. Patting Gayl on the head, she raised her arms, inviting Gabrial to clamp her around the midriff. She was thin, a mere thread of life. It was all Gabrial could do not to break her bones. Outside, but still some distance away, he heard the squeal of the Veng approaching. Only two had survived the goyle wars, but they made enough sound for six. Gabrial yanked Pine up and was gone in a blur, leaving not one but two females roaring in his wake. For he had hit the sky and banked away south, against Grendel's advice.

He had gone seaward in search of Gariffred.

He found the drake soon enough. Gariffred was circling the barren cliffs, unmoved by the ringing chorus of seabirds who were squawking their murderous threats at him. He had no fire to frighten them with—that was still a few days ahead—but his size alone was enough to scatter them off their settles whenever he swooped in close. Now and again, he would skrike back, mocking them, though his "roar" was barely a tone below theirs. Every show of aggression, fake or intended, would be drowned in a new cacophony of screams, futile cries that occasionally ended in bloodshed. For the drake had to eat, as any dragon did. If a bird, in panic, crossed his path, his young but exceptionally agile claws were more than capable of stealing it out of the sky. He was spitting the feathers from a kill such as this when he heard Gabrial calling him down to land. He dutifully obeyed, gliding onto the windblown headland beside his blue guardian.

Gabrial released his grip on Pine, dropping her, unscathed, onto all fours.

At the same moment, Gus landed close by. "Gabrial? What's happening?"

"There's no time to explain. Circle above me. Call if you see any Veng approaching. I need to commingle with Gariffred."

Gus growled at the thought of Veng. He hated the Veng. Most dragons did. "And the girl?" He gestured her way.

"I'm trying to save her. I'll signal to you when I'm done with Gariffred. Get him away from here, clear of the water. Take him to the Hom man, Rolan, if you like. The drake's auma healed Ren once. Maybe it can help save Rolan."

A softened expression swept across Gus's blunted snout. An unspoken bond of gratitude passed between him and the blue. With a downbeat that had Pine covering her ears, he lifted off, almost blowing Gariffred over.

Gabrial righted the drake and pressed his thoughts into

the young one's mind. At his age, this was easier than trying to speak. *Gariffred, listen. I must find Ren. If I don't, the Veng might come and hurt Pine. Gariffred, look at me. Right into my eyes. Do you know where he is? Can you i:mage his location?*

Graark! went the drake, trying to break eye contact.

But Gabrial's glamoring hold was strong. *Gariffred, concentrate. Show me. I promise you, no harm will come to Ren.*

And slowly, as he had done once before, the drake began to form a picture. Using that peculiar power all dragons had of turning their thoughts into floating i:mages outside their heads, he drew what looked like a mountain peak.

It was undefined and fuzzy at its base, as if it were poking through a layer of cloud. A high mountain, then. Gabrial quickly looked over his shoulder at the mountain range he'd left behind, focusing his gaze on the tallest peak, the one the dragons called Skytouch. The shape of the mountaintop matched the drake's i:mage. Skytouch was also where Grynt had his eyrie. Was it possible that Ren was hiding there, waiting for a favorable moment to transfigure into Graven and strike at the Prime?

Hrrraarrgh! came a deep-throated cry from above.

Gus, with a warning.

The Veng were coming.

Gabrial ground his fangs. They must have tracked his flight from the cave, after all. "Gariffred! Come to me! Now!" he bellowed.

The drake had drifted back toward the cliff. He was stumbling on the uneven ground, crying at Pine in a manner that begged her not to leave. The girl had gotten to her feet and was now well out of the blue dragon's reach. To Gabrial's horror, she was balanced on a rock at the edge of the land, her lank hair blowing sideways in the breeze. "Girl!" he called, in the best Hom voice he could.

She looked into the sky and saw the two Veng coming. A faint smile passed across her lips. Then, without a care, she looked down at the water, opened her hand to let a flower fall—and jumped.

6

It seemed to take an age for her body to disappear, as if the sky in its mercy wanted to cushion her against the drop. Gariffred skittered to the cliff edge, squealing, his wings extended, dragging the grass. The first of the Veng flashed by. The speed at which it cut across Gabrial's path blurred his eyes bright green for a moment and stopped him taking off in search of Pine. By the time his vision had cleared, the other Veng had landed close to Gariffred. It barked at the drake to make himself scarce. Gariffred put his foot into a hollow and tipped back on to his skinny haunches, hissing at the Veng for all he was worth. Allowing no margin for age or naivety, the Veng poured its flame over Gariffred's head, then sent a sharp burst in Gabrial's direction, a warning to the blue to stay back.

"Hurt him and I'll kill you," Gabrial roared, his claws plowing deep into the ground. Thankfully, the thrust of heat had done no more than scare the drake and bowl him aside. His body scales, not yet fully hardened, looked to have suffered some minor scorching: the Veng equivalent of a reprimand, a cuff. To Gabrial's relief, the drake took to the air and faded out of range.

The Veng peered casually over the cliff, giving no hint of what it could see.

"The girl. Is she dead?" Gabrial pressed. In his mind, he pictured her floating, star-shaped, her tiny frame lapping with the shape of the waves, a better i:mage to carry back to Gayl than a body smashed against unforgiving rocks.

"I can't see her," the Veng said sourly. It graarked at its companion to check.

Gabrial twitched his nostrils. It couldn't *see* her? Maybe Pine had plummeted deep underwater? Though that was unlikely, for the cliff was not sheer at this point. But if she'd hit the rocks, her body would be seen. Even if she'd slipped between the pointed crags that stood like guards against the foaming tides, her body would have bled. The scent of fresh blood would be easy for the Veng to trace. He watched the second one roll in midair, then dip out of sight beyond the cliff. A beat passed, yet no word came from it. Gabrial glanced at the sky and saw Gus circling. There was now no sight nor sound of Gariffred.

With his hopes for Pine dashed and his loyalties divided, Gabrial was now anxious to make a move. "I need to leave," he said, flicking out his wing tips. "The Prime is in danger. I must speak with him on a matter of great urgency."

"You're going nowhere till we find the girl," said the Veng.

"She's dead," snapped Gabrial. "You saw what happened. She took her life. Not even by my order. She couldn't survive a drop so deep. Now get out of my way. There's nothing for you here. Trust me, Veng, the longer I delay, the more you'll have to answer for later."

The Veng gargled. Not a good sign. They were known to possess a considerable range of intimidating noises, and this didn't sound like a yielding reaction. The moment Gabrial opened his wings, the Veng roared again. Its fire blazed so close this time it caused a heat mist to form in the blue dragon's eyes. As he blinked to cool them he noticed Gus had dropped lower in the sky. The roamer had his claws out, ready to attack.

The Veng that was searching for Pine reappeared. It flew over, giving a brief report. *Nothing. She must be hiding.*

The Veng confronting Gabrial growled suspiciously.

At that moment, Gariffred glided by, intent on doing his own search of the cliffs. The Veng in the sky closed in to shadow the drake's movements. In desperation, Gabrial said, "For the last time, hear me. I need to take Gariffred to Skytouch right away. He . . . he knows something about the boy."

Foolish. Even as the words were leaving his mouth, Gabrial wished he could bite through his tongue.

The Veng wound its slender neck forward. It opened its long, ferocious jaws. Strings of gluey drool wound down off its fangs, fangs that looked sharp enough to perforate rock. The shields came down on its slanted eyes. Veng shields were nothing more than a hard transparent membrane, a heat-resistant battle aid evolved over centuries of selective breeding. The membranes were clear at birth, but the Veng had learned to stain them a subtle shade of green by draining blood into them from nearby cells. The resulting "eyeless" appearance struck fear into their foes, which more than compensated for the slight impairment of vision. Even Gabrial, who had seen the effect many times, felt his primary heart skip a beat. The Veng lashed its tongue. A sign of its desire for answers—or conflict. "Where is the Hom boy? Speak or you die."

Gabrial closed his mouth. It would have been so easy to bow to the Veng and simply share Gariffred's i:mage with it. Had Grendel been beside him, she would have pressed this course for the sake of Gariffred's safety, if not his. But nothing in Gabrial's bloodline would make him back down from a head-on threat, even with an opponent as deadly as this. And so he raised his battle stigs and heard himself saying, "That's for me to know and you to find out, *sier pent.*"

The Veng reared back, offended by the slur (Gabrial had called it a "green fish"). But instead of launching an immediate attack, it snapped an order at its companion. Before Gabrial could work out what was happening, Gariffred was in the second Veng's clutches. It had pulled the drake clean out of the sky and now had him pinned to the ground by his neck.

"Tada!" Gariffred cried, squirming under the Veng's cruel claws.

Gabrial was helpless. And the facing Veng was quick to confirm it. It whipped its tail into the air and said, "One step, one puff of smoke, and his scrawny neck cracks. All I have to do is drop my tail. Now, *where is the boy?*"

"I knows where," said a voice.

If Ren himself had drifted by on a bed of cloud, Gabrial could not have been more astounded. Pine had suddenly reappeared. She must have climbed back on to the headland somehow, though Gabrial had seen no sign of it. For all he knew, she could have popped up out of the ground like a flower. Who knew what powers she'd inherited from Gayl? She was showing no cuts or other injuries. And her robe, though marked with some rips from previous adventures, was still intact. The thought crossed his mind that she could be a spirit returned from a very disagreeable death, though she didn't float over the ground like a vapor, and vapors—in his admittedly limited experience—didn't come bearing gifts. Pine was carrying an egg, carefully balanced on an upturned palm. A seabird egg. White. A little larger than usual. She offered it up to the bemused Veng, who seemed temporarily immobilized by this bizarre apparition.

Once again, Pine spoke in perfect dragontongue. "Look, Veng. See. Watch."

She wafted her fingers over the egg.

"It's coming," she whispered.

"What's coming?" snarled the Veng. Gabrial heard it suck in through its spiracles. It was filling its fire sacs, ready to incinerate her.

"Your death," she said.

And she closed her hand around the egg, and broke it.

7

When he would come to think on this later, Gabrial would remember being as mesmerized by Pine as the Veng clearly was. As her fingers ruptured the shell, he expected something marvelous might happen. That rays of light would emerge from the egg, or a perfect flower spring up from its center, or that he might see a featherless bird squirming for breath in her small, pink hand.

But nothing quite so wonderful happened. The egg cracked. Its gooey innards ran down Pine's arm. A splash of yolk hit the gap between the Veng's nostrils.

Then came an instant of absolute calm.

No predictor of the carnage about to follow.

As silent as a winged seed, Gus swept down. Not even a shadow preceded him. Only the seabirds spotted his descent. They scattered from their settles as he tilted into his final glide, thinking, perhaps, that he was coming for them. But Gus had a bigger target: the Veng that was holding Gariffred.

He closed in on it at incredible speed, moving his huge bulk fully forward to generate the critical momentum he needed. The Veng must have felt the sudden change in pressure, for its auricular flaps sprang tautly open just a heartbeat before the giant dragon struck. By then it was too late.

Gus's brawny talons had slammed into its back, clamping it by the shoulder joints, the place where the thickest frame of the wing joined the spine of that serpentine body. At the same time, Gus adjusted his wings to maintain his forward thrust and plucked the Veng away from Gariffred as easily as he might take a rabbit off a hilltop. A bold maneuver for a dragon of his size. But what came next almost made his spiracles burst. The Veng wasn't particularly heavy—of all dragon breeds, they were the lightest—but the strain of lifting it into the sky from such a shallow angle required every drop of oxygen-rich blood Gus's primary heart could pump to his wings. But pump it did. With every beat, he took the Veng higher. Until a crosswind came to assist his endeavor and he was able to bank back seaward with his quarry. It would be there, over the rugged black cliffs, that the grisliest part of his attack would play out.

The Veng was not slow to respond. Raising its horns to their optimum angle, it bent the yellow tips upward to point roughly at Gus's throat. Of all the regions on a dragon's body, the underneck was one of the most vulnerable, for the suppleness required to twist the head meant that the scales there had to be flexible. The Veng were experts in ripping through this layer. In two slick movements, it opened the cone on each of its horns and flicked out a set of poisoned vanes. It then jabbed its head up with such ghastly force that one horn broke against Gus's jawbone. The other horn missed his head by some way. But the Veng had a marker now. On the next thrust, it crunched through a poorly sealed overlap and lacerated the soft tissue underneath the scales. It could not go deep without breaking its own neck. But it ripped and pierced and ripped again, and even allowed itself a cry of victory as Gus's blood fell in warm splatters over its back.

Its tail was hard at work as well. Due to the angle at which the Veng was being carried, the toxic, claw-hammered isoscele was too low to strike at Gus's belly. But the tail was thrashing the air nonstop—not in desperation or distress (that emotion had been bred out of the Veng centuries ago) but in the hope of intertwining with Gus's tail. The Veng had some nasty tricks in their armory and knew how to use every part of their bodies to inflict as much damage as possible on an enemy. Experienced fighters could "thin" their tails by freakishly stretching the extensor muscles until the last few segments effectively formed a cable. When used in a whipping motion, the elongated tail was then capable of cutting through a neck or a leg many times its own thickness. It could also be used to strangle tissue, to cut slowly, squeeze painfully, in the Veng's favorite way. One of their much-feared "reprimands" was to sever an opponent's tail as near to the isoscele as possible—never cutting right through, but leaving the triangular end piece dangling. The embarrassment of suffering a blow like this was often more agonizing than the pain of the wound or the length of time it took for the injury to heal.

So when, by a stroke of mischance, Gus felt the Veng's tail lock around his own, he knew he must act faster than his foe. It was bad enough to have his tail trapped, but that would be a mere inconvenience in comparison to actually losing his isoscele and, with it, his best directional aid.

So as the Veng's horns struck his throat, he in turn pulled violently sideways and tore the beast's wings away from its body, breaking the shoulder joints and ripping through the entire wing canopy, right down to the dorsal bones. The Veng screamed like nothing Gus had ever heard, a sound more chilling than the numbing cold of its cruel poison, which was already spreading through his chest. With the worst of the foul deed done, Gus switched his feet quickly and broke the Veng's neck in a single twist. The beast went silent and limp, but even then, its tail would not let go. As Gus tried to drop the body into the ocean, its dead weight hung off him, threatening to drag him into the water. With one last surge of power, he swung his tail and hurled the dead creature at the cliff face. It came free of him at last and smacked into the rocks, before tumbling sideways and plunging into a spuming wave that drew back from the shoreline foaming green.

One threat resolved.

The rest would be down to Gabrial.

8

The moment Gus struck, Gabrial knew he would be forced to attack the Veng in front of him. It was sure to react. And it did. The only advantage it awarded Gabrial was its momentary indecision about where to strike first: the annoying Hom girl or the squealing wearling. It leaned toward Pine, but that was a mistake; it should have been watching the blue.

Gabrial came for it with teeth, not fire. The Veng already had its eye shields down, and any blast of flame at this short distance was likely to flare and injure them both. The key to winning was to stop the Veng taking flight. A Veng in the sky was twice as hard to kill as one on the ground. They were swift through the air and incredibly agile. A roamer the size of Gus would have had little chance against one in open combat. Even Gabrial, who'd famously taken down a goyle mutant, knew he would need a good deal of luck to survive any form of aerial clash.

So he rushed for its throat, clamping it between his powerful jaws and sinking his fangs in as far as they would take. In his head, he could hear the snarling words of his tragic patron and mentor, per Grogan. *Bite and bite hard. Until you feel your fangs grinding against each other.* That's what the old dragon would have said. *Cut right through and be sure of your kill.* In training, Gabrial had been given sheep to bite on. Their throats were like wet sand compared to this Veng.

Only one fang punctured it—and that went in through a breathing hole. The bite caused some serious damage all the same; the Veng's roar of pain was testament to that. Warm blood flowed between Gabrial's fangs, thickening to a gush as he bit down harder. All this time, he was pushing forward, flinging his head from side to side with all the force he could muster. From the start, he'd had the Veng badly off-balance, and though it was putting up dogged resistance, it had little chance of landing a blow while Gabrial was driving it back toward the sea. Back away from Gariffred. Back away from Pine. Straight for the cliff edge.

And over.

They fell, still clamped together, and only broke apart as they bounced off a rounded saddle of rock. Gabrial got lucky then. He had caused no injury to the Veng's wings, and as soon as it was free, it tried to open them, to fly. It flicked a wing out and swiftly extended the poisoned barbs that ran the entire length of it, including the hidden spur that lay in the bony joint halfway along the main arm. But the other wing was hampered by rock. The Veng had fallen into a chasm, not quite big enough to trap it, but awkward enough to prevent a quick escape. It had no choice but to fold its wings down and scull the water at the base of the chasm, while it struggled to get a grip against hunks of stone scoured with layers of sea thorn and slime. In a raging burst, it came up suddenly, rasping a host of murderous noises from the seat of its throat and the ragged, blood-drenched hole in its neck. It clambered upright and looked around, and soon saw Gabrial waiting for it.

Gabrial lashed his tail across its breast, a swipe so strong that the Veng was batted clear of the shoreline and into the open sea. There it floated in its own blood, steam pouring off its grayish underbelly, claws contracting in no fixed pattern, one leg twitching in spasmodic bursts. Not dead yet, but gravely winded, all bar its head just under the water.

Gabrial knew he must finish this now. If he let the Veng recover, it would come for him, no matter how bad its injuries might be. Veng battled to the death, and he must do the same. One more hit while it was dazed should end it.

He flew the short distance to where the Veng floated, flashed his tail, and struck at the head in a hard chopping motion.

A crown of water splashed into the sky. But something was seriously wrong about that. His isoscele had traveled farther than it should have, as if he'd cut through a drift of snow. He looked down and saw blood still pooling on the water.

The body had disappeared.

The Veng had dived.

In an instant, Gabrial knew he'd been tricked. The Veng had lured him into a trap. Suddenly, the thing leapt out of the water, grasped one foot, and pulled him down. Gabrial beat his wings hard, whipping the sea into a clattering fury. But there was little hope of flight with such a weight against his leg. He crashed below the surface, rigid with fear, bubbles streaming from every spiracle. Water was not a good fighting ground for dragons. But if it favored one class, it favored the Veng. They were excellent swimmers and not called "green fish" for nothing. Water dulled their natural speed of attack, but they could easily outmaneuver most marine creatures. Gabrial was no match for them in these conditions. He was in desperate danger and he knew it.

The first strike punctured his wing. It was a truly surreal experience to be tumbling through water with a foe so deadly and not be able to roll on command or hit at will. The usual tactics did not apply here. The best immediate defense was avoidance. Through the murk, he saw the Veng's isoscele coming, squirming toward his head like a dart. Just in time, he turned away and felt a thud as the point arrowed into his wing. A cold pain lit up his shoulder. The isoscele had ripped through one of the sails that made up the canopy of his wing. He saw the wound edges flapping but could only guess at the damage, not truly feel it.

More strikes followed. But they were all minor. A scrape of claws along the neck. A bite to the foot. He realized the Veng was playing with him, wearing him down, waiting for him to run out of breath before it went in hard with its poisons and spikes and all the rest of its toxic arsenal.

He had to surface. Had to. But how? Every time he pushed toward the murky light, the Veng circled and took another piece out of him. Like all dragons, Gabrial could hold his breath for long periods. But the effort required to repel the Veng was eating into reserves he didn't have, whereas the sier pent was sure to have plenty in its air sacs.

Time was running out.

Think, Gabrial. Think.

Then, an idea came to him. Once again, it was the voice of per Grogan he turned to. He remembered a story the old dragon had told about a foolish roamer who had fallen into an ice-cold lake and tried to use its fire to warm the water. The flame had boiled a small part of the surface and created a scalding veil of steam. The steam had spread under the roamer's scales and burned some parts of its body so badly that it never walked properly again.

Fire. Every dragon's sacred gift.

But would it work underwater?

For the love of Godith, it was worth a try.

As the Veng came again, Gabrial opened his fire sacs and blew with all his might. A stranger outcome he had rarely seen. Instead of pouring forth in a golden wave, the fire died at the end of his snout, displacing an ongoing surge of ripples that raced one another to reach the surface. The Veng saw what was happening and must have thought the blue had gone mad. Fire? In *water*? Its eye ridges flipped to a mocking angle, and it dived straight forward, into the swell. That was the start of its downfall. Gabrial closed his eyes and sealed down his scales as the first throb of heat surrounded him. Despite blowing forward, he felt the burns worst on his undersides and tail, and in every scratch the Veng had landed. At one point, he thought his wings would ignite. He immediately swam for the surface and broke through just before the Veng managed to. The sea was boiling, rushing in circles from the heart of the disturbance, carrying steam flurries all the way to shore.

Now the Veng was in desperate trouble. It was gasping badly through the hole in its neck. Red welts were showing in places where its bright green scales had lifted. One of its bloated eye shields had popped. Briefly, Gabrial pitied it. But as soon as the Veng laid its good eye on him, it spat out a roar and came for him again. Wild with pain, it launched itself forward, straight into Gabrial's powerful claws. He seized it by the neck and with one wrench opened up the rings of bone that supported the network of throat muscles, making the bite wound larger again, large enough to flood the Veng's airways with water. Then he plunged the head below the waves and held it there until the beast stopped thrashing.

The Veng sank painfully slowly. And with it went Gabrial's hopes for the future. The last of the Wearle's security force was dead. And though there had been provocation in plenty, there was nothing to prove it, no clear defense for his actions. When news of the killings reached Prime Grynt, Gabrial, Grendel, Gus, and the wearlings would all be branded traitors. None of them would leave this planet alive. They were outlaws of the Wearle and would be called to justice. There was only one option open to them.

Flee.

9

But a swift escape was not going to be possible. Despite the Veng's strike, Gabrial's wing was not badly damaged and he was able to fly to the clifftop again. There he was met by a troubling sight. Gus was stretched out sideways on the ground, his chest rising and falling faster than it ought to. The big green roamer was cradling Gariffred, who looked disoriented and a little cold. Pine was nowhere to be seen and Gabrial could find no hint of her scent. He figured she'd made a run for the mountains. But the girl was the least of his worries now.

He limped forward, blood dripping from a bite to his foreleg. Shaking a piece of seaweed off his snout, he ran his gaze over Gus's body. The roamer had suffered no obvious injuries other than a serious wound to the throat. The gash was doing its best to close and bleeding had slowed to a trickle. But a dark gray pus was already congealing around its edges. The scales nearby were also losing color. A sign of deep Veng poisoning.

Gus opened his arms and encouraged Gariffred to wriggle free. The drake nestled under his guardian's breast. He had seen enough of the world for one day.

"You need to go," said Gus, wincing as he struggled to open his jaw.

"Gus . . ." Gabrial wanted to tell him to rest. The effort of speaking had made the wound swell and broken some of the healing webs. But there was no point asking Gus not to talk. By right, he needed to say his piece. No dragon liked to switch to thought exchange when they had little time to live.

"Go," Gus croaked. "Take the drake. Leave me. A sweeper could come over at any time. Then they'll all be here."

Gabrial shook his head. "I can't leave you. Not like this."

Gus retracted his claws, grimacing as the poison did its work. "You can. You must. Burn me and fly to Grynt."

The blue glanced briefly at the mountaintops. If Gariffred's i:mage was accurate, Grynt might be overthrown by now—or lying dead in his eyrie, slain by a boy with the power to transform into a black dragon. The thought sent a chill down Gabrial's spine and made him worry for Grendel and Gayl. But surely if the Prime had been attacked, there would be battle cries ringing out from the mountains? Yet the skies were clear and calm. That once again begged the puzzling question: What *was* Ren doing on the peak of Skytouch?

"Tell the Elders it was me who attacked the Veng. Tell Grynt you tried to stop it."

Gabrial snorted softly, irritating a freezing cut in one nostril. The Veng venom had not gone deep in him, but it would still be a while before his natural defenses brought it under control. “They’d never believe me. Besides, what reason would you have to take both of them on?”

Gus made a slight movement in his back. “The rumor going around the Wearle ought to do it.”

Gabrial’s eye ridges stiffened. “What rumor?”

“You obviously haven’t heard,” Gus said, coughing up a swab of yellow mucus.

“Heard what?” said Gabrial, distracted by a sudden flare of screeches. He swung his head fast toward the sea. For one panic-stricken moment he thought the Veng had survived and was about to mount a surprise attack. But it was only the seabirds, squabbling for space as they returned to their settles. He panned the sky warily all the same. Gus was right. If they stayed here much longer they would be seen.

“They think one of us killed Gallen.”

Gabrial swung his head back, his stigs bristling. That was a name he thought he’d heard the last of. The Veng commander had died in Gabrial’s fire when the blue had mistaken him for an enemy goyle. The memory of it still spiked his sleep.

“They found his body in the forest,” Gus said, his claws bunching against the pain. It was hurting him now to squeeze the words out. “Burns all over him. Dragon scars. The only ones near him at the time he died were you, me, and Garodor. I’m guessing it was you who took him down, but I’m happy to accept the blame for killing that piece of callous—”

At that moment, Pine reappeared. She came hurrying over the ground like a wisp, crossing the humps and hollows with ease, her white knees showing just below her robe.

She skidded to a halt in front of Gabrial. He was ready with his tail and stopped her on the point of his isoscele.

She raised both hands in surrender. In the left, she was holding some long-stemmed plants with drooping red flowers. In the right was a clutch of large green leaves.

"*You* have a lot of explaining to do." Gabrial's weighty isoscele raised Pine's chin as high as it would stretch. He dented her skin to show he meant business, while allowing her just enough freedom to speak.

"I picked furzlewort and hoddleroot," she said in dragontongue, though these were not Hom words Gabrial recognized. "And here be redsel, fresh—for him." She rustled the flowers and tilted them at Gus.

Gabrial glanced at the weedy stalks. The healing dragon, Grymric, often talked about the soothing power of plants. But even Grymric, with all his years of experience, had found no remedy for Veng poison.

"He's dying," the blue growled.

"Then I would save him," said Pine. She lifted the thin band of hair above one eye ridge. The fang in the center of her mouth glinted.

Gabrial rolled back his upper lip and showed her what a real fang ought to look like. "Why is Ren on Skytouch?" he growled. "You know something, don't you? What's he planning?"

She gave a little gasp as he pricked her for an answer. "Why do you hurt me so? I came to you with healing. These flowers are my trust. Do harm on me and your roamer will die."

"Answer me," he growled, making her bleed.

"Whitehair seeks the truth," she squeaked. "No more do I know. I swear to you fair on the spirits of the Fathers." If it were possible to grit one tooth, she was doing it.

"Truth about what?"

"This." She flicked her gaze sideways, inviting him to look at her arm. As she closed her eyes in concentration, her delicate skin began to glaze, until the entire length of her arm was covered in tiny dragon scales. Shining silver-green juvenile dragon skin that would have looked well on any wearling. It made Gabrial wonder just how far the auma would travel. What if she could change her whole body like this? What would happen in her heart if she did? How long before her blood ran green, like theirs? And then what would she be, Hom or dragon?

With a rumble of annoyance, Gabrial lowered his isoscele. What choice did he have but to let her try to save Gus? "If he suffers, girl, I'll have your head."

To his amazement, she stuck out her tongue. "And I might yet have yours, beast."

Wisely, she did not persist with her petulance and quickly knelt beside Gus instead, laying the redsel flowers at his head. She called Gariffred to her and instructed him to watch.

Picking two leaves off the hoddleroot pile, she crumpled them into her mouth and chewed them as well as her tooth would allow, then spat the pulp into her open hand. "Now you, pupp." She mimed the chewing and spitting for Gariffred.

Graark, he went, to show he understood.

With Gabrial in close attendance, she fed Gariffred the furzlewort and hoddleroot leaves. While he was mulching, she began to pluck the redsel flowers off their stalks, separating out the spiny seedpods that nestled just below the flower heads. Deftly, she cracked the pods open and spilled the tiny black seeds they bore into a pleat of her robe. When every pod was emptied, she tipped the seeds into a pile in one hand.

By then, Gariffred was ready with the leaves. Pine shuffled closer to Gus and sprinkled the seeds into the wound at his neck. He made no complaint, prompting Gabrial to wonder how close he was to death. The amber shine had gone from Gus's jeweled eyes. His tail was barely flicking. He had hardly breathed in the last few moments.

The girl signaled to Gariffred and pointed. The drake adopted a vomiting stance and hawked the contents of his mouth over Gus's neck. Gabrial looked away in disgust. He had seen Grymric applying poultices to wounds, but nothing quite as repellent as this.

Pine leaned forward and spread the goo over the wound with her hands. She patted it into place, covering all the pus and making a seal for the seeds. She stroked Gariffred to say he'd done well, then told him to stand back.

"You too," she said to Gabrial.

For once, he obeyed her and pulled the drake away.

She moved around to the tip of Gus's snout. Still on her knees, she clamped his head between her hands and began to sing. A lilting tune with a tender cadence; it could have charmed the wind.

It wasn't long before Gabrial understood why he'd been ordered back. Out of nowhere, a spasm ran through Gus's body. His claws slid out and clutched the erth like dry roots starved of water. His tail thumped the ground, showering small stones across the headland and leaving a permanent rut in the soil. At the same time, he cried out and tossed his head, heat blowing from his froth-corrupted lungs. Pine held on bravely and sang more sweetly. The tail moved again. It swept the ground in a mighty arc, almost catching Gariffred's toes. Gabrial drew him farther back, hardly able to believe what he was seeing. A huge convulsion had taken hold of Gus. His free wing had unfolded to half its expanse and was jabbing the air in violent spasms. His tail was still flaying the grass. Then, in one explosive burst of power, he somehow struggled to his feet. Pine was thrown clear, but got up unhurt. Gus steadied himself, snorting lather from his nostrils. He tottered sideways briefly and almost collapsed. He blinked several times, looking dazed and haunted.

Pine slowly approached him again. She caught hold of his head and slid her hands flat along his shuddering snout until they were resting just under his ears. *"Galan aug scieth,"* she whispered, meaning "we are one"—not in body, but in common purpose.

Gus nodded faintly. So too Gabrial. There on that clifftop his mind was decided. Hom and dragons *must* find a way to share this world and live together in peace. But it could not happen here, in this mountain domayne. Grynt would never be persuaded, not while he thirsted to spill Ren's blood. So Gabrial called Pine over and humbly thanked her for saving Gus, then bade her look out to sea with him. "What lies beyond the water?" he asked. The horizon was far away, bare of land.

Pine crouched down and picked a flower. "I know not," she said, "but if you go there, you must take me with you."

Gabrial stared ahead, tight-lipped. Far below, on the edge of his vision, he could see the body of the Veng he'd killed. It had floated to the surface like a castaway leaf. A grim and ugly sight it was. That deed was going to haunt him all his days. But Pine need not be a part of it. "What of your tribe, the Kaal?" he asked her. "Is it not your wish to return to them?"

She stood up like a slip of light and wedged the flower under one of his scales. "You are my tribe now, skaler."

And she patted his breast and turned back inland.

10

As Gabrial turned to follow Pine, he heard a sharp cry from above. His gaze flashed skyward. Just as Gus had feared, a sweeper had seen them. It was flying high with the sun at its back, cutting a stitch between the clouds. It banked seaward and circled over the area, tilting its inquisitive head as it swept across the cliff line. It had the seen the bodies, scented the blood, identified the dragons on the ground—and in the water. The idiot girl was even waving to it! Gabrial felt a giddy rush in his ears, magnified by the thump of his primary heart. He had been a sweeper once. He knew the role well. If the dragon in the sky stayed true to its orders, it would save an i:mage of this scene to memory, then turn toward the mountains and report to the Elders. It would be over Mount Vargos before Gabrial could catch it. Too late by then. Maybe too late now.

"Do you recognize it?" he said urgently to Gus. The sweeper was circling a second time, not exactly in a hurry to go. Gabrial followed its flight path around, trying to read the intent in its eye.

"It looks like Gruder," Gus replied, still reeling from Pine's dramatic cure. He set himself down with a weary thump. "Myverian bloodline. Not a fighter."

That didn't do much for Gabrial's fears. A nervous type was more likely to bolt.

"Call him," Gus said. "Call a greeting."

They watched Gruder disappear behind a cloud.

"Will he respond?" asked Gabrial. "How well do you know him?"

"I don't. But if he flies to Grynt and reports what he's seen, the Wearle will descend upon us in force. Then it's either fight for our freedom—or drown."

Gabrial's eye ridges stiffened, prompting Gus to say, "I heard you ask the girl what lies across the water. That may be our only hope of escape. But you can't attempt a flight across an unmapped distance with a hole the size of my snout in your wing. A rip like that needs time to repair. One thing is certain: You'll never lift a full wing again if you don't get that sweeper on the ground. Call him."

"What do we tell him—assuming he lands?"

Gus grunted in thought. "We'll think of something."

Quite what Gus supposed he would say Gabrial could only wonder at. But he did as the big green dragon had asked and put back his head and bellowed, *Guh-raaar!* toning it to sound as if they needed help.

Gruder circled a third time, taking another long look at the carnage on the rocks. Then, to Gabrial's relief, he altered his wing shape and glided in. He landed on a hillock just in front of Gus, scattering loose dirt as his wings gathered down.

He was a rather elegant dragon, as slight in his build as Gus was burly. He had dark green tufts all along his jawline and two bent fangs that poked out of his mouth when it was fully closed. "What happened here?" he asked, his voice as frail as cracking ice. He looked at them all in turn, his gaze hovering longest over Pine and Gariffred. The drake had wandered back into her company and was gleefully nuzzling her out-stretched hand.

"The Veng attacked us," Gus said bluntly, raising his head to show his wound. It was blackening around the edges, but not in an adverse way. Pine's poultice had split down the center but was largely intact. "We killed them in self-defense."

Gruder blew a thin line of smoke. He was one of those dizzy-eyed dragons who was never far from a puzzled expression. "But why would they attack you? What reason would they have?" His quizzical gaze drifted back toward Pine. She had found a dead tree branch and was dragging it around for Gariffred to chase. "Why is the Hom girl playing with the wearling? I thought she was our prisoner?"

"Not anymore." Gus raised his battle stigs.

Gruder stumbled away a pace, his wing tips shuddering. "What's going on here? What have you done?"

"Gus, back off," Gabrial growled. He stamped the ground to claim the sweeper's attention. "Listen to me, Gruder. We mean you no harm. I was ordered to kill the girl in the hope of drawing Ren out of hiding. The Veng got involved and everything turned hostile. They bullied the drake and provoked a battle. Gus was poisoned in the fighting. The girl is running free because she saved his life with seeds and a poultice. For that reason, we are bound to let her go. Now that you know the truth, you have two choices: either you report us both to the Elders—or you help us to get away unharmed."

"Get away? You're leaving?"

"We have no choice."

"But if the killing was justified?"

"Grynt won't believe us. And if he did, he'd never free the girl." Gabrial took a step closer to the sweeper. "All we need is time. Finish your circuit, then go to the Elders and make your report. Tell them you've seen two Veng, dead, on these cliffs, but with no apparent reason why. By the time they bring the Wearle to investigate, we will be gone. Will you do that for us?"

Gruder inhaled a ball of smoke, his bent fangs dragging at his lower lip. "You can't *leave*. The Wearle needs you. If the black dragon rises . . ." He stopped himself there. "Besides, where would you go with a damaged wing?"

"He's right," Gus said to Gabrial. "You came to Gariffred hoping for a lead on the boy. More than once, I saw you looking at the mountains. You have unfinished business. You have to go back."

"How?" said Gabrial, puffing air through his spiracles.

"Tell Grynt I started the fight and dragged you into it. You'll need to invent some minor details and slur my name from here to the scorch line, but they'll believe it, especially if Gruder backs you up." He threw the sweeper a semi-threatening look.

Gruder gulped and gave a swish of his tail. "I'll do it. I'll help."

Gabrial sighed heavily. "If the truth comes out, you'll be branded a renegade."

"I don't care. I hated them," the sweeper cut in. "After the Veng destroyed per Grogan in the quarry, they made me search for his heart. When I found it, they gave it to the traitor, Givnay. Grogan was my teacher once. The best per I ever had. I can't forgive Gallen for making me dishonor him." He glanced across the water. "I'm glad they're dead. It's a good plan. You can rely on me."

"It's a dangerous plan," said Gabrial. "And we haven't heard all of it yet." He turned to Gus. "I assume you won't wait here for Grynt to find you?"

Gus fanned his impressive claws. "I'll fly the girl across the water and take my chances. If Godith is smiling on me, I might yet live long enough to see my scales turn red."

Gabrial glanced at the ocean's horizon. "You know Grynt will condemn you and your family name? You'll never be allowed to return to Ki:mera."

The big dragon gave a casual sniff. "I came on this mission to see something different. I like it here. Clean air. Fresh water. A whole new world to explore. On Ki:mera, I'm just another roamer." His gaze drifted back toward the mountains. For the first time, sadness blurred his eyes. "This is going to happen, Gabrial. This is my sacrifice, for you—and for Gariffred. I ask only one thing in return. Look after the Hom they call Rolan. If he's dying as Grymric claims, hasten his end. He was brave for us once. He must not suffer."

Gabrial gave a faint nod. "I also have one request of you."

"Name it."

"Take Gariffred with you."

"What?" Gruder's ears pinged back in shock. "You can't desert a *wearling*. That's worse than abandoning Grendel."

Gus raised an eye ridge. "The sweeper has a point."

"I don't intend to desert him," Gabrial argued. "I simply want him out of harm's way. I will find him when it's safe to do so. Besides, he's never been accepted into the Wearle and Grynt refuses to listen to our pleas to have him formally Named. I want Gariffred to have the chance to explore. He's an Erth dragon. His destiny is here. Grendel will be angry, but that's for me to deal with."

As he spoke these words, a ripple of light flared in the distance. Somewhere over the mountaintops, the thick gray clouds were slowly parting, squeezing sideways in two unnatural arcs. A sign of a fire star opening. A black shimmer ran down its invisible center, forming what looked like a giant eye. As it grew in size, it threw out volleys of purple rays that made the snowcapped mountains shine. Then the sky folded and was calm again. Gabrial sank back on his haunches. That could only be Garodor leaving. The thought of his departure left a nervous hollow in the blue dragon's breast. If anyone in authority would have understood this situation, it would have been the De:allus. At least he was safe and on his way back to Ki:mera.

As for Ren, all Gabrial could hope for now was that the boy's intentions were honorable. If the darkness inside him gained control, the whole Wearle was potentially at risk. If the black dragon rose, what then for the colony?

What hope for peace on Erth?

11

Shaking his dark thoughts aside, Gabrial dispatched Gruder into the air again, telling him to sweep the area until Gus was ready to leave. He then called Gariffred to him and told the drake that Gus was going to take him on a great adventure. They would fly across the water in search of new lands. When they found them, Gariffred must i:mage them as strongly as he could so that Gabrial could come and find them as well. It was a big game of "seek," the blue dragon said. He stroked Gariffred's back. The game might last for days, he told him.

"When you reach cloud cover, let him fly ahead of you," Gabrial instructed Gus. "Stay out of bad weather if you can."

Gus looked up. The sky was turning uniformly gray. There was no real hint of rain, but there was a wintry feel in the air.

"Carry him when he gets too tired," said Gabrial. "If you haven't found land by sunset, turn back."

Gus nodded. "And her?"

Pine was wandering vaguely in front of them, drawing an ear of grass through her fingers. She stopped a few paces away and pushed her lank hair behind her ears.

"I must return to the Wearle," Gabrial said, pitching his voice across the gap to her. "It's too dangerous for you to stay with me. If Gus permits, you may fly with him. Or you may go to your people. Choose."

Pine flicked the grass away. "I choose Gus."

The big roamer shrugged and opened his talons.

"But I will not be carried like a hopper in his claws."

Gabrial grunted. The girl certainly had nerve. "Lower a wing," he said to Gus.

Gus extended the wing nearest her until it just touched the ground. The whole canopy was so large it completely shadowed Gariffred. Pine sprang up it like a mountain goat.

Without further ado, Gus took off, barking at Gariffred to stay close to him.

Watching the drake depart was the hardest thing Gabrial had ever had to do. But this was not a moment for mawkish regrets. He had spent too long on these cliffs. Grynt must be wondering about the outcome of his orders. And he needed to be told what had happened to the Veng. It was time to return to the mountains and face him.

Although he would never admit it, a small part of Gabrial was slightly disappointed to find Prime Grynt still very much alive. His response to the news was predictably irate.

"DEAD? *Both* of them? How?"

Gabrial turned his face from the heat. "I did as you

commanded and took the Hom girl to a high place—the edge of the domayne, the sea."

"Why there?" Gossana asked, her tongue snipping at the edges of the words. "Isn't Skytouch high enough for you?"

She had settled on the terraced side of the eyrie, poking a small fire with her isoscele. She flicked a probing look at Gruder, who was standing to attention just behind Gabrial. The sweeper, aware of her penetrating gaze, managed to keep his head held high and his stance solid.

"There are unmapped caves in the cliff face," said Gabrial. "I thought Ren could be hiding among them. When I arrived, Gariffred was there with a roamer called Gus. The drake became upset when he realized what was going to happen to the girl. His squealing maddened the Veng. One of them pinned him to the ground and threatened to crush his neck. That provoked Gus to attack."

"And what were you—the drake's guardian—doing?" asked Gossana, weaving her words among the trails of smoke. "Appealing for mercy?"

"Not mercy—restraint."

The female dragon stretched her neck so she could better see the hole in Gabrial's wing. "Yet you fought alongside this renegade, Gus. Hard, by the look of it."

Gabrial's reply was clipped. "The Veng *threatened* Gariffred. I had no choice. Kill or be killed. Isn't that the Veng way?"

Grynt snorted noisily, fire pocketing deep in his throat. "You," he said, aiming his gaze toward Gruder. "What did you see of this?"

"He didn't arrive until it was over," said Gabrial. "He helped me—"

"I'm asking HIM!" roared Grynt. "Well, sweeper?"

Gruder stared straight ahead, speaking his report as if it were painted in blood on the wall. "I saw no fighting, Prime Grynt. Only the bodies. And Gabrial, injured. Naturally, I came to assist him."

"Naturally," Gossana repeated. "And the gallant Gus—where is he now?"

"He fled." Gabrial lowered his head. Even now he wasn't happy promoting this lie, inventing the "minor details" that would blacken Gus's character. "When the fighting was done, we argued. I said he should come to you and give himself up. He refused. He flew across the water, taking Pine with him. I was too injured to give chase."

"And the boy?" said Gossana.

That was unexpected. Gabrial shook his head, unbalanced by the question. Should he tell them about Gariffred's i:mage? Would they believe it if he did? "What does Ren have to do with this?"

Gossana fanned her sawfin scales. The movement blew a lick of fire in Gabrial's direction. "Was the boy not the reason for this luckless jaunt? Are you telling us that 'Ren' did not appear? That he did not leap heroically out of a cave and play a part in the slaughter or make any attempt to save the girl, even after she was . . . taken hostage?"

"No," said Gabrial. "I saw no sight of him."

"You swear to that?"

"I do." Gabrial laid his isoscele against his heart.

Gossana let out a false sigh. "Then this is a worse disaster than ever. Not only are our last two Veng wiped out, but our worst enemy is still at large and half our Hom 'bait' has gone missing."

"Listen—" Gabrial began to say. He had decided he must tell them about Gariffred's i:mage. The threat of Graven, though still unclear, hung like a dark cloud over his hearts. For all he knew, the boy was lurking invisibly in the shadows, hearing all of this. But Gossana only had ears for her own words.

"All is not lost, however. I suggest you try again, Prime Grynt. We have the man 'Rolan' in our grasp, do we not?" Her throat hardened around the name as her callous gaze locked onto Gabrial once more. "And this time, as the blue is clearly unfit, I suggest it should be *you* who carries out the threat. Take the Hom to the peak of Skytouch yourself. If the boy will slide out of his shell for anyone, it will surely be you."

"No. Please, hear me," Gabrial said.

But this time it was Grynt who cut him off. "Get out," he

snarled. "You're confined to the inner domayne until I decide what to do with you. Sweeper, go back to your duties. NOW!"

Gruder gave a shuddering nod. He licked his troublesome teeth, then took off with Gabrial close behind him.

"Well?" said Grynt, watching them wheel away. "Speak up, Matrial. What is it you wish to say? Something is bubbling under your tongue. I hear it louder than a wearling's fart."

"Isn't it obvious?" she said.

"If it were obvious, I wouldn't be ASKING you!"

She gave a penitent nod. "He's lying. They both are."

Grynt stared at the gray sky, simmering. "Why? What reason would they have?"

"To protect the Hom—and this bond they claim to have with them. Gabrial has clearly set the girl free. And I think he knows where the boy is hiding. They're plotting against you, Grynt. Don't you see it? First they remove the Veng, then you."

Grynt extended his claws, making them squeal against the cave floor. In a deep voice laced with bitterness, he said, "Go to the cliffs yourself, alone. I want a full report on what you find there. Get me proof of Gabrial's deceit."

Gossana rose to her feet. "It will be my pleasure, but I hardly think it necessary to dig for the truth. They will show themselves as traitors if you do as I suggested." She made eye contact. "Strengthen the guard around the eyrie. Then have the man, Rolan, brought to you—and kill him."

12

“Taken him? What do you mean, Gus has *taken* him?”

The sheer thrust of Grendel’s voice laid Gabrial’s stigs flat. Breaking such devastating news to her was never going to be easy, but he’d hoped for a little less fury than this. The golden braids along her face had almost combusted when she’d learned that the drake had been spirited away.

“I thought he’d be safer, away from Grynt and Gossana. Maybe even from Graven.”

“Safe? In the company of a renegade?”

“That’s making it sound far worse than it is.”

“Oh. So what you’re really telling me is you’ve wrapped Gariffred up in your little plot and condemned him forever if the truth comes out!”

“Grendel, it’s not like that.”

“It’s exactly like that. Why did you drag him into it? Gariffred didn’t kill the Veng, did he?”

“They attacked him,” Gabrial retaliated. “Believe me, you would have admired his courage. Another year’s growth and—”

“He’d be dead.” Grendel was close enough now to bite the end off Gabrial’s snout. “Hacked down or poisoned, ready to shed his tiny fire tear. When are you going to learn that fighting is not the answer to everything?"

Gabrial put his head back, counting the jags of ice growing from the cave ceiling. "I didn't know what else to do."

"Of course you *knew*. You should have brought him back."

"Into a Wearle that doesn't want him? And won't formally Name him?"

"*I* want him! Me. His mother in all but blood. Don't I get a say in our wearlings' future?"

"I'm sorry," the blue said, sighing as he bowed to her, "but at the time it seemed like the only option."

"Ohhh!" Grendel swept away in despair.

"This colony is falling apart," Gabrial argued. "We should leave while we can. Find new lands. Settle. Build. Other families from other colonies have done it."

"And put ourselves at war with Grynt?"

"It's our right to roam; Grynt won't come after us."

"Of course he will. He's the Prime of a colony sent here by the Higher. Ultimately, he has to answer to them. He'd have every right to outlaw us, Gariffred included, and call for reinforcements from Ki:mera. Not that he'd need them. Even without the Veng, we'd be heavily outnumbered. What's you, me, Gus, and a couple of wearlings against a wyng of . . . twenty roamers?"

"I don't think the roamers would fight for Grynt. Not against us."

"You don't think . . ." she muttered quietly to herself. "That's precisely right, Gabrial. You just don't *think*. I want Gariffred found. I want him with me."

Gabrial shuffled his feet. "Technically, he is."

"What?"

"The Elders don't know he's with Gus; I didn't tell them."

A look of thunder passed across Grendel's face. Again, she came close enough to steal his breath. "If Grystina were alive, she would probably have taken your head off by now. And I still might. You think the Veng were savage opponents? They are nothing compared to me. I want Gariffred back in the safety of the Wearle. You have five days. After that, I go to Grynt and tell him everything you've just told me. Grynt may not think highly of Gariffred, but the drake is still part of this Wearle, *his* Wearle. He could have you arrested for sending Gariffred away beyond the care of his guardians."

"Mama . . ." The wearmyss, Gayl, wandered into the argument. She pawed at Grendel, clearly upset by the raised voices.

"Shhhh, little one," Grendel reassured her. "Tada is hurting from his wound. It somehow seems to have affected his *mind*."

Gabrial snarled lightly and rustled his wings. "I need to see Grymric urgently."

That seemed to come as no surprise to Grendel. "That's

the most sensible thing you've said all day. Ask him for an herb that can keep your battle stigs locked down."

"In five days," he countered, "you'll see I was right." He looked at Gayl. She still had Pine's flowers draped around her neck. "When you're ready, tell her Pine is well and with Gus. It's because he wants to protect the girl that he's accepted the blame for slaying the Veng. She saved his life on those cliffs, Grendel. And now I'm going to try to save Rolan's."

And without another word, he turned toward the light, caught what he could of the wind, and flew.

"Tada!" cried Gayl, scampering after him.

"Gayl, come here," Grendel sighed, turning her head to one side to think on all that Gabrial had said. When she glanced at the cave mouth again, it was empty. "Gayl?" she muttered, looking all around. "Gayl? GAYL?!"

Half a wingbeat took her straight to the edge. She looked down the craggy mountainside, worried for a moment that the wearmyss had fallen.

But Gayl, like her brother, had found her wings.

She was a hazy dot in the murky sky, on a gliding descent that would take her across the great ice lake—following the scent of her guardian, to the cave of the healing dragon, Grymric.

13

"Gabrial!"

Grymric was pleased to see the blue—at first. Then he noted the hole in the wing and his aging eye ridges creaked around the edges. When Gabrial presented with a serious injury, it was usually a sign of trouble within the Wearle.

"You're hurt," he said. "I'm surprised you're flying. Is that a fighting wound?"

"Better you don't know the details," said Gabrial.

Grymric cast an anxious glance outside. "Not goyles again?"

Gabrial shook his head. "Personal dispute."

Was that worse than a goyle threat? Grymric decided it was better not to ask. "Well, turn to your side. Let me view the wound properly."

"It's nothing. Just a tear. It will heal itself soon. I'm not here about the wing. I've come to take the Hom man away. Where is he?"

He leaned sideways, peering deeper into the cave. Toward the back, half lit by the light from a small fire, lay the man Ren had called Rolan Woodknot. He wasn't moving or making any sound.

"WAIT!" Grymric shifted his wiry frame to block Gabrial's forward step. "What do you mean, 'take him'? Take him where?"

"You need to trust me, Grymric. We don't have much time."

"He's weak, Gabrial. Moving him could kill him."

Gabrial stared into the healer's eyes. "He'll be thrown off a mountain if I don't get him out of here. Grynt's orders."

Grymric swished his tail, sending a pile of leaves into the fire. "But that's barbaric. Why would Grynt do that?"

"He thinks it will flush Ren out of hiding. Let me by, Grymric. Grynt's roamers could turn up at any—"

At that precise moment, Gayl landed awkwardly in the cave mouth, overflapping so much that Gabrial was fooled into thinking that a much bigger dragon had arrived. He swept around and roared a ferocious warning, a hooked flame spiking out of his throat. Luckily, it curled over Gayl's head, close enough to cause the young dragon to squeal but high enough to leave her physically untouched. Gabrial quickly sucked back, reducing the flame to a puff of smoke that escaped through his teeth as he clamped his mouth shut.

"Gayl?" he spluttered when the shock had passed. "What in Godith's name . . . ?" He looked at the sky and wished he hadn't. Grendel was arriving fast.

She banged down, issuing a screech so piercing it made poor Grymric's teeth vibrate. His precious leaf collection was immediately scattered; it was soon raining herbs all over the cave.

Gabrial had never seen Grendel so enraged. She looked ready to carve him open.

"It was an accident," he said, wisely stepping back. "She surprised me, that's all."

Grendel punched a fireball out of her nostrils. It burst in a weak flare against his chest. He backed away again, careful not to growl.

"Why did you call her?"

"I didn't. She followed me."

"Are you planning to send her away as well? Are you going to give Gayl to another of your *dark wyng*?"

"No!"

He shied away as more fire flowed from her snout.

"Grendel, he meant no harm," cried Grymric. "Not to Gayl, anyway." He placed his isoscele between them, urging calm.

Grendel retracted her fangs and turned to the healer. "How much has he told you?"

"Some details. Not all. Things I don't understand and probably shouldn't be a party to. Listen to me, both of you. This is a dangerous course you're on. If one of you is openly defying the Prime and you cannot find kindness between yourselves, what hope do we have for the future of the Wearle? I beg you to be of one heart. Gabrial, you cannot move this man. His wounds are bad and his body is not repairing well. One of his arms has withered. I don't know how to help him. But I'm certain of one thing: Physical upheaval will be too much for him to take."

Gabrial turned his back on them both and quickly walked over to Rolan. The fire flickered almost to nothing as he said, "I promised Gus I would kill him if nothing could be done."

"No," said Grymric. "He may be Hom, but he's in my care. I can't just stand here and see him slain."

"Then let me take him. I tell you, Grynt is coming."

"You know I can't allow that either."

"Then it has to be death." The blue raised his isoscele.

"STOP!"

The male dragons looked warily at Grendel. Her bitterness had morphed into a glare so imperious that Gossana herself would have bent a knee. "There is another way." She turned to Grymric. "Do you have an herb that can make him seem dead? So that he won't feel any pain?"

"There are certain . . . supplements," Grymric said. He felt his throat pinch. "But feeding anything to him is difficult, and I could only guess at the dosages. The Hom body is not like ours. It takes time for herbs to work and—"

"We don't have time," Gabrial cut in, continually checking the sky for roamers.

"A poultice?" asked Grendel.

Grymric shook his head.

"Then he's doomed," she said bluntly. Her face grew serious. "Very well. Do what you have to, Gabrial. But hear me well: My threat still stands. Gayl, come away."

All through this conversation, the wearmyss had been at Rolan's side, sniffing the body as if she'd like to sink her fangs deep into it. Grendel was on the cusp of calling her again, when out of nowhere Grymric said, "Cold flame might do it, though it could just as easily finish him off. Why, Grendel? What were you thinking?"

She turned her head suddenly and looked at the sky.

"They're coming," said Gabrial, his battle stigs rising. In the distance, still quite small, three roamers were flying in an arrow-shaped formation on course for the cave.

"Do it," said Grendel, flicking back her head. She looked harshly at the blue. "Cool him. Quickly. Then kill the fire and get to the rear of the cave."

"Why? What—?"

"Just DO IT, Gabrial—and don't start anything!"

14

Although he had no idea what Grendel was planning, Gabrial bundled Gayl out of the way and did as Grendel had instructed. Cold flame was a peculiar anomaly that all dragons knew how to produce. It was really nothing more than a fast exhalation of icy breath, called a flame because it colored the air blue as it streamed from the nostrils. Gabrial ran it all over Rolan, choosing only to miss the exposed face. The man looked gaunt enough without the need to have the warmth frozen out of his expression. When it was done, Rolan looked little different, though his skin had changed to a pale shade of yellow and crack lines were forming in the joints of his toes. The rise and fall of his chest could no longer be seen.

Gabrial backed away into the shadows, allowing Grendel close to the body. Before he could stop her, she had raised her isoscele and with one swoop cut off the withered arm. The stark ferocity of the act stunned Gabrial to the core. But all he could do was retreat into the shadows. The first roamer had landed. In the flurry of its entrance, Grendel calmly bent down and whispered an instruction into Gayl's ear. Then she drew a measured breath and turned to the front of the cave again, where Grymric was already speaking.

"What's the meaning of this?" he demanded, though the words came out as a shaky squeak.

The roamer, a large purple dragon with dark golden eyes and rows of blue studs along his robust jaw, closed down his wings and strode purposefully forward. The other two perched where space would allow, just outside on the lip of the cave mouth.

"My name is Garrison, subcommander to the Prime. I am here on his orders. The Hom prisoner is to come with me." He bowed as Grendel came into view. She raised her head to tower over Grymric, even though they were of similar size.

Grymric began with a sigh. "The Hom prisoner—"

"Is dead," Grendel cut in. "You are welcome to what's left of him, though I doubt that Prime Grynt will find it particularly . . . appetizing."

She looked down to her left. Gayl emerged from the shadow of her mother's tail, the severed arm dangling from either side of her jaws. She opened them and snapped them shut again, to catch the arm better between her small fangs. A bone crunched. A sorry chunk of limp flesh separated off.

Garrison dilated his nostrils a little, trying not to show any sign of disgust. "By order of the Elders, I would remind you that eating of Hom is forbidden."

"Only while they're alive," said Grendel.

The commander made a sound that resembled a huff. His eye ridges shrank a fraction. He held Grendel's stare for another moment, then bent his head toward the arm. A slightly imprudent move at best. Gayl's warning hiss was so intense that Grymric gave a start and one of the guards outside lost his grip on his perch. He flapped wildly to regain his hold while the other barked a scornful reprimand at him.

Garrison was somewhat less startled. He drew back his head, casting a repugnant glare at Gayl. "I must see the remains, to know they are genuine."

That surprised Grendel. She hadn't expected to be challenged. Here, for once, was a dragon who was *thorough*. His persistence was almost admirable. Keeping her composure, she said, "Are you asking me or my wearling to vomit?"

The scales around Garrison's throat showed a slight blush of green. "If I do not have proof to take to Prime Grynt . . ."

"Proof?" snarled Grendel. *"Proof?"*

To her right, Grymric shuddered. The young matrial was sounding more like Gossana with every breath.

"Are you accusing me of deception?" she growled. "When my wearlings are both officially Named, I will be the queen of this colony. You would do well to remember that, Commander."

Garrison bowed, his expression impenitent. He took a pace back, his head so low it almost scraped the ground. His resolve, though damaged, was not entirely crushed. "I can scent a male dragon elsewhere in this cave."

"That's . . . Gabrial," Grymric jumped in. "He came to me with an injury. I've given him something to make him sleep."

"Injury?" That sparked fresh interest from Garrison.

"Some minor wing damage. A clumsy accident . . . apparently."

"Accident?" said Garrison.

Grymric did his best not to gape. Why did it always fall to him to defend the dubious activities of others? "I could wake him if . . . ?"

The bluff hung in the air for what seemed like an age, until Garrison finally twisted his snout and, still looking pointedly at Grendel, said, "Thank you, healer. That won't be necessary." He glanced down at Gayl and back again at Grendel. "You might like to teach her that it's better to pin her prey to the ground and rip it."

Gayl was gnawing the arm as if she'd like to swallow it whole.

To help her cause, the hand dropped off. Grendel swept it into Garrison's feet. "Thank you for your valuable insight. Take the hand as proof to Grynt. Your duty here is done."

Garrison gave a nod so faint that the dust motes between them barely moved. He gathered up the hand and quickly departed, calling the two guards after him.

Moments later, Gabrial emerged from the shadows. The first thing he heard was Grendel ordering Gayl to drop the arm. The wearling at first refused, but proved no match for her mother's stare. Glumly, she put the arm down.

Grendel thumped it out into the sky. "Let the crows have that," she said, wrapping her tail around Gayl briefly. "You will never eat Hom flesh again."

Graark, went Gayl, spitting a shred of dead skin. It wasn't clear if she had understood the ruling or not.

"Grymric, you need to see this," Gabrial said urgently. He was standing over Rolan again. Barring the loss of the arm there was no real change in Rolan's body. But in the pale blue light of Gabrial's gaze, something was glittering on the man's face.

"Is that . . . a *fire tear*?" Grymric gasped.

"If it is, then he really is dead," Gabrial whispered. He looked up at Grendel. "The cold was too much."

"Then burn him," she said. "If Garrison comes back, there must be nothing left."

"But that's dragon auma flowing out of him," said Grymric, still mesmerized by the tear. "I've never seen anything quite so extraordinary."

"Gayl, NO!" Gabrial cried suddenly.

Too late. Gayl had stepped up to Rolan's face and casually licked the tear off. It was gone in a gulp. The wearmyss wrinkled her snout and idly walked away.

"What does that mean for her?" Gabrial said in a panic. "Grymric, what has she taken in—dragon or Hom?"

"I . . . I don't know," said the healer. He opened and closed his mouth several times. He looked worriedly at Grendel. "I don't know," he repeated. "Possibly both."

"Then the Hom lives on in our wearling," she said. She stared at Rolan's face, committing it to memory. "What's done is done. Burn the body. Grynt can find another way to get to Ren."

15

"A hand?!"

Prime Grynt's rush of fury had turned his face the same purple as Garrison's chest.

"I asked you to bring me the complete man, not a *sample* of him!"

Garrison raised his head. "I attempted to. Grymric and the matrial claimed he had died."

"Matrial? Grendel was there?"

"With her female wearling, yes. She—the matrial—had allowed the wearling to feast on the body. I brought a small part of what was left."

"You saw the remains?"

"An arm, nothing more."

"Idiot! How do you know he was dead? How do you even know the arm came from that Hom?"

Garrison lowered his gaze. "Why would a dragon of my rank challenge the word of a queen-elect?"

"So you might execute the orders of your PRIME!" The force of Grynt's reprimand carried a storm of hot dust across the cave. He turned away, blowing short bursts of steam. "Grendel can never be queen. Her wearlings are adopted. She's not worthy of that title."

Garrison's expression suggested otherwise. "The matrial is greatly admired for her commitment to Grystina's line."

"What's that supposed to mean?"

Garrison stared dead ahead. "I merely say what I hear. The Wearle still mourns Grystina's death."

Grynt gave a derisive grunt. "Well, hear this and hear it well. *I* give the orders to the Wearle, not Grendel. Was the blue with her?"

"Yes. Sleeping."

"Did you check?"

"No."

"Did you listen for his *snoring*?"

Garrison sighed quietly. "No."

"Then how do you know he was ASLEEP?!" Grynt kicked a rock against the wall in frustration. "What's the matter with the dragons in this colony? I chose you to be my commander on the ground because I believed you were intelligent! Garodor himself put your name forward. Yet you've been misled by a bumbling healer and a female barely old enough to shed her birth scales. And her wearmyss!"

"Matrial Grendel is very astute," said Garrison, struggling to keep his voice level. "I was chasing my isoscele from the moment I engaged her in conversation."

"Astute," Grynt repeated with a scornful hiss. "Gossana's right. They're plotting against me. That blue is dangerous."

Garrison tapped his claws together. "With respect, I

think you're mistaken. I have heard no rumors of a conspiracy. Gabrial is highly thought of since the goyle attacks. But there is no indication that the roamers look to him to be their leader. I would know of it. I swear the Wearle is loyal to you."

Grynt gave another contemptuous snort. He circled around to Garrison's other side. "Earlier today, Gabrial and a roamer called Gus slaughtered the last two Veng in the colony, claiming they'd acted in self-defense."

That froze Garrison's breath. "The Veng are *dead*? That's how Gabrial was injured?"

"Well, he didn't roll off his settle in his sleep!"

Garrison's eyes darted in thought. "Where is Gus now?"

"Across the sea, if you believe the blue's account."

"But that's an unmapped area. We've no idea if there's land within reach."

"Then he'll return," snarled Grynt. "And when he does, he'll be dealt with. Severely. In the meantime, you are going to obey your orders and bring me this BOY. You know the Hom settlement beyond the scorch line?"

"Yes. I was there once with Veng Commander Gallen."

"Good. The Hom are a scourge. I want them destroyed."

"Destroyed? Is that wise?" Garrison looked up in shock. "I was in the forest when the boy laid down his terms. If we harm his people—"

"You think Graven will *rise*?" Grynt said scornfully.

Garrison turned his face away.

"Go to the settlement and flatten their dwellings. Drive them out. Kill any that resist. No, wait—spare just one." Grynt hardened his stare to a point. "Gallen spoke of the boy's mother in his final report. A wild woman. Do you recall her?"

Garrison nodded. "She was the one who struck Gallen and was injured."

"Good. Find her and bring her to me—all of her."

And with one last snort, he pressed his foot against Rolan's hand and crushed it.

16

Gossana's plan to get proof of Gabrial's deceit was simple. She would ignore the blue and his arrogant "queen" and concentrate on the idiot, Gruder, instead. It would be an easy task to intercept him along his sweep of the domayne, force him to the ground, and glamor him. Ruthlessly. There were few things more enjoyable than watching a feeble mind give up its secrets. His confession was really just . . . a glare away.

The obvious place to wait for him was on the headland where the Veng had been killed, thereby fulfilling Grynt's order in the process. But Gossana cared nothing for the sier pent class (or orders, for that matter). She cared even less to see their bodies torn apart and bathed in blood, carrion birds squabbling over them like wearlings, scraping at the scales for the flesh beneath.

So she headed out toward the scorch line instead, on a shallow trajectory that glided her over the sprawling forest where the Veng commander, Gallen, had met his end.

In less than twenty wingbeats, she was at the line. It was quiet. Not even a sheep was grazing. She cast her gaze both ways, extending her optical triggers to their maximum. No sunlight had broken the cloud for days, but she could see through the overcast well enough.

No sign or scent of Gruder yet.

But something interesting did prick her nostrils: Hom blood, relatively fresh.

In the flatlands beyond the last slope of the hills lay the small Hom settlement where the upstart, Ren Whitehair, and his irritating tribe of accomplices had come from. Until this day, Gossana had never ventured beyond the central hub of the colony. She took no interest in the mappers' reports of the "features" that lay beyond the mountains. Endless fields. More clusters of trees. Deep valleys. The occasional river. A tremendous profusion of fauna and flora. *Fauna*. What a ridiculous word. These natural "wonders" bored the matrial. The quickest route home to the flame-carved labyrinths of old Ki:mera was all she truly cared about. Open landscapes baffled her.

Yet, for want of some amusement, and to satisfy her glint of curiosity, she decided to follow the scent of the blood. In a matter of moments, she saw a Hom body. It was lying on the hillside, just the wrong side of the scorch line. A male, she thought, though it was hard to tell; the body had been quite badly . . . mangled.

She circled once, before landing a few strides away from the corpse. Still no sign of that idiot sweeper. Any self-respecting Hom could have been halfway to Vargos by now.

But not this Hom. It really was a mess. A starving wearling wouldn't leave its prey this badly damaged. Which begged the question, what had done this? And why had it been left on the wrong side of the line? Was it supposed to be some kind of *taunt*?

She poked an open wound with a claw. The jab disturbed a cradle of flies. They swarmed around her head like angry rain. She snorted and flashed her tail at them, barely harming a single fly, bar one that managed to buzz up a nostril and was vaporized the instant she blew it out.

Issuing an angry growl, she picked up the body and hurled it well back into Hom territory. It landed with a juicy splat.

Near to another.

Gossana adjusted her optical triggers. No doubt about it. Two bodies, not one. *Pah, what of it?* she asked herself. What did she care that two Hom were soaking into the hill?

Curious all the same. What were those bodies *doing* there?

With a furious huff, she took to the air and went to investigate.

That was when she saw a third body. It too was lying on open ground, as far distant again as the first two bodies had lain apart. Then she saw a fourth. And another ahead of that. Someone (or some *thing*) had laid a trail of death on the ground. And Gossana, for whatever reason, followed it. It would lead her to a place she would never otherwise have dreamed of visiting.

The home of the Kaal.

The Hom settlement.

17

Not once did it cross the matrial's mind that following the trail could be a dangerous endeavor, or indeed a trap. She was aware that the arrogant boy, Ren Whitehair, had threatened the Wearle with swift retaliation if the dragons refused to let the Kaal roam freely across their land. But even with all Ren's dubious tricks, what could a bunch of poorly armed men do against a dragon of her power?

She glided stealthily over the encampment. It was nothing more than a tightly grouped knot of round-shaped dwellings. To her surprise, every one was discolored by burning, all the roofs opened up like sores. Yet there was no activity. Barring the straggle of bodies to the scorch line, she could see no Hom.

Thinking they had seen her coming and were hiding, she dropped low and swept over the settlement at speed, building up a rolling downdraft of turbulence. Dwellings leaned. Dust clouds billowed. An old wooden water trough somersaulted noisily across the clearing. Gossana herself squealed loud enough to make a Hom ear bleed. But no Hom came running in terror from their homes.

In frustration, she landed. The ground felt unusually lush underfoot, but she paid no real heed to it. Instead, she swaggered into the clearing, blowing fire from each nostril in turn, lighting up threads of thatch in the air.

Some kind of Hom was here, she could smell it. A more animalistic scent than she remembered, but close enough to their revolting sweat to make her nostrils contract in disgust. Compared to dragons, all species stank. But if she could *scent* a presence, why couldn't she *see* it?

Finally, something did appear, but it was like no Hom Gossana had previously encountered. It had the same basic shape as a man, but was smaller, crouched, much rounder in the shoulders. It wore no robe and had a stringy tail that it held in a half curl away from its body. Its upper limbs were limp and long. The legs were so bowed it was a wonder it could stand. Yet the body was lithe, the feet and hands both powerfully clawed. It was covered in a skin of smooth brown hair.

"Turn," Gossana snorted, though she doubted the beast would comprehend. It was facing away from her, its head part-hidden in a shale of dust.

But it did hear. And it did turn. And when the dust cleared and she saw its face, her misplaced bravado quickly deserted her.

Attached to its head was the upper part of the skull of a dragon. Scraps of dead tissue were clinging to its crevices, blood smears lining the dark eye sockets. One of the fluted nostrils was broken, the other plugged with leaves and dirt. A more unsettling sight Gossana had never seen. But what disturbed her most about this grisly apparition was that she recognized the basic shape. For this was no ordinary dragon skull. It was long front to back and could have been easily mistaken for a female. But the tooth pattern gave it away. The fangs were greater in number than most dragons would possess and arranged in a double row toward the front. The skull had come from a Veng-class beast.

Gossana suspected it was Gallen.

She backed off, roaring fire at the thing, carpeting the ground between them in flame. Two things happened as a result. The creature unexpectedly jumped—higher and quicker than she could have predicted, using its tail to bounce off the erth. At the same time, she heard a great scream of pain and the ground she had flamed came alive. A whole host of creatures similar to the skull wearer split away from her with fire running up their backs. She saw one of them fall as a leg was consumed. The creature gurgled low in its chest and opened a pair of poky brown eyes. It died making a chattering sound, revealing a row of square-shaped teeth that seemed too big for its blunt-nosed face.

A victory for Gossana, but momentary at best. The creatures were soon swarming over her, skipping up her tail and covering her back as lightly as a breeze. She reared and shook most of them off, stamping out one that landed by her feet. It burst like an overripe berry, the wet shell of its body gumming to her claws. She used it to slap the next assailant, almost taking its head off its shoulders.

They went for her wings, but she was wise to that. One vigorous flap saw most of them thrown. Those that clung on began to rip at her sails or gnaw down the joints with their powerful teeth. One of them seemed to be poking her ear. She blazed in anger and tried to fly, but so much ballast had destabilized her shape. She fell awkwardly on to her back, kicking like a wearling on its first failed attempt at takeoff.

And then, just as all seemed lost, terror raged down from the sky. Grynt's commander, Garrison, swooped on the settlement, flaming the land all around Gossana. Five, maybe six creatures died in his fireball, melting in an orange river of ruin. On his second pass, he snatched two creatures off her back, crushing them as easily as she had stamped one flat. He let their blood rain over the clearing before dropping what was left of them back to the ground. The creatures fled in ripples after that, no match for a dragon in flight. As Gossana righted herself, two more dropped off her back. She dispatched them with a swipe of her tail so vicious that both were cut through at waist height.

Garrison slammed down next to her. "Matrial, are you hurt?"

"Of course I'm hurt!" she roared. Several sections of her wings were in tatters and the left side wasn't folding as it should. One leg had been badly chewed. Around the back of her head, her famous sawfin array was cracked.

"Can you fly?"

"Yes, yes," she said irritably. She twitched and shook herself. Her right ear was throbbing.

"What are you doing here?" He sounded annoyed with her and was making no real attempt to hide it.

"There were bodies," she snapped. "A trail of Hom. All the way to the scorch line."

"I didn't see them," he muttered. But he had approached the settlement from another direction and could have easily missed them. "A trail? They baited you?"

When she didn't answer, he turned his attention to the dead around him. "What are these creatures?" He rolled one over, puzzled by the general hairiness of it. Eyes close together and darkly round, a hooded bone structure protecting the eyes, a wide mouth almost plucked of hair, a tiny flattened nose. It resembled a Hom with his face punched in.

"How should I know?" she griped. "They came for me when I landed. They were hiding on the erth—in the erth—I don't know."

Garrison studied the creatures again. He could see how they might blend subtly with the land. But to lose themselves in dirt and not be readily detected by a dragon? That made them a significant threat. "I give thanks to Godith that I arrived when I did."

"I don't need males to fight my battles," Gossana carped. "And if you dare speak informally to me again, I'll be picking my teeth with your severed claws. Why are *you* here, anyway? You don't look like a sweeper."

"I've been sent to take a Hom woman hostage. Have you seen any Hom—other than bodies?"

"No," she said brusquely. She twitched again. Her ear was prickling deep inside the void. A revolting trail of slime was running through half her head, it seemed.

Garrison looked around him, recording an i:mage of the abandoned dwellings. "Perhaps the creatures drove the Hom out." He felt a small sense of relief at that. He had no regard for the Hom, but it troubled him that any dragon, especially a Prime, should want to wipe out an entire colony of intelligent beings. "No matter. My duty is to you now. I must protect you and guide you back to safety."

"I suppose so," she grumbled, still unable to bring herself to offer any gratitude.

"When you're able to, please fly ahead," he said. "I'll— Wait. What's that?"

"What's what?" she huffed.

He walked a few paces, kicked a body aside, and picked up the skull. "This is Veng." He almost dropped the skull in shock.

Gossana wriggled her ears again. What had these disgusting creatures done to her head?

"This is from Gallen," Garrison muttered. "But that would mean the creatures have crossed the line and been in the forest."

"I don't care if they've been to Cantorus and back," Gossana railed, swiping at one of the dead for good measure. "Just do your duty and escort me back to Vargos."

"Yes," he said, more attentive to her now. "You must see the healer. Many scales are broken."

"I don't need that idiot's herbs." She winced as she tested her wings, twisting her neck as far as it would turn. There was a soreness in her back, somewhere forward of her wings.

Garrison approached at a courteous pace and looked over the ridge scales that ran up her spine, zooming his gaze so he wouldn't have to touch her. He didn't like what he saw. The creatures had torn some scales clean off and stabbed the soft tissue underneath. Green blood trails were flowing down her sides. "They've ripped a patch off your lower neck," he reported. "There's something in the skin crust. A dart made from wood. It looks deep and the angle is shallow. I'm not sure I should attempt to remove it. The healer—"

"Oh, just pull it out!" she snapped. "I can't be squirming all the way back to the mountains."

"It may be painful. I'll have to use my teeth."

The dart's shaft had splintered in the skirmish. But even a wearling, with their small claws, would have had difficulty getting a purchase on it.

Gossana took a breath. "Just do it," she hissed.

And so Garrison leaned forward and carefully placed his jaws around the dart. Thankfully, the shaft was stout enough not to split against his fangs. He closed his eyes tight and pulled, successfully releasing the dart.

Gossana burst forward as soon as it was done. "At last. Now get me away from this stinking place." She tested her wings again. They were shot with holes, but she had enough resistance to be able to lift.

Garrison spat out the dart. "Let me sear the wound." It was a common service offered during battle if a dragon couldn't cauterize an injury themselves.

"Don't be ridiculous," Gossana said proudly. "It's a scratch, that's all."

"But, Matrial—?"

Too late. She was in the air before he could reason with her.

He spat again, to be rid of something foul on his tongue. Only then did he dare to glance at the dart. The tip was barbed and glowing.

It had scratched Gossana's skin all right.

But a scratch was all it took to leave a trace of poison inside a body.

18

When Garrison arrived to give his report, he again had to endure the Prime dragon's wrath. The commander had returned without a hostage and brought news of another threat to the Wearle. None of this sat well with Grynt. But on this occasion, his anger was transmuted into clear and decisive orders.

"Send word around the colony that all roamers, including any mappers beyond the scorch line, are to be recalled to the inner domayne."

Garrison nodded. "I'll see to it immediately."

"Wait. How many sweepers are patrolling the line?"

"Two, since the goyle attacks."

"Double it to four. Concentrate them in the area where Gossana was ambushed. Then assemble a wyng of fighting dragons, as many as you think you need, and take them to that forest."

Garrison looked up.

"Burn it," said Grynt, his words condensing on the air.

"The whole forest?"

"All of it. Every twig. I want the scent of that place stinging my nostrils by nightfall. Let's flush these creatures out."

"But we don't know for certain they came from the forest. We've never seen them on any of our territories before and—"

"BURN IT!" Grynt roared. "Or it will be your skull they'll be taking next. Do I make myself clear, Commander?"

Garrison gave a solemn nod. "May I say something else?"

Grynt glared at him impatiently.

"I have concerns about Elder Gossana. She was wounded by a creature's dart."

"Then she'll mend. What of it?"

"I believe the dart was poisoned. In my opinion, she should speak to healer Grymric. I tried to persuade her to go to him as we flew in. She refused."

"That is her right. Gossana needs no instruction from you."

"Of course." He tipped his snout. "But the injury was deep and already festering. When I left her at her cave, she was giddy and talking in occasional riddles. She shakes her head wildly as if the poison has gone to her brain. I'm not sure she's in control of herself."

Grynt sighed and drummed his claws. "How old are you?"

"Thirty-two at the next orbit of Cantorus."

"Exactly," said Grynt. "A mere wearling in comparison to Elder Gossana, who has lived through one ancestral war and borne four young who have gone on to build some of the sturdiest bloodlines on Ki:mera. You think a dragon like that can't cope with a scratch from some long-haired Hom?"

Garrison tipped his snout again. "I do not wish to denigrate the Matrial's lineage or underrate her personal strengths. But the Hom are sly and this . . . tribe was clever enough to trap her. How can we be certain their poisons won't harm her? Healer Grymric has studied the flora of this world and may know—"

"Enough," snapped Grynt. "Gossana's no fool. She will rest for as long as she needs to and let her restorative powers do their work. If you're that concerned, send Grymric to her, not the other way around. Send Grendel too. If either of them object, say I've ordered them to stay together for their own safety until we've investigated this new breed of Hom. You'd better post a guard. Well? What are you waiting for?"

"One more question: Why was Elder Gossana at the scorch line?"

"I have no idea," Grynt said tiredly. "Now go."

Garrison left immediately, plotting a course for Gabrial's eyrie high on Mount Vargos. There he found Grendel pacing the cave mouth, restlessly swishing her elegant tail.

"What do you want?" she said as he landed. Her words were quick but not aggressive.

Garrison gathered in his wings but didn't sit. An indication he would not be staying long. "I bring orders from the Prime. You are to join Elder Gossana at her eyrie."

"And why would I do that?"

"Earlier today, the matrial was attacked by a strange breed of Hom. I fear she's been poisoned."

"What?" Grendel immediately stopped pacing.

"Prime Grynt would like you to attend her while we investigate. Is Gabrial here?"

"No, he's with Grymric."

"Ah, yes." Garrison recalled their earlier meeting.

"Why? What do you want with Gabrial?"

"I need him for my wyng."

Grendel stared across the misted mountains. "Fighting's not an option for Gabrial right now. Besides, he's injured."

Garrison nodded quietly. Somewhere in the space between those sentences lay a truth not yet spoken, he thought. "Not badly injured, if I remember. I'm sure a dragon as sturdy as Gabrial won't let a nick get in the way of his duty—especially when he hears the Wearle is under threat."

And with that he exited, setting a course for Grymric's cave.

19

The healer was not exactly pleased to see him.

"What does Grynt want now?" Grymric's voice, like his body shape, radiated anxiety. It was sometimes said that whenever Grymric spoke it was as if he was trying to fend off disaster. And so it was now. "If you've come back looking for proof of the prisoner, we burned his remains to ash."

"I'm not here about your Hom." Garrison dropped his wings to a close. "I bring a message from the Prime. You are required at Elder Gossana's eyrie."

Grymric fought off a twitch above one eye. Only dragons with a death wish called on Gossana. "Why? What's the matter with her?"

"I believe she has a fever."

Gabrial emerged from the back of the cave. "Fever? How so?"

Garrison held the blue's gaze for a moment before addressing Grymric again. "A word of warning: She's slightly delirious. She might not be entirely . . . welcoming."

"Is she ever?" the healer chuntered. He fussed about the cave for a while, gathering herbs with which to treat a fever. Then, poking his head between the two much larger dragons, he said, "I may be old, but I'm not a fool. I want no part of whatever's going on. Gabrial, you need at least another day before you do anything you might . . . regret."

And with a shuffle and a huff, Grymric left them to it.

"Well?" said Gabrial, repositioning himself in the open space to Garrison's left. "You haven't come here to talk about Gossana."

"Actually, I have," the commander replied. "But that can wait for a moment. Please, lower your isoscele. I'm not here to challenge you. Surely you've done enough fighting for one day?" He squinted at Gabrial's injured wing. "Clumsy accident you had—though I suppose such things are to be expected if you cross the path of the Veng."

Gabrial glanced outside, half wondering if they were truly alone. "Is this an interrogation?"

"No. Though I'd like to know what really happened on those cliffs. I share a common lineage with Gus. It pains me to hear him accused of crimes against the Wearle. I don't believe for one moment he struck without cause."

"He didn't. The Veng threatened Gariffred."

Garrison nodded. "And is it true that Gus fled?"

"Not exactly. He was happy to accept the blame and leave. He took the girl, Pine Onetooth, with him."

"Why?"

"She healed his injuries."

"How?"

"Flowers. Magicks. I don't really know."

Garrison wrinkled his snout in thought. "Are you planning to join them—when you're mended?"

The blue dragon stiffened his jaw. "That would be an act of treason, Commander."

Garrison stretched an idle claw. "Leaving the Wearle of your own free will, even if others join you in peace, is no violation of our laws. No one can stop you going across that sea. But the Veng slayings do complicate matters. When news of that incident spreads, the colony will suspect you of challenging Grynt's leadership, no matter how much you try to deny it. Even if your loyalty to Grynt were shown, the problem of Gus will not go away. The idea of being a fugitive will prey on his mind. It will eventually draw him back to the mountains to settle any score he thinks he has. I can prevent that happening."

"Isn't it your duty to bring him to justice?"

Garrison gave a self-contained *hmph.* "These are difficult times, Gabrial. Traitors. Mutants. The shadow of Graven lurking over the colony. We need unity. Understanding. Strength. That's not what I'm seeing from Grynt or Gossana."

"Are you suggesting a dark wyng should overthrow them?"

"No . . . but if things *were* to get out of control, I want to know I have your support."

"Why me?"

"You're the queen's guardian, and the key to securing peace with the Hom. The roamers are fearful of the boy's threat. If any dragon can settle the Wearle, it's you."

Gabrial flicked his isoscele, first one way then the other. "Why should I trust a dragon who answers directly to the Prime?"

Garrison peered outside for a moment. The gloom that seemed to have been gluing the world together was now at its dullest. Even the fog that normally hung in the vales had retreated from the brooding pressure of the sky. The grayness was crushing everything it touched. "Right now, I should be burning down the forest that lies near the scorch line, slaughtering countless innocent species and making a terrible scar upon the land. Instead, I find myself sitting here, trying to secure an alliance with you. I'm prepared to fight anything that would harm us, Gabrial. And mark me well, that includes the Hom. But by the grace of Godith, I cannot bring myself to inflict needless destruction on a world as full of beauty as this."

"Then why has Grynt ordered it?"

"Something is lurking in or near those trees."

Garrison explained in detail what had happened at the settlement.

The first word to come out of Gabrial's mouth was "Hairy?"

"Like Hom, but more agile. They have a sad look about them."

"Why would they attack us?"

"That is still to be determined."

"Do we know their numbers?"

"No. We can't even be certain they populate the forest."

"Then how did they get Gallen's skull?"

"I assume they came to the burn site and took it. What I find odd is that none of the sweepers, you included, has ever reported seeing these creatures."

"Could they have come from farther out?"

"Possibly. We need to be wary of them. When I arrived at the settlement, many of the creatures were invisible to me. When I questioned Gossana about it, she said they were hiding in the erth. How, I cannot say. Grynt has asked me to double the sweeper patrols and call back the mappers, but I think we should be more active than that. Tomorrow, when you're fit, I want to take a wyng and explore the whole area around the Hom settlement."

Gabrial blew a long line of smoke. Talk of the settlement had made him think again about Ren's whereabouts. Surely, if the settlement was under threat, the boy would go to the aid of the Kaal? His mother, Mell, was still there, after all. "What about the forest? Will you defy Grynt's order?"

Garrison glanced outside. "I can't burn a forest while its trees are wet."

Gabrial switched his gaze to the cave mouth.

The dark Erth skies had heard Garrison's anguish.

It had started to snow.

20

The snow came down suddenly, as if the weight of gray had proved too much and the sky had no choice but to shatter its debris over the land. Flakes as large as tertiary scales set fast where they fell, repelling the threat of any warm surface. All that melted was the color of the land. White became the new silhouette. Snow redrew the contours of the mountains.

"I must go," said Garrison, poking his long snout into the flurries. "Grynt will see this and modify his orders. I need to know what he's planning. Will you think on what I've said?"

The blue gave a silent nod.

"This world has much to offer us," said Garrison. "One day, Grendel and your wearlings will rule it. I trust you and I will stand proudly beside them. For my part, the bond begins now."

With that, he touched his isoscele to his breast, then launched away smoothly from the cave, punching a temporary hole in the storm before the flakes closed in to shield him from view.

He did not, however, go straight to Prime Grynt, but elected instead to trace a path around the bulky northern face of Mount Vargos and stop off at Gossana's eyrie. He touched down in a drift to one side of her cave, cupping his wings to stabilize his landing. The snow was already deep enough to trudge through. He nodded at a jaded guard who was huddled on a tapering settle near the entrance. The guard shuddered in response, loosening a dusting of snow off his shoulders. The only parts of him visible were his dark green head and thick black claws. He looked like an over-large wearling about to break out of an over-large egg.

The eyrie was crowded. Grendel and Gayl were there, and Grymric was just inside the cave mouth. He appeared to be waiting for the storm to abate.

"How is she?" Garrison asked.

Grymric looked anxiously behind him. Gossana could be seen by the light of a fire. The old matrial was lying on her belly with her head stretched flat to the floor. Her intimidating eyes were firmly closed. "You should have told me she'd been darted," said the healer. "Her limbs have been weakened by poison. Grendel has sung her into a sleep."

"Can you help her?"

Grymric looked into the stippled white sky, counting falling flakes for a moment. "I've treated the wound, but the dart was not the problem. Shortly after Grendel began to sing, Gossana started raking one side of her head just behind the ear. Look closely and you'll see fresh cuts. If Grendel's song hadn't calmed her down, I think she could have sliced her neck wide open. It's one of the most unsettling sights I've ever had the misfortune to witness."

"There was a problem with her ear," Garrison said, focusing his gaze on the wounds Grymric spoke of. "She complained about it twice before we took off."

"Did the creatures do anything to her?"

"I don't know."

"Then we can only watch her and wait. There's nothing more I can do. But make no mistake, her condition is serious. I fear for her life. The Prime must be informed."

At that moment, Grendel came forward. "Oh, the dour commander again."

Garrison bowed politely. "I came to inquire after Gossana. The Prime will be pleased with your efforts to calm her."

"Hmph," went Grendel, blowing an unintentional smoke ring. "Grymric tells me you've been talking to Gabrial?"

Garrison gave a slight nod. "Like me, he's concerned about the new Hom threat. I've asked him to join my wyng when he's ready. Where is Gariffred, by the way? I see the wearmyss is with you, but not—"

"He's asleep, in the eyrie," Grendel said curtly.

"Unguarded?"

Grendel narrowed her eyes. "The drake's snores would drive away a whole wyng of goyles. Anyway, I suspect Gabrial has returned to the settle by now."

Garrison gave a faint bow.

He left quickly after that, instructing Grymric to keep him informed.

And then he did go back and report to Grynt.

The Prime dragon, who seemed to be living in a perma-nent state of thwarted fury, laid out more orders. "The snow won't last forever. As soon as it melts, you light those trees."

Garrison found himself praying for a lengthy winter. "And in the meantime?"

"Organize patrols to watch the domayne. The creatures can't move without leaving a trail."

"And Gossana? The healer fears for her."

That did seem to cripple Grynt's rage. "She'll recover," he said with a grumpy sniff, and he retired to the back of his cave.

21

To the amazement of all concerned, by the next day, Gossana *had* recovered. When Grendel awoke the following morning, she was startled to see the older matrial standing over her, eyeing Gayl. The wearmyss was still asleep at that point, neatly wrapped up in her mother's tail. It needed two requests from Grendel for Gossana to draw back. Only then did Grendel nudge the youngster awake.

Gayl wandered to the back of the cave to defecate. Meanwhile, Grendel rose up and said to Gossana, "You're well. That's good."

Gossana flicked her head as if she hadn't quite heard or understood. Her slanted eyes followed Gayl into the shadows.

"What is it?" said Grendel, blocking the wearling from Gossana's sight. Her gaze flickered forward, gathering up the light. Snow was still falling. The guard's breath was blowing across the cave mouth. For some reason, Grendel found that comforting.

"It was talking," Gossana said, shaking her head as if the cold had gotten to her.

"It?" said Grendel. "Do you mean Gayl?"

"Hom words," Gossana said, snarling lightly. She stepped away swishing her tail.

Grendel furrowed her brow slightly, making the dew on her ridges fizz. She thought back to the incident with Rolan's "fire tear." Was Gayl speaking Hom a result of that? "We all growl in our sleep," she said. "Gayl spent some time with the girl we were holding. She learned some Hom words from her, no doubt."

"They hunger," said Gossana, clearly not listening.

Grendel shook her head in confusion. *They?* Was Gossana talking about wearlings? They always "hungered." It reminded Grendel that Gayl hadn't eaten for the best part of a day. A fact the youngster would soon start to make plain.

At that moment, she heard a flutter of wings and saw Grymric speaking with the guard. The healer came in. He too looked stunned to see Gossana on her feet, even if the matrial's famously harsh eyes had greeted his arrival with a swift change of color.

"Well, well. This is a welcome . . ." He was going to say *surprise* but thought better of it. "Matrial, may I ask how you're feeling?"

Gossana gave a violent twitch. She thumped her tail and looked again at Gayl. The wearling had wandered to her mother's side and was, as predicted, calling to be fed.

"Grendel?" said the healer, making signs toward Gossana.

"Confused," Grendel whispered, putting her head close to his.

He nodded. "But physically improved."

"Apparently."

"Feed," said Gossana, making Grymric jump.

"Yes, yes," he called. "I'm sure the roamers will bring something soon." It was routine, when dragons were being protected, for others to hunt on their behalf.

But Grendel, who had never liked the practice, didn't want to be listening to a baying wearling on top of having to deal with Gossana's odd behavior. A hefty mouthful of succulent meat might hasten the matrial's recovery, she thought. Or at least shut her up for a while. And so she said to Grymric, "While you're assessing her, I'm going out."

"What? Where?"

"Only to hunt."

"Is that wise? Will the guard allow it?"

"I'm the queen-elect, Grymric; I make my own decisions. I'm here to help with Gossana's recovery, not because I feel threatened. I don't need Grynt's protection." She bared her impressive fangs. "I'm not going far."

And before the healer could protest any further, Grendel was at the front of the cave. There followed a short-lived exchange with the guard. Then, with a *whup* of her wings, she was away, unaware that Gossana had watched her exit with the sort of precision that bordered on obsession.

Grymric, however, had noticed the look and felt a long shiver of fear run through him. There was something not right about that stare. It was almost as if Gossana wasn't there and something *alien* was looking through her eyes.

"Matrial, may I examine you?"

He stepped into her space, bowing politely as she rose up.

He could never have seen the blow coming. She hit him so hard with the side of her tail that he spat two fangs through his upper lip. He slumped over, making no sound. The thud of his body against the rock was glossed away by a whistle of wind.

It was Gayl who alerted the guard. Her screech brought him clumping into the cave mouth. He stood perplexed for a moment. But as he twisted his neck to look at Grymric, Gossana plunged her isoscele into his throat and screwed it hard to be sure of ripping the breath right out of him. His eyes froze. The snow clinging to his breast flowered green. Gossana withdrew her isoscele. The guard wobbled once and tipped over the mountainside, helped by a push from Gossana's tail.

She immediately looked for Gayl.

But the wearmyss was already gone.

Gayl had launched herself into the open sky, her small, inexperienced wings bravely battling the frigid snow and the crosswind driving it in grueling swirls. She was strong, but not as strong as Gossana. When a set of firm claws grasped her underbelly, Gayl must have been briefly relieved. But there was no gentleness in that grip. No attempt to support her against the storm. Gossana had followed her into the blizzard and was already rising away from the mountains with Gayl as her captive.

"Mam-maaa!" the wearling wailed.

But all she heard was Gossana's strange voice.

"They hunger," the matrial said again as she beat a path toward the forest.

And together, they disappeared into the white beyond.

Part Three
The Islands

22

Given the tenderness of his age, Gariffred was a powerful flyer. He had needed Gus's help to rise to a suitable cruising height, but once "launched" on a level course, he was clever with the wind and the updrafts of air coming off the sea. Yet, the farther from the mountains they went, the more Gus realized the wearling's prowess would be of little benefit. The sun had dropped low enough to kiss the horizon and was spreading its light across a body of water that refused to reveal any place to land.

It was time to make a critical decision.

If he chose to take the drake between his claws, Gus knew they could still turn around and reach the domayne under cover of the night. He could end this bold "adventure" right here. Conflict and shame awaited him in the mountains, but was that any worse than the agonies of guilt and responsibility that were weighing heavy on his hearts right now? He had placed his absolute trust in Pine, hoping the girl would lead them somewhere. From the outset, she'd seemed certain land would come. *There! That way! Turn, skaler! Turn!* Her spirited directions had spurred him on. But the risk of failure was growing too great. He dared not ignore the drake's needs any longer. They must turn back, before the ocean claimed them all.

He swept over Gariffred and told the young dragon to close his wings.

The drake flapped on, wheezing audibly through his spiracles. His will to keep going was admirable to watch, but his upstrokes were falling short of their best. Suddenly, he missed a beat on one side and dropped through the cloud layer, out of control. He flapped hard to avoid going into a spin, but that moment of panic had sapped his reserves. With a tired *gra-ark*, he dropped his wings. Gus was quickly in position to clamp him. The big dragon immediately soared higher, praising the youngster for flying so far, unaided. The drake certainly had Astrian auma in his blood.

Meanwhile, Pine was shouting again. *There, skaler! There!*

Where? Gus could see nothing but open sky.

He felt Pine twist her body and got the impression she was looking around. At the same moment, something small and colorful flashed across his vision. More important, a line of light, like the opening to a fire star, seemed to ripple the air in front of him. For an instant, he froze, as if time itself had stopped momentarily. Then he was bursting forward again, flying at speed with all his sensory awareness intact. Gariffred was firmly in his grasp; Pine was still riding on his shoulders.

But all around them the world had changed.

The sky claimed his attention first. The rush of air through his spiracles was warm and pure, free of the clogging microspores he was constantly filtering out in the mountains.

It tasted sweeter on his tongue and had a thinner composition, but it was breathable and seemed to want to work with his body in a way he had never experienced before. He felt a renewed strength in his wings and thought them a little less cumbersome to lift. Every stig on his head pinged taut, while his optical triggers whirred with the sort of pinpoint accuracy that wearlings enjoyed when they first saw sunlight. Even his tired old scales began to recharge themselves in fresh clean patterns, enhancing the dormant purple in his system, buried underneath the dominant green.

But the strangest sensation was in his fire sacs. The change of atmosphere had made their membranes quiver. It was almost as if the air flowing through them was keen to cause a minor ignition, to learn how that part of a dragon worked.

And now he noticed the sky was *orange*—a pale reflection of the water below, which had lost its opaque density and was flowing clear and shallow to a bottom.

And in the water, there was land. Lots of land, in island clusters. Wherever Gus looked, he saw dabs of green melting into the distance. Every shape the eye could invent. Plump bays and twisting river inlets nibbled at the intricate array of coastlines. Most, but not all, were heavily wooded.

From above, each isle appeared quite flat. But as Gus descended and panned his gaze wider, the islands spooled up out of the ocean to show themselves at varying heights. He swept over the first, scanning for any signs of life. He saw and scented no animal auma, not even on the open patches of green. The only feature that caught his eye was an area of crusted orange stone. It appeared to be ordinary bedrock, pocked by a network of odd-shaped holes. Here and there, stones were stacked in chaotic layers, forming high towers that listed so badly they must have been held together by faith. One of them rocked as Gus swept by.

He chose his landing site with care, dropping Gariffred by a pool of water on a stretch of land where the ground was level. There was a catchment where long-leaved plants with speckled red fruits sprouting fresh from their cores were growing around the edge of the pool. "Eat nothing," he said to Gariffred, bending his body so that Pine could slip easily off his back. Then he flew to the nearest, highest point—a huge, unnatural arc of stone that looked like a giant bone stuck in the ground.

"Girl, what is this place?"

"I know not."

She dipped her hand into the pool from which Gariffred was drinking. The water sparkled bright and clear in her palm. Gus gave a start when he saw the drake glugging. But the wearling was suffering no ill effects, and after a flight like that, he needed water more than he needed caution.

"You must know," Gus continued. "You were the one who led us here."

Pine glanced out to sea. "Nay, skaler. The islands spoke. They drew us here."

Gus sighed heavily. *The islands spoke.* This was no time for stupid Hom games. He looked around for dangers, his big broad nostrils sifting messages wrapped in the breeze. Something small and warm-blooded was near. Something lively that could make its way at speed. In and out of these holes, perhaps? He trained his gaze on the nearest run of rocks. "How did we come upon this place so suddenly?"

Pine knelt beside Gariffred and picked a white flower with a bold orange center. "There was a slit," she said.

"Slit?" he repeated.

"A line between worlds."

Gus tightened his claws and thought about the flash he'd seen. For some reason, his mind was trying to tell him that a brightly colored *bird* had crossed his path. His second heart stuttered. The air immediately swept into his nostrils, found his beating center, and calmed it. "We passed through a fire star?"

"Nay, skaler. We passed through a *slit.* The Fathers of my tribe knew the lines well—and the spirits that commanded them. In the days before now, they used them often."

Gus snorted in disbelief. Slits? Spirits? The girl had lost her mind.

He stared at the uniform orange sky, lit by no sun he could see. None of this was making sense. Every fire star he had ever passed through left a trace when it opened or closed. The sky here had healed in an instant.

For the first time, it struck him that they could be lost.

Pine stood up with a small cache of flowers. She wiped one hand down the side of her robe. "They know," she said.

It took Gus a moment to realize her gaze had settled behind him. He swept around awkwardly, dislodging crystals of stone off the arc. And there was the source of the scent he'd detected.

Popping their heads out of every other hole were a bunch of nervous, brown-eyed creatures. They were so like the orange rock in color they could have been natural extensions of it. Gus was stunned. The beasts resembled dragons in every way, but dragons stripped of all traces of ferocity. Their eyes were so appealing he couldn't bring himself to raise a roar, let alone spout a line of flame. His mouth fell open and the creatures all dipped back into their holes, frightened, no doubt, by the sight of his fangs.

He flew to the ground to stand beside Pine. She scolded him for scaring the creatures off. But one by one, they popped up again. Following a little chatter between them, one creature, about twice the size of Gariffred, climbed out and settled on a chunk of stone. Gus was naturally wary, but the creature posed little threat. Its tail possessed no isoscele. Its feeble claws could serve no purpose other than to help it scratch or climb. Likewise, the wings were less sturdy than a dragon's and almost transparent. And all that differentiated this individual from most of its companions was a set of white frills around its ears. Gus thought it might be a female.

Pine clicked her fingers, trying to encourage the creature to her.

It crouched low and began to creep forward. But as Pine reached out to stroke its snout, Gus flipped his tail across her chest and said, "Wait. What are these beasts?"

"Dragonkind," she sighed. "What else?"

That's what Gus intended to discover. If they *were* of dragon origin, these things, they ought to know his words. He repeated the question for them, applying force to his words but finding it strangely difficult to growl.

What are you? We? What are we? What?

The words bobbed between the heads in a form of dragon-tongue far less guttural than any dragon would have used. But the creatures had grasped the sense of the question.

The brave one sat up and bowed. "We are Worvonn," it said.

That was how it sounded to Gus, anyway.

"War-*Veng*?" he said in reply, trying to put a meaningful slant on it, even if it did offend his tongue to mention the foul sier pents again.

He need not have worried; Pine had heard it right.

"Nay," she tutted. "Blow the dust from your skaler ears and listen." She wriggled clear of his tail and stretched out a hand. The "beast" nuzzled it gently. "The creature calls itself 'Wyvern.'"

23

Wyvern. The name ran well off the tongue, but it still meant nothing to Gus. He had never heard of such a creature. No per had taught him that a species like this could even exist. He wondered what the Elders of Ki:mera would make of it. The De:allus would be blowing their scales with excitement. But to any normal dragon, the beast was a weird anomaly. A glitch in Godith's magnificent design. It was pleasant to look at, but a mutant all the same. A distortion of nature.

A freak.

By now, more Wyvern were out of their holes. Initially, they were all as cautious as the first. But when Gus allowed Gariffred forward, they clustered around the drake in total wonder. They wanted to touch his perfect scales. And see his powerful claws extend. Most of all, they wanted to hear his voice. His gentle *graarks!* caused much delight. One creature broke a fruit from its stalk and offered it to Gariffred, nodding to say he should take it. Gus had other ideas. "No!" he barked, making the Wyvern scuttle back. One or two flew to the stone pillars, to settle on top to watch. The fruit bearer looked puzzled. It sniffed the fruit and expressed its confusion to the others on the ground. Then they all did a very odd thing. They rose up on their hind legs and looked at the sky.

Instantly, a breeze swept over them, making their delicate ears vibrate. Whatever was in that breath of wind seemed to determine their next course of action. The Wyvern with the fruit quickly stripped it of its peel, unwrapping a capsule of soft orange berries. It bit the capsule in half and swallowed as many berries as it could, licking off several that stuck to its jaw. Then all the Wyvern picked a fruit and offered it up—not just to Gariffred, but to Gus and Pine as well.

Pine took one gratefully. She peeled it, ate it, and licked her one tooth clean of its juice. Gus refused the fruits he was offered on the grounds that "real" dragons only ate meat, but he did let Gariffred take one. The Wyvern with the white frills came to help. "Like this," it said, showing Gariffred how to peel it. Gus watched the drake snap his jaws around the fruit (sending berries everywhere) and found himself praying that the wearling would not turn Wyvern orange. What kind of color was that for a dragon? Grendel would never forgive him.

His thoughts began to turn to more practical matters. When it came to it, what *was* he going to eat? He could survive without a kill for many days, but it was preferable not to for a dragon of his size. And where would be safe for the drake to shelter? He'd seen no caves among the rocks he'd scanned. The Wyvern clearly liked their holes and no doubt Gariffred would like them too, though Gus could not allow the drake to go down them; anything might lie inside those tunnels. All of this begged a far bigger question: *What exactly were they going to do here?* Fascinating as the islands were, Gus couldn't conceive of a less likely environment for a Wearle to inhabit. Where were the ledges, the caves, the mountains? No dragon could settle in a place where it did not feel it owned the sky. That sent a painful jolt to his hearts, and another when he recognized what the jolt meant. He had glimpsed a miserable future. One in which his only prospect was loneliness.

"Who is your Prime?" he asked, floating his gaze across the whole troop. Was there a system of command, he wondered? Hierarchy? Bloodlines? Enemies? Guardians? Who controlled this colony? Most of the creatures were now happily going about their business, which seemed to involve collecting more stones to add to the pillars.

"Who leads you?" he asked, rephrasing the question. The word *Prime* had seemed to confuse the Wyvern.

"We have no leader," one replied.

"No leader," said another.

"We are what we are," another joined in.

"We are Wyvern," they chattered.

Gus rolled his shoulders. Well, at least he'd sparked some interest.

"What are *you*?" said the one with the white around its ears. Gus was certain now that this was a female. She came up close and stroked his tail.

"I am dragon," he said in a low rumble.

The frequency of sound just made her head wobble. She twizzled her ears and appeared to be confused. Her eyes turned a curious shade of green. "No," she said.

No? Gus snorted hotly, making the Wyvern wings flutter. Some held them out for another blast. They seemed to like the flow of warm air.

"We know dargon," she said. "You are not dargon."

Dargon? Was this mutant mocking him now?

Pine sauntered up. "Look, skaler. The Wyvern like flowers!" She had a garland around her neck, made from the many types of flower head the Wyvern had brought to her.

"Forget flowers," he said. And at last, he managed a minor growl. The sky seemed to darken a little in response, as if a small cloud had chosen to shade him.

Pine sighed and put a hand on a Wyvern snout. "Do not listen to the skaler. He is old. His bones creak."

"Skaler," they said, happily sharing the word among them. "He is skaler."

"No!" Gus repeated, loud enough to make the colony cower. "I am DRAGON!"

So hard to shout. It would have been easier to push a stone between his teeth. What was happening here? He looked at the sky as though it were his enemy.

All the Wyvern looked up too.

Another breeze swept over them, slightly stronger than the last.

"You must come with us," the female said.

"Where to?" said Gus.

"We will take you to the dargon."

"Dargon?" said Pine, jumping in before Gus could chew off his tongue. "Did you hear the skaler right? His name is Gus. He is DRAGON, not dargon."

Again, the Wyvern looked at the sky.

"We understand," they said. "L'wen-Gar was mistaken."

They all stared at the female Wyvern. She, L'wen-Gar, wiggled the ear that had (apparently) done the mishearing.

"He is DRAGON," said the group.

Pine nodded, pleased they'd gotten it right, if only to stop Gus stomping on something.

But the confusion was not quite over yet. "He is dragon; the dargon is dargon," they said.

Gus blew an exasperated sigh.

But Pine was deeply curious now. "The dargon is on this world?" she asked.

"Aye," they said, making her laugh. They were learning her words and using them. She liked that.

"And you would take us to it?"

"AYE, PINE!"

She clapped her hands lightly.

"Where is this 'dargon' creature?" snarled Gus. He glared at Pine, faintly disgusted by her easy acceptance of their familiarity. He also checked quickly on Gariffred. The drake was still eating fruit and paying no real attention to the argument.

The Wyvern looked at one another and reached a decision. One of them said, "L'wen-Gar will lead you."

And they parted to make a pathway for Gus.

A pathway that led to the arc of stone.

24

L'wen-Gar flew the short distance to the arc, where she waited in front of it for someone to join her. Pine removed her garland of flowers and declared herself ready. L'wen-Gar opened her wings and flew through the space.

She disappeared in a shimmer of light.

"WAIT!" Gus bellowed.

The Wyvern community leaned back like blades of grass in the wind.

Pine dropped her shoulders. "You tire me, skaler. What now?"

"It may be dangerous."

She looked at the arc. "'Tis a portal, surely?"

And that division of the sky was a slit, thought Gus. *And look where that brought us.* "We don't know what's on the other side." There was grass and erth and sky beyond the arc, but that was clearly not where it led.

"Then I would go through it and see," Pine huffed.

"It might be a trap."

Pine opened her hands. "Why would these creatures bring harm on us?"

Why would they not? Gus had heard many sobering tales

of Wearles being attacked in places they had tried to colonize. Why should these islands be any different?

He was about to inflict this wisdom on Pine when L'wen-Gar fluttered back through the arc armed with nothing but a puzzled expression.

"See?" said Pine. She kissed her fingers and patted Gariffred, then walked through the arc with L'wen-Gar at her side. Gariffred graarked in shock when Pine shimmered out of sight. Even Gus could feel his primary heart thumping. If the girl did not return . . .

But she did. At least, part of her did. An arm came through the arc in midair and a finger on the end of it beckoned them forward.

Gus rumbled quietly and told Gariffred to stay close.

Together, the dragons went through the portal.

Gus had raised his entire array of battle stigs in case they met danger on the other side, but all they found was more of what they'd left behind. Flowers, fruits, another large arc. The landmarks were very different, however, particularly out at sea.

"This is a different island," Gus muttered.

Pine tutted loudly. Of course it was! You didn't go through a portal and not expect change.

"Why couldn't we fly to this place?" Gus asked.

"We have traveled far," L'wen-Gar said. "Our wings are not strong enough to fly here."

Gus could understand that. He'd noticed from the start that the Wyvern wings were almost stunted, useless for anything but fluttering, really.

"The arcs take us anywhere we wish to go."

And yet the light has stayed the same, thought Gus. Again, he wondered where this world hid its sun. He cast his gaze around. "Where is the dargon creature you speak of?"

"Not here," said the Wyvern.

Gus looked hard at Pine. Was this a trap after all?

Pine raised a hand for calm. "Then why did L'wen-Gar bring us to this island?"

"So the dragon will not fear the power of the arc."

Gus immediately broadened his chest. "I fear nothing," he rumbled, pushing his snout so close to L'wen-Gar she was forced to squeeze down to nearly half her size.

"Oaf! Don't fright her!" Pine complained, kicking him in the belly (for all the good it did). "She means to show you the portal is safe, no more!"

But L'wen-Gar, to her credit, had not tried to run. Her eyes widened and she rolled them skyward again. A breeze came over her, rustling her wings as she spoke back to Gus. "The Aether says you fear yourself, dragon. You fear your power. You have . . . killed."

Gus pulled away slowly. Somewhere deep inside, he was trembling. "Aether?" His gaze blazed across the sky.

Pine rested her hand on L'wen-Gar's back. "Gus will not harm you. Yes, he has killed—to protect the little one. But dragons oft speak louder than their size. Pay the beast no heed."

Although she looked grateful for Pine's advice, L'wen-Gar pulled in her snout and whispered, "There is more. He fears the dargon."

"What?" said Gus, snapping back into the conversation. "How can I fear what I've yet to see?"

"The Aether is never wrong," said the Wyvern.

"Take us," said Pine. "Through this arc here." She walked to it. It was much like the one they had just come through, the same rough size, constructed from stone. "We would see this dargon the Aether speaks of. Show us, L'wen-Gar."

The Wyvern nodded. "It rests high, in a cavern."

Gus raised an eye ridge. So there *were* caves here.

"Many of us attend it," she said.

"Do you serve it?" said Pine. "Is the dargon your master?"

"We have no master," L'wen-Gar replied.

Except the mysterious Aether, thought Gus, glancing at the sky again.

"The dargon is sick," L'wen-Gar said.

"What ails it?" asked Pine.

"We do not know. We wish to heal it, but we cannot. It is dying."

"You have flowers," Pine said. "Leaves. They cure."

L'wen-Gar shook her head. "The darkness is too great."

"Darkness? What darkness?" Gus turned his head. Words of that texture made his scales lock down.

"The darkness that binds it in misery," said the Wyvern.

There was silence then. Gus swallowed hard. One thing he hoped he'd left behind in the mountains was the disturbing rumblings about Graven rising. What if the dark one was hiding here, ready to launch an attack on the Wearle?

"Take us to it," Pine said bravely.

"No," said Gus. "I won't put Gariffred in danger."

He glanced down at the drake. Gariffred was switching his gaze among the three of them, largely immune to what was being said.

Pine turned to L'wen-Gar again. "Is there an island where the wearling will be safe?"

"I'm not leaving him," Gus snorted.

Pine crossed her arms and sighed. "Then stay and eat fruit, if you fear this thing so." Tossing her hair off her shoulders, she swept toward the arc with L'wen-Gar at her side.

"Wait," Gus said tiredly.

Pine put a hand on L'wen-Gar's shoulder.

"All right. The drake can stay. But if anything happens to him, I'll, I'll . . ." Why couldn't he say it? *I'll slay them all.*

Pine got the point. She repeated her earlier question to L'wen-Gar.

The Wyvern replied, "All the islands are safe, Pine Onetooth. I will call others to play with the Gariffred."

She dipped her head into the nearest hole and made a whistling sound. Moments later, another group of Wyvern had surrounded the drake, looking as awed as the last lot Gus had seen.

"They will take him undererth," L'wen-Gar said.

"Into the holes?" Gus didn't like the sound of that.

But the drake was gone before he could argue.

Gus turned and studied the arc. On any other terrain, he would have marked this point so he might find it again with ease. He recorded an i:mage, but with no celestial object to orient by, coming back was going to be difficult—by flight anyway.

He was still grumbling about it as they shimmered through the space and came upon a very different tract of land. Here, at last, was some height. L'wen-Gar had brought them to a rocky plateau opposite a compact gathering of trees. Rising out of the trees was a mound of stone. To call it a mountain would have been an injustice. To Gus, it resembled a giant row of teeth all fused sideways into one. From left to right, each "tooth" stood a little higher than the last. Every peak was bluntly rounded, except the one nearest the end, which sported a solitary spike. The rock itself was old and predictably orange. Gus could almost hear the different strata groaning. The whole row was marked with clefts and fissures where water had worn the stone away. Gus saw the cave L'wen-Gar had spoken of before she could point it out. A black hollow punched into the hard edifice, wide enough to admit a large dragon.

Punched was genuinely how it looked. The cave was just below the treeline, and only visible from here because the trees in front had been broken down. Something had crashed through the tops at speed, likely aiming for the cave and the shelter it might bring.

Pine, when she saw it, leapt to the wrong conclusion for once. "There must be a skaler in there," she whispered.

But Gus knew otherwise. "That's no dragon," he growled. And though the sky continued to work against him, he lit a small spark in his fire sacs and bared every fang and claw he possessed. His battle stigs rose again. Blood powered into his giant wings. "I can smell it," he snarled. His fearsome nostrils doubled in size, their linings ready for the stream of heat.

"Smell what?" said Pine as he rose for takeoff.

"Goyle," he said. "I smell *goyle*."

25

The slap of Gus's wings was like the crack of thunder. L'wen-Gar, who was already shying from the sound, was nearly blown off the plateau as the roamer launched. Pine, more used to the rolling surge of a dragon propelling itself into the air, had chased up to Gus and screamed at him to wait. He couldn't hear her, and wouldn't have obeyed if he had. He had fought against goyles in the mountains, seen dragons killed and maimed by them. Rumor had it they were the agents of Graven, and the sworn enemy of the Wearle. He was going to that cave no matter what. He was going to kill the "dargon."

Pine was lucky to get on to his back. She jumped for the nearest leg as he rose and only just made it, nimble as she was. He inadvertently helped her by pulling up the leg as he would for flight, but she still had a dangerous climb to his shoulders. She was twice nearly crushed as his wings beat down. By the time she had reached her "riding" position, seated between his largest ridge scales, she was in no mood for his bellicose behavior.

"STOP, SKALER! THINK!" She tugged at one of his primary stigs.

"Do that again and you'll die," he warned her. "It's a long way down from here, *One-Fang*."

He twisted the stig and sent her sliding. Cussing in a manner that would make the sky blush, she kicked herself upright and scrambled back into position. "STOP!" She beat a fist on the back of his head. It had no more impact than a small hailstorm.

He dipped suddenly, making her stomach vault. He was just above tree level now, blowing away the top layers of leaves as he hurtled over them. He was closing on the cave at frightening speed. Pine was terrified he might plunge, blazing, through the hole and they would both be consumed in a back draft of fire. But at the very last moment, he flipped his wings and turned away, issuing a warlike scream. He was calling the goyle to come out and fight.

Once again, Pine tried to reason with him. "STOP, SKALER! WE DON'T KNOW IT'S A GOYLE!"

"It is," he said. His olfactic glands were not misleading him. He swept around, giving out another scream.

Pine looked down as they banked. A few Wyvern were standing on the short patch of rubble that sat like a bib around the cave mouth. More were spilling out of the hole and fluttering away like seeds on the wind. All were wide-eyed with terror.

"THEN WHY DOES IT NOT ATTACK THE WYVERN? THEY ATTEND IT, BUT IT DOES NOT HARM THEM. WHY?"

"I don't know!" Gus growled. He sucked a huge pocket of air into his throat and flung his head from side to side.

Again, Pine had to work to hold on. "WHAT AILS YOU?"

"My FIRE! I have no FIRE! This world has stolen it!"

He circled and began another descent. She could see he was planning to land this time. Fire or no fire, he was going to storm in and challenge whatever lay in that cave. She saw one last chance to halt his aggression.

"IF THIS WORLD HAS TAKEN YOUR FIRE, IT MUST HAVE TAKEN THE GOYLE'S ALSO!"

Rendering both a little less dangerous, she hoped.

But Gus had an easy answer to that. "A goyle does not *have* fire."

With a thump, he landed on the threshold of the cave, sending loose stones racking down the hill.

Pine closed her eyes, recalling the battles she had seen above the settlement. Gus was right. The goyles relied on a vile spit that burned like fire and ate away flesh. In that sense, the thing might have an advantage.

"Get off me. *Now.*" Gus's claws were fully out.

"Aye," she said, knowing exactly what she had to do.

She stood up tall, ran the length of his snout, and jumped.

Into the cave she went, still running. At every step, she could hear Gus calling her back. But she needed to get to the goyle before he did.

She did not have to travel far. The cave was larger than it looked from outside and was lit by a multitude of glowing flutterflies. They were present in every notch of stone. And there, taking up most of the floor, was the beast the Kaal had called a darkeye. A hideous black monster, half the size of Gus, with a scale-free body and stigs like branches cut from a tree cursed by evil. To see a living one this close made Pine catch her breath. Its eyes were like mud shaken up in water; no light shined from their fixed black cores.

But L'wen-Gar was right. The beast was dying. It barely had the strength to raise its head. When it saw what stood before it—a plain Hom girl—it put its head down again and groaned.

"I know what you are," she panted in dragontongue. She put a hand on her bloodstained robe. Not many days since, she had been invaded by the auma of a "goyle" and would have died if Ren had not come to her aid. She was free of the darkness now, but the memories of it lingered in her sleep. She looked over her shoulder. Gus was closing in with menace in his hearts. Even without its fire, an irate dragon was a herald of death.

"There is a dragon coming to kill you," she said. "I can help you, but you must—"

Too late, Gus was there.

"Stand away!" he bellowed.

"NO!" Pine whipped around to face him, spreading her arms in a gesture of protection.

Gus lifted his isoscele. It was straining him to twist it into a position from which he might land a decisive blow. But in truth, all he really needed to do was drop that weight on the sick creature's head to knock any life force out of it.

He swung the heavy isoscele forward.

"NO!" Pine screamed again.

And on that word, the cave light faded.

Every flutterfly had shut off its glow.

Pine gasped. Panic seized her heart. Suddenly, she found herself in total darkness, between two creatures capable of the most dreadful malevolence. Could the goyle see Gus? She wasn't sure. But any moment now, the inborn light from the dragon's eyes would give Gus enough shine to mount an attack. And surely after this he wouldn't hesitate.

She heard him snort. He was confused and unnerved. But in the end, it was the sound the darkeye made that turned out to be the most frightening of all.

"Gurrrsss," it cried. A stressed gurgle from a damaged throat.

Gurrrsss. Gurrrsss. The cry echoed all around the cave.

Pine counted her breaths. Shaking, she turned. There was something about that noise. Something . . . "Again," she panted.

"Gurrrsss," the thing said.

Behind her, the dragon growled.

Pine gulped; the light from his eyes was coming.

"Say 'dragon,'" she blurted.

The darkeye opened its mouth a fraction. The needle fangs, so deadly in battle, glinted weakly in Gus's light. "Darrrgon," it said.

"Dargon," Pine whispered. She whipped around to face Gus. "Harken, skaler. The creature knows it is dragon, but labors to say it. It knows you also. It speaks your name. Gurrrsss. Gurrsss. It *knows* you. GUS."

Before he could react, she knelt beside the "dargon" and asked it one more question. "You were dragon once. How were you named?"

It gagged as though it might spit bile.

Pine bravely held her position. She stilled her shaking fingers and laid a hand on its blunted snout. "Tell me," she said, with gentleness.

"Gaarrrnunn," it hissed, writhing away from her act of kindness.

"No," Gus said, shuffling back. His tail anxiously swept the floor. "No, it can't be. No. No. No."

"Garnun," said Pine, angry now that Gus was retreating. "You know this name, don't you? It pricks your ears true. Tell me, skaler. Who is Garnun?"

Gus's face was a sea of distress. Despite the lack of light, Pine could see his color draining.

"Tell me," she demanded. She had never seen a dragon look so shocked.

Gus shuddered from nose to tail. "Not Garnun," he said. "It's trying to say Garon."

The darkeye let out a faint moan.

"Garon?" Pine repeated.

"A dragon from the first Wearle," the roamer stuttered. "His name is Garon. He's Gabrial's father."

26

A moment of deep, deep silence passed.

By the end of it, the flutterflies were glowing again and Gus had lost his appetite for killing; he was already stomping out of the cave.

Pine took one more look at the goyle, then jumped up and hurried after Gus.

By the time she'd caught up, he had dropped to his haunches outside the cave mouth, his jeweled eyes staring at everything and nothing.

"Tell me," Pine said. "I would know about Garon."

Gus shook his head.

"Tell me, you lump!"

She hit him to jolt him out of his slump. But she had tested his patience once too often and he roared back, knocking her down to the ground, his face just a muggy breath away from hers.

"Go on, eat me," she taunted him. "I pray to the Fathers my bones rip your throat!"

He squeezed his claws into her robe for a moment. Then, with a snort that nearly blew her one tooth out, he released her and pulled away.

Pine breathed in relief. That was a little closer than she cared for. She stood up, shaking grit off her robe. Gus's sweat was clinging to her hair. "Was he noble?"

"Who?"

"Garon!" she tutted.

"There is no *Garon*. The goyle took his auma. It has to die."

"You would offend your friend Gabrial by slaying his father?"

"If Gabrial were here, he'd kill that thing himself. It's a mutant. A servant of Graven. It's evil."

Pine walked around and put herself in front of him. "I know about goyles."

"You know nothing, girl."

"I do," she insisted. "I was slain and reborn with the auma of a goyle. It can be conquered. Ren Whitehair knew."

"Ren Whitehair is an enemy of the Wearle."

"As are you—but I do not stand here in judgment of you, skaler."

He growled in frustration and looked away.

Again, she put herself directly in his eyeline. "Your loyalty to the Wearle is no slight on me. I know you would fly with them again if you could. Help this beast. It was one of you once. If we save it, your honor can be restored."

By now, L'wen-Gar had crossed the valley to be with them. All around, the Wyvern were quietly returning, slipping past Gus to go into the cave. He thought he could hear them singing to the goyle. Singing! In the presence of something that vile.

Pine sat on a rock and explained to L'wen-Gar: "The creature you call 'dargon' was once dragon, like Gus. In this form, he calls it by another name: 'goyle.' But its true name is Garon. Garon is father to a dragon called Gabrial. Gabrial, likeways, is guardian and father to the little one, Gariffred."

"Then, the dargon is a great-father," L'wen-Gar said.

"Yes," said Pine. She felt Gus wince. This was painful for the roamer to hear. "Garon was changed into the shape he is now because he ate the blood of an evil black dragon. The blood was cast in rock and Garon did not know what he was doing. He did not know that darkness would befall him. Until then, his auma was pure."

That brought an angry snort from Gus. "How would you know? How can a mere Hom girl know anything about a dragon like Garon?"

"Because I have ears," Pine said curtly. She looped her hair behind them as if to prove it. "When I was held in Gabrial's cave, I would hear the blue wake from sleep sometimes, vexed by unsweet dreams about his father. He would speak them in frightened whispers to Grendel. I learned that Garon was kind of heart, yet as brave as any skaler could be. There lay the core of Gabrial's terror. When he learned what had happened to his father's Wearle, he wanted to believe that Garon had died fighting goyles. The fear that his father might have turned into a mutant would always wake him. Here, in this cave, is the truth of it."

"A truth he must never learn," said Gus. "I'm telling you, girl, that beast must die."

"The Aether will not allow killing," said L'wen-Gar.

Gus tightened his jaw. "I want my fire restored."

"Let her be," said Pine. "Can't you see the Aether is displeased?" A dark orange cloud was hovering over Gus. "There is no badness in this world. Aught that would threaten it is swiftly tamed. You have no fire, the goyle has no spit. You must learn to be at peace with that."

"How can you talk of peace," Gus railed, "when that thing in there is writhing in torment? The fact it speaks its name is no comfort to me. If badness is not allowed in this world, why is Garon still sick? If the auma of the goyle can be tamed, why haven't they crushed the evil out of it?"

"We have tried," said L'wen-Gar, gazing at the sky. "With Pine Onetooth's help, we will try again."

"You know a way?" asked Pine.

"Perhaps," said the Wyvern. She pointed at the bite marks on Pine's hand.

Until that moment, Pine had given little thought to her wound. Now, for the first time, she looked at the marks and wondered at their unusual pattern. What had been a gooey mess had quickly healed into three clear lines that ran in parallel waves across her palm. Gus looked at the pattern and grunted scornfully. *Gayl should be taught to bite harder*, he growled; any competent dragon would have taken Pine's hand off.

But Pine was intrigued. "This means something to you?"

L'wen-Gar nodded. "There is a place we know where the stars align thus."

Pine clicked her tongue in thought. "You must lead us to it. The dargon also."

"What?" Gus almost splintered a nostril. "You want to *move* it? How?"

Pine glanced at his huge, strong feet.

"No," he snorted, backing up. "The only way I'll put my claws on a goyle is to tear it into tiny pieces."

"The Aether will not—"

"I know!" he snapped. He looked furiously at Pine. "This is madness. I want Gariffred brought to me. Now."

"And then?"

Gus rose to his full height. "We find that slit and go back. I can't stay in a world where I can't burn evil—and neither will he."

Pine did her best to scowl. Realizing the Aether would not approve, she apologized silently, then turned to L'wen-Gar and said, "Bring the little one to us. We will wait here for you."

L'wen-Gar nodded, glad to be away. She disappeared down a hole, leaving Gus to vent his anger on Pine. "This is not going to happen, girl. The wearling is mine to protect. If you stand in my way, I will . . ." Still the words of violence would not come. In frustration, he swept his tail across the ground, almost catching a Wyvern that had popped up from a hole to see what all the fuss was about. "How can you ask me to aid a beast whose kin slew one Wearle and many of another?"

"You must learn to forgive," she said, holding her nerve in the face of his snarls.

He turned on her again, generating just enough heat to make her flinch. "Dragons do not forgive their mortal enemies."

"Then dragons are no better than goyles!" she hit back. "Garon is fighting the darkness within. Why would you let it take him when there may be a way to heal his pain?"

"You really expect that fiend to regenerate just because we show it *mercy*?"

"My heart begs me to try," she said. "Look into my eyes and answer me this: If you were in his place and he in yours, would Garon have tried all ways to save you?"

A good argument. One that ran a spike through Gus's breast. While the question pecked at his brain, Gariffred popped up out of a hole. "I can't put the drake in danger," Gus growled, but his tone was gentler now.

Pine stroked her hand over Gariffred's head. "I swear on the souls of the Fathers of the Kaal, no harm will be done to the drake."

Gus snorted quietly. There was nothing of meaning in that vow. What dragon would put its trust in the spirits of the Hom?

Nevertheless, he admired the girl's faith. He sighed and gave a reluctant nod.

"Gus will bring the dargon out," Pine said to L'wen-Gar. "Will you guide us to the place of stars?"

"We must wait for night," the Wyvern said, nodding. "Until then, rest."

27

In time, night fell as it usually did with a slow shift from light into darkness. Yet there was no hint of a setting sun. It made Gus wonder how the island world worked. Where did its gentle warmth come from? What turned its sky this strange shade of orange? What *was* the mysterious Aether?

He was dreaming on these things, when Pine tapped his shoulder. They were still by the entrance to Garon's cave, which was lit by the glow from the flutterflies and the few faint stars that had blossomed above. The Wyvern choir was still in voice.

Pine's touch made him snort and her draw back. A dragon's waking breath was not the most pleasant of odors.

"Come, skaler. It's time."

Gus rose sluggishly and looked around him. The Wyvern were awake and active. Their gauzy wings glowed in the dark, making it easy to pick them out. To his surprise, their eyes shined a pale shade of blue, not unlike his in dim conditions. "Where's Gariffred?" he asked. Panic gripped his hearts when he realized the drake was not among the Wyvern, a feeling that grew a magnitude worse when Pine said casually, "In the cave with—"

"WHAT?!"

Gus exploded past her, scattering the Wyvern that had gathered around the entrance. To his relief, he found Gariffred at the first bend of rock. L'wen-Gar and two of her kind were with him. The drake was unharmed, but his eyes had a forlorn look about them. Gus immediately knew what it meant.

"Has he seen it?"

L'wen-Gar gave a wary nod.

Pine hurried up. She wrapped an arm across Gariffred's back. With her shoulders set firm, she faced the big roamer. "I showed him the goyle so he would know what it is—who it is."

Gus rumbled like a bruised volcano. But the deed was done, the drake unharmed. There was nought to be gained by taking Pine's head off. He checked his anger and pushed her away. "Wait for me outside."

Pine wisely said no more. She guided Gariffred into the night, leaving Gus to do what he must.

Gus took a breath to steady his nerves. No per on Ki:mera had ever given counsel on a situation as challenging as this. He prayed it would not be a false endeavor.

Battle stigs bristling, he moved cautiously into the cave, into the chamber where the creature lay. Every wall was lit by flutterflies. Garon was awake and making shadows, clearly aware that something was happening.

Gus laid his isoscele over his breast. He took another deep breath and spoke. "My name is Gus. I was born of the line Karnayen. I fly with your noble son, Gabrial. You have my word on his trust that I mean you no harm. I am to take you to a place where you might be healed. But first I must bring you out of this cave. It may cause some discomfort. I beg you, do not resist."

With that, he put his jaws around Garon's neck and began to drag him toward the exit. Brutal, perhaps, but the only way. There wasn't room in the cave to lift him. And Garon was too weak to crawl.

At the very first contact, the goyle in Garon began to fight back, writhing and thrashing as best it could remember and the Aether would allow. The barbed tail rapped Gus more than once, but failed to leave a single cut.

Once outside, all opposition faded. Garon merely gave an exhausted groan as Gus let go of him to turn and reposition. For one heartrending moment, the goyle's blank eyes set their sights on Gariffred. The wearling crunched his claws into a ball, but his soulful *graark* suggested he had seen through those vacant mirrors and found a shred of light inside.

"Get on," Gus said to Pine.

He dropped a wing and she scrabbled straight up.

To L'wen-Gar he said, "I can't lift off with the creature in my claws. I'll need to snatch it up. Be ready to lead."

And with a *whup* of his wings, he launched off the slope, using the air rolling up from the valley to aid his forward thrust. "Gariffred, follow!" he commanded the drake. He waited for the clap of Gariffred's wings, then banked back sharply and in one swoop seized Garon off the ground, turning Wyvern heads in awe. "Which way?!" he bellowed to L'wen-Gar, his mighty wings working at full capacity.

"Across the valley to the arc," she called. "The Aether knows our purpose. It will take us straight to the place of stars."

That was good enough for Gus. No time to wonder how these gateways worked; his task was simply to get the goyle through it to whatever lay beyond. He sped forward, keeping a tight grip on Garon. The arc was in his eye line, glowing softly to guide him in.

"Hold on!" he cried to Pine. "This is going to be tight!"

He checked on Gariffred and saw that the drake was in his slipstream, a little way behind but well on track. A small rush of pride ran through Gus's breast. That drake was worthy of any dragon's care. If they survived this adventure and rejoined Gabrial, the blue would hear well of his son's heroic progress.

Whoosh! L'wen-Gar flashed through the portal. Gus was not so neat. The far point of his right wing clipped the stone and dragged some surface crystals off, but it wasn't enough to break his momentum.

One by one, they all landed on a high sloping plateau, a ramp to a vast array of stars. Even before he set the goyle down, Gus could feel a sense of wonder flowing through his hearts. He'd never seen so many glittering points of light so close. He could almost reach out and pluck one. It made him think of the Aurauma Fantalis, the fabled web of celestial energy that surrounded Ki:mera. The stars that shined there were said to be the souls of dragons, dead. Common dragons were not permitted to fly there, for the Aurauma was a place of infinite power and inexplicable mystery, the legendary eyrie of Godith. Gus felt his throat harden. If this place was anything like the Aurauma, something extraordinary was about to happen.

"What do we do?" he barked as more and more Wyvern came through the arc. The singing started up again. But Gus was happier for it now. At least it was keeping the goyle calm.

Pine looked at L'wen-Gar.

L'wen-Gar said, "The Aether has called Pine. Pine must answer."

Pine looked again at her scars. They were glowing, and changing color too. Instinctively, she raised her hand.

To Gus's amazement, the stars began to stir.

"That's impossible," he muttered. He took a step back.

Graark! The drake rose up on his toes.

"Seren is coming," L'wen-Gar whispered.

"What?" said Gus.

All around him, the Wyvern song had changed to a chant: *Seren. Seren. Seren. Seren.*

And the stars were quickly changing their pattern, realigning themselves to the shape of Pine's extraordinary wound.

As Gus looked on in awe, the stars swirled and came together in a single ball of light.

The Wyvern gurgled in delight. *SEREN!*

"It can't be," Gus breathed. "That cannot *be* . . ."

For he knew about Seren. All dragons did.

Seren was the star at the center of Ki:mera.

The so-called beating heart of Godith.

28

Gus's mind was in turmoil. This didn't make sense. Even if this *was* Seren pouring its energy over the plateau, how would the Wyvern know the star's name? From an early age, all dragons were taught that Seren was the absolute center of the universe. *Their* universe. How could the bright star possibly show here? On a world so very different from his?

Seren or not, the star was shining directly on them, its rays inspecting every living thing present. Pine was the first to feel its power. The girl arched backward as a ray much brighter than all the rest struck her. It raised her aloft with her arms outstretched, her robe and lank hair streaming out behind. Gus could only look on, spellbound, as she slowly began to transform. Jagged wings grew out of her back. Her eyes took on a slanted shape. Stigs emerged above her ears. For a few spectacular moments, Pine was turned into a unique winged creature. But the changes did not last. The wings faded, the stigs retracted, and the eyes returned to their rounded shape. She was set down gently, but flopped in a heap at Gus's feet. His hearts beat a note of concern. But her pale Hom face was perfectly calm. And when she'd landed, three shafts of light had gone into her hand. It seemed to Gus that she had been explored (or educated), to see how she might be . . . improved. Was this the future of her species, he wondered, because Gayl had given her dragon auma? If so, what did that mean for the boy, Ren Whitehair, who had more dragon auma than Pine did in his veins? Some of it from the dark dragon, Graven.

Like this goyle.

The strange rays now fell on Garon, bathing him in a halo of Wyvern orange. At the same time, a voice entered Gus's mind.

You seek healing.

Gus steadied himself. He could feel the power of the star inside him, touching his mind in a way he would never be able to explain. Suddenly, a monumental idea struck him. What if this *was* the Aurauma Fantalis and the Aether was simply the Wyvern name for it? That would mean the island world was somehow linked to Ki:mera. But why should that not be so if Godith was everywhere and part of everything . . . ?

This creature has been trapped by darkness, he replied. *He was dragon once. I wish him so again.*

You care for him.

This was not a question. In his mind, Gus could see an extraordinary i:mage of the star's light exploring his third heart. His spiritual center was being tested, his motive for bringing Garon here verified. At the same moment, he had another intuition of a small, colorful *bird* flashing past him, just like the event he'd experienced when the slit had opened between Erth and the island world.

And then the voice said something . . . odd.

Do not fear him. He is the way.

Without the need for Gus to express another thought, the starlight lifted Garon clear of the plateau and turned him back into his dragon form. The Wyvern gasped. Gariffred turned at least three circles. Gus, for his part, could only swallow. There in the sky was Gabrial's father. Bold. Blue. Utterly magnificent. As perfectly composed as a dragon could be. But for one thing.

His eyes were black.

Gus feared right away that the healing had failed. He saw the star pulse and felt the contact wane. It seemed to him that the goyle had reversed the situation and drawn on Seren's power to satisfy its needs.

What's more, the creature was looking at Gariffred. Its powerful gaze singled out the wearling, as if the drake was the sworn enemy, the one real threat to the goyle's dominance. Its jaws opened. Its claws spread. And though no light poured out of its eyes, Gus saw Gariffred held quite motionless and knew that the creature was in the drake's mind.

Later, in his confusion and torment, Gus would curse himself for not doing more. Though he'd flared into action to protect the wearling, and Pine had tried to assist, neither was any match for Garon. He bowled them aside with a mighty roar. By the time Gus was on his feet, Gariffred had collapsed, the sky had grown dark, and Seren's light was breaking into star clusters again. Gus saw the blue dragon phase. In a blink, it was gone, on a direct course for Seren's last position.

Straight for the heart of Ki:mera.

Part Four
Goodle

29

Skytouch, a few days earlier

"De:allus Garodor. You sent for me?"

The novice roamer, Goodle, folded down his wings and dug his claws into the glistening ice, punching through multiple layers of snow to find a suitable foothold. To the less experienced eye, it must have looked as if he was doing his best to throttle the mountain peak. But landings had never been Goodle's strength. And they certainly didn't come much harder than this: ice, altitude, howling winds, and a precipitous slope just begging him to take a humiliating tumble. Thankfully, he'd set down without a real wobble and without spraying snow all over the De:allus. And on the plus side, it wasn't every day a roamer like him was allowed to perch at a higher level than the Prime, whose eyrie lay far below. But why had he been called to Skytouch? he wondered. He looked nervously at Garodor and prayed he had done no wrong.

"I understand your name is Goodle?"

"Yes, De:allus."

"From the Aldien bloodline?"

"Yes."

Garodor nodded. The soft rays of yellow from his haunting eyes were struggling to penetrate the burgeoning gloom. A snowstorm was building. He would not be sorry to miss it. "I've known Aldien dragons before," he said. "Intelligent, but not ambitious. Isn't that how you're described?"

The blue hung his head. Was this a test? Perhaps he *had* done something to offend the Elders? "I am loyal to the Wearle and try my hardest in everything I do, De:allus. May I ask why you've summoned me here?"

Garodor rolled his shoulders to even out the stiffness in his wings. He'd been sitting in the cold for a good while now, thinking about this unique planet and its troubled history. About the traitor, Givnay, and his knowledge of fhosforent. About memory stones and the Kashic Archive. About Ren Whitehair.

About what lay ahead.

"The Prime wants me to have an assistant. I've studied all the profiles and chosen you."

It took an extended moment for these words to seep into Goodle's consciousness. For a fraction of that interval, Garodor wondered if he'd overestimated the blue's intelligence or if water was condensing on Goodle's brain, causing some sort of vocal malfunction. Finally, there came a response: *"Me?"*

The blue's squeak of surprise sent a small avalanche sliding down the mountain. He had to scrabble a little to hold his position.

"Would that appeal to you?"

Would it *appeal* to him? Goodle was almost fainting with excitement. "Why, yes! Yes, of course!" The De:allus rarely worked with dragons outside their own order. To be asked to assist one as senior as Garodor was a giant leap in status for an ordinary roamer. "De:allus, it would be an honor. What would you like me to do?"

Garodor blew out softly, dotting the air with warm, red cinders. "Would I be correct in thinking you like solving puzzles?"

"Yes!" cried Goodle. This was wonderful! The surprises just kept on coming. Suddenly, this wintry peak didn't seem so cold or so bleak anymore.

"Then you'll be good at analyzing patterns."

Goodle nodded fiercely. "Oh, yes. Once, I looked at the Telaurean constellation when Cantorus had risen to its highest southern aspect and saw—"

"Yes, yes, Goodle. There will be other times for stars."

"Sorry, De:allus." Goodle hardened his gaze, trying to strike a proper balance between eagerness and elation. "You have a puzzle for me?"

"A very demanding one. I warn you, the work may be tedious. It will require a great deal of concentration. And there is some chance of danger."

That pricked Goodle's bubble of enthusiasm. He had to work hard for a moment to stop his emotions from going into a spin. "I've faced danger before," he said, stiffening the scales on his chin to prevent a ripple running down his throat. "Will I need to fight?"

"No," Garodor assured him. "The danger, if any, will come from the puzzle itself. Do you remember this?"

He held up a glowing orb. A thread of light was dancing at its center.

Goodle's blue eyes widened. "Is that the memory stone found in Gabrial's eyrie?"

Not long ago, Goodle had been given the awkward duty of standing guard at Gabrial's eyrie while Gabrial had been confined to his cave. During a visit from Garodor, Gariffred had come forward with three small pieces of rock he'd found. When joined together in the right manner, the pieces had made this stone.

"Yes," said Garodor, handing it to him. "You may recall it was removed from the Kashic Archive by Elder Givnay."

Goodle nodded, trying not to flinch. He didn't want to be involved with anything to do with that traitor. But to show weakness now would displease the De:allus. He kept his head up and listened.

Garodor said, "I'm going to use my powers of transference to share its contents with you. The stone contains a partial record of Erth's history, recorded by an old De:allus called Grendisar. I want you to roam the Kashic Archive and locate the Cluster this memory stone came from. Find every link to it, no matter how small. I want you to piece together everything you can about this planet and our involvement with it. It won't be easy. Some stones might be hidden or partially encrypted. You'll need my code to unlock them. I'll transfer that to you as well. Be aware, this is a secret mission. You must share your findings with no other dragon but me. No one. Do you understand?"

Goodle nodded, ice crystals dancing on his steamy breath. Garodor was right: Trawling the Kashic Archive collating snippets of information was the perfect task for an Aldien dragon. But as errands went, it was a strange assignment. Until this moment, Goodle had assumed that Erth was only recently discovered. How much history could there be of this planet?

He was about to ask that very question, when he heard another dragon approaching. It was Garret, the Wearle's chief mapper. Now, for the first time, Goodle realized why they were meeting here, on Skytouch. "We're going home," he muttered. "Back to Ki:mera."

"You sound disappointed," Garodor said.

A tiny part of Goodle *was* disappointed. He wasn't entirely happy on Erth—the goyle wars and these troubling rumors that Graven had risen in the Hom boy, Ren, served to keep him awake most nights. But to leave while the Wearle was on battle alert felt a little like failure. He prayed that this task with the memory stones would prove to be of worth.

Garret landed smoothly, reading the icy terrain with ease. Like all mappers, a calm air of confidence radiated off him. He'd clearly been summoned to help De:allus Garodor reverse the coordinates of the fire star that had brought the two Wearles to Erth, the same portal that would open a pathway back to Ki:mera.

"De:allus. Goodle." Garret greeted both dragons with a nod of respect. "Just the two of you, I take it?"

"Yes," said Garodor. "I've asked Goodle to assist me with a project I'm working on; we'll be phasing into the same patch of sky. Will the wind be a problem?" It was moderate, despite the high exposure, but lively enough in gusts to rock a dragon of Garodor's size.

"No," said Garret, "but it's going to snow soon and you should phase before it does. Here are the coordinates."

Right away, Garret produced a stunning i:mage of the precise region of sky they needed. Erth's star system was beautifully mapped in three revolving dimensions of green. At the spatial center of the map were the vital points of red that would open a "rip" in space when Garodor poured his auma into them. Creating a fire star required the mental powers of at least two dragons highly skilled in the art of physical i:maging. But once a portal had been initiated, space "remembered" the site of the rip. It was then a relatively simple matter for a competent dragon to reopen it.

As Garodor's gaze locked on to the coordinates, the sky began to rumble and the first hint of a dazzling white line appeared.

"Goodle, are you ready?"

"Yes, De:allus." Goodle snapped to attention. His physical form was about to dissolve into the dark energy of the universe. A dangerous experience if you didn't concentrate.

"Merge with my mind so I can give you the information you need. Stay fixed and I'll take us through together."

"Yes, De:allus."

One interesting thing about journeying through a fire star was that it could be done on a group basis. A whole Wearle could pass through the portal together if the individual dragons were to put their trust in an experienced leader. Goodle had arrived on Erth in just such a manner, by joining his consciousness to the extraordinary mind of the old Prime, Galarhade. The rest of the Wearle had done the same. It must have been a terrifying moment for the Hom when sixty dragons had materialized in the same zone of sky, right over these mountains. On Ki:mera, dragons popped in and out of space all the time and no one even raised an eye ridge.

Putting his functional senses to sleep, Goodle quieted his mind so he might commingle easily. But straightaway, he sensed that something was wrong. As he melded with Garodor's consciousness, he thought he felt another presence ripple between them. But if Garret wasn't traveling, how could that be? In that instant, Garodor transferred the contents of the memory stone. It came to Goodle in a powerful rush, as if the De:allus had felt an urgent need to unload everything before they reached Ki:mera. And what a load. Goodle's head was swiftly overcome with the incredible notion that Erth was not a new colony, that other dragons had visited the planet before the two Wearles he knew of. That—

Fzzzt!

The edges of the fire star fizzed with energy.

Space warped. Time rippled apart.

And horror of horrors, Garodor cut the mental connection.

Goodle, not without reason, panicked.

Great Crune! What was the De:allus DOING?

BANG! A crack like a thunderbolt. A searing burst of light. The harsh tug of G'ravity. A feeling of being one with the universe.

Goodle was through the fire star and spreading his wings.

That was the second time he realized something wasn't right. The Ki:meran sky was always colored a faint shade of purple.

The sky he was crossing was definitely blue.

For a moment, he thought the portal had rejected him and spat him back to some far-flung corner of Erth. But when he looked down, all he could see was a rocky terrain drained of every color but a pale blue gray. He flapped toward the highest rocks he could see and landed on one to get his bearings. It was daytime, but when he stared into the sky, he could see the faint lights of Ki:mera in the distance. He knew right away what had happened. The power of the fire star, combined with his cry, had displaced the phasing point and taken him to Crune, the smaller of Ki:mera's moons.

Garodor was nowhere to be seen.

Goodle's heart sank into a dire rhythm. Crune had a breathable atmosphere, but in the circumstances, that was cruel consolation. The whole moon was a dry, infertile rock, with no food source and probably no water. He couldn't leave; there was simply nowhere to go. The nearest Ki:meran labyrinths were far across open space, impossible to fly to. And he couldn't phase across a distance that great without creating another fire star, something he alone wasn't capable of doing. Whichever way he looked at it, his future was grim. He was going to die here alone, pining for his home world. All he had was this pointless memory stone with its ridiculous scripts about Erth. In frustration, he hurled it against the rocks and watched it split into its parts again.

That was the third time he knew that something wasn't right.

The stone opened and a vapor emerged.

The spirit of a long-dead dragon had risen.

His name, as Goodle would shortly discover, was Grendisar.

30

"Vapor, be merciful!"

It was rare to see a dragon cower, but acts of bravado were not generally advised in the presence of vapors. Although Goodle had never encountered one before, the rules about vapors were clear. Flying away angered them. Any use of flame was likely to get you turned into a fireball. Legend even had it they could kill your shadow, then *become* your shadow so they might haunt you for the rest of your days. The best a dragon could do in such a situation was apologize for disturbing the phantom, ask for its mercy, and hope it went away.

(The mercy part was especially important.)

Yet this vapor didn't look *particularly* menacing. It had the bulging yellow eyes of a De:allus, for a start. It was also very old. Even in its wraith-like form, its body color was leaning to red, a shade associated with dragon longevity. And from the way it kept looking at its limbs, it seemed more fascinated with its feat of materialization than with any desire to do Goodle harm. A few muddling moments went by. Goodle shifted his weight from one foot to the other. He swished his tail quietly to check that his shadow was still intact and wondered if he couldn't just . . . creep away? To his left was a decent-size rock. If he could shuffle over and crouch behind it . . .

"Ah."

Too late! The vapor had spoken! Goodle froze with one leg off the ground. What did "ah" mean exactly? Ah, he'd been spotted? Ah, the vapor was glad to be alive? Ah, it was in pain? Ah-ha, a shadow to gobble? What?

"And who would you be, young dragon?"

The voice wafted across the space between them.

"I am G-Goodle, from the Aldien line."

"Is something amiss with your voice?"

"No," Goodle squeaked.

"I would see a healer all the same. Sounds squeaky. Probably needs more grit. Well, now, where are we?" The vapor poked a nearby rock.

Goodle gasped as the claw went straight through the stone and emerged cleanly on the other side. "Crune," he gulped.

"An interesting choice," the vapor said, sending a puff of dust into the air. "Still, always useful to get one's bearings."

Goodle nodded and finally put both feet on the ground. He cautioned himself that it was early days yet, but it seemed as if the spirit was going to spare him. Bravely, he tried to ask a question. "Vapor, if I may—?"

"Vapor?" it said in a voice that almost blew its head apart. Every time it turned or extended a limb, the lines of its body would separate briefly before catching up with the flow of movement. It was making Goodle feel quite queasy. "Well, yes," the thing muttered. "I have been dead for . . . well, I don't know how long precisely. Perhaps you do? I assume it was you who took the memory stone out of the Archive?"

"Not I," said Goodle, feeling the need to bow. "It was shown to me by Garodor, a dragon of your class. If I might ask, I saw the stone in parts once before. Why is it you've only emerged now?"

"An excellent question," the vapor said. "I suspect I miscalculated the holomorphic loop and the stone required a more energy-dependent exit strategy."

Goodle looked puzzled.

"A good thump; I was stuck."

Goodle nodded. Now he got it. He steadied his hearts and asked another question. "Forgive me, are you . . . *Grendisar*?"

"Indeed I am," the vapor said proudly, shaking his phantom wings. "You know my work?"

"Some of it," Goodle muttered, searching through the information lodged in his head. The entire contents of the memory stone were there, plus some analytical data from Garodor himself. "You were on Erth long ago," Goodle said, as i:mages, scripts, and theories began to accumulate at the forefront of his mind. "You believed that Graven's heart was banished there, smashed into fragments and scattered among a flock of . . . of *crows.* And Garodor believes that Graven's blood is . . . Oh!"

Goodle staggered back as if the ground had cracked open. His tail swept fretfully over Crune's surface.

"No, that can't be. The fhosforent was *his*? It was Graven's *blood*?" His eyes stared wildly. "That's why we saw goyles. The mutants were made in Graven's i:mage. Then it's true. He is risen. He—Hhh!"

While Goodle had been ranting, the vapor had come close enough to touch his misty isoscele to Goodle's head. It felt as if a cold spike had entered Goodle's mind, and everything he knew was flowing out through it.

"Hmm," the vapor murmured excitedly. "Yes, yes. Fascinating. Of course. Of course. De:allus Grinwald always used to say that if the heart was shattered there must be blood. I suspected if that were so it would seep into the crust of the erth and be lost. Dear me, how wrong I was. I should have guessed the blood might crystallize. And like any mineral, dragons would ingest it. And now it has made traitors of once-noble dragons and even drawn the Hom into its web of darkness. Hmm. I see from the memories of De:allus Garodor that the boy you seek is carrying what remains of Graven's heart. Fascinating. Fascinating. We will try to avoid Ren Whitehair for now, lest his impulsions vary our course."

"But, De:allus Grendisar, no one knows where the Hom boy is. How can we avoid him if—?"

"Of course we know where he is," Grendisar snorted, an act that made his facial features blur. "Has your brain begun to leak out through your ears?"

Goodle hoped not. That wasn't on his list of vapor atrocities, though it probably ought to be.

Grendisar went on, "What would you do if your mother had condemned you to a life of eternal darkness and now you were risen again?"

"I . . . I would seek her out—I think," Goodle muttered.

"Quite," said Grendisar. "And where would you go to seek her out?"

Goodle turned his head and stared at the web of lights in space. Suddenly, it was all becoming clear. He understood now what had slipped alongside him at the entrance to the fire star. It was Ren, riding his strange invisible horse. That's why Garodor had broken the link so urgently. He must have detected Ren's presence as well.

"He's there," he breathed, hardly able to stop himself quaking.

"Indeed," said Grendisar, as if it was nought but an interesting anomaly. "Like us, the boy is eager to learn the truth. Or he wishes to wreak some kind of devastation—that is yet to be established. But the evidence is perfectly clear. He has broken through the boundary between two worlds. The boy you call 'Ren' is in Ki:mera."

31

"Now, then. How shall we cross this void . . . ?"

Grendisar tapped his claws together, producing a cloud of reddish fuzz. He was on a high rock, staring far across space at the strange maze of lights that was the dragon world, Ki:mera. At the center of the maze winked the bright star, Seren, which was lighting the world with a faint purple glow.

". . . Ah, I think I have it."

Without warning, Grendisar suddenly took flight. Goodle arched his neck to watch the vapor flowing over him. To his relief, Grendisar reassembled on a rock just behind him.

"Wait!" Goodle cried.

Grendisar was holding up the memory stone, turning it deftly as though he were on the verge of disappearing—fittingly, in a puff of smoke. Having found someone—or rather some *thing*—to talk to, Goodle did not want to feel marooned again.

Grendisar squeezed his eye ridges together. "You have your own notion of how to cross the void? Splendid. Speak up. Do not be afraid to share your calculation."

Goodle shook his head. "I trust your judgment in these matters, De:allus. I simply ask that you take me with you. Please?"

Grendisar paused, looking as puzzled as a vapor could look. "Is our mission not mutual? Of course you must come!

If my conjectures are correct, we can use the ancient forces embedded in the stone to phase ourselves straight into the Kashic Archive." He gave a mischievous grunt. "We might even sneak past that crusty old Curator. Now, there's an adventure, don't you think?"

"About that," said Goodle. "About . . . the adventure. What did you mean when you said that Ren might be seeking the truth?"

But now that he thought about it, Goodle was beginning to realize he didn't have to ask for an explanation. The principal facts were all in his head. As he shuffled the underlying details in his mind, the full pattern of Garodor's misgivings began to fall into place. The entire mystery was built around one suspicion: *The discovery of Graven's blood—the fhosforent—had not been an accident.* Some unidentified power on Ki:mera had reignited Grendisar's theory that Graven's heart was hidden on Erth and had sent the first Wearle to investigate. But how did they know where to find the fhosforent? And more important, why did they want to raise the dark dragon? To wreak some kind of revenge on Godith? Who was really behind all this? And what of Ren, the real thorn under the scales, dragged into the drama by a wearling's bite? He was dangerously unpredictable and, worse, still at large. Who in the world could count themselves safe while a brash Hom boy was shielding the deadliest auma known to dragonkind?

"Ah-ha," said Grendisar, too deeply embroiled in his calculations to be bothered with Goodle's murmurings. "I have set the coordinates. We are ready to phase."

He threw the stone to Goodle. A map, not unlike the kind of thing Garret had i:maged on the peak of Skytouch, was buzzing around it.

"Open it once more, if you please."

So Goodle did as he was asked and clicked the stone open, using the coding shared by Garodor. Waves of energy began to radiate from its interior. Before long, Goodle was bound in a halo of light.

"Excellent. Excellent," Grendisar said. "Wake me when we reach the Archive."

With a *whoosh*, he collapsed his shape to a single rotating spark and whizzed into the nuclear core of the stone, dancing with the sparkling atoms there.

Goodle allowed himself a gulp. Then he closed the stone carefully and concentrated hard on his journey's end.

The Kashic Archive.

BANG! For the second time that day, he was moving across the universe.

With a skidding jolt, he stopped.

Immediately, a voice boomed, "WATCH WHERE YOU'RE PHASING!"

Goodle opened his eyes. He had reached the Kashic Archive, but he wasn't inside it as Grendisar had hoped. He was on the great stone plateau at the starlit entrance. The way in was blocked by a giant of a dragon.

He was as red as Hom blood and almost as thin.

His name was Gorenfussental the Twenty-Third.

Better known by his dignified title: the Curator.

32

For the third time that day, Goodle found himself addressing a dragon of much higher rank. "Forgive me, Curator. I . . . misjudged my coordinates."

"I'll say you did," the Curator growled. "Nearly took my eye out with your isoscele! Why do you underscaled miscreants have to PHASE everywhere? What's wrong with flying? You've got wings, haven't you?"

Goodle straightened them against his back.

The Curator leveled his bony neck, making the hinged scales crackle and pop. He was easily twice the size of Goodle, though most of that was measured from top to tail. Gorenfussental and his illustrious ancestors had been managing the Archive since the dawn of time (allegedly), and each new descendant was longer and thinner than the last. No one really knew why. Goodle had heard it said that the records of dragon history were growing so fast they were stretching each curator's mind to the limit, and therefore a longer one had to be found if the one in charge looked in danger of exploding. He suspected that was a myth put about by the pers, though he wouldn't have been in the slightest bit surprised if the twenty-third curator had blown his stigs right here. Despite the fawning apology, Gorenfussental was still grumbling.

"Young dragons. Always jigging in and out of intraspace. Wouldn't have happened in my day. No wonder you've all got bellies the size of Crune." He nodded at the memory stone. "Returning that, are you?"

"Yes," Goodle said, fanging his lip. The mention of Crune had made him nervous. The Curator, if he wished, could open any stone. Thankfully, he was showing no interest in this one. Goodle wondered, in passing, if it was a crime to harbor a vapor inside a memory stone. He'd never *heard* of a dragon being charged with that offence. He rather hoped he wouldn't be the first.

"Well, leave it over there with the others."

Goodle looked over his shoulder. Memory stones of many different colors were stacked in a shallow depression of the flame-carved rock that made up the outer wall of the Archive labyrinth. Like all the great edifices of old Ki:mera, the main façade of the Archive had been formed from a refired *graig*—one of the millions of rocky "fragments" that together made up Ki:mera's mass.

A philosophical debate had raged for centuries about the origins of the graig. From the De:allus point of view, Ki:mera didn't make sense. De:allus Garodor, no less, had lectured at the prestigious Labyrinth Scientii on what he called *Improbable G'ravity and Inverse Contrastructure.* He, Garodor, was the main proponent of a highly contentious theory that challenged the accepted view of Ki:mera's creation. It basically suggested that far from pouring Her gush of fire into a limitless void and i:maging Ki:mera from nothing, Godith had blown apart an existing planet, leaving Her divine light at its core.

It wasn't hard to appreciate the logic in this. Stripped down to its basics, Ki:mera was little more than a spherical collection of millions of misshapen rocks: the graig. Some pieces of graig were entirely free-floating, suspended in Ki:mera's deep G'ravitational field. They were known as *darn.* But most rocks were joined to at least one neighbor by a multiplex of winding bridges or conduits, many reaching farther than a dragon eye could see.

Viewed from space, the whole world was a tangle of cavernous, three-dimensional labyrinths. A gigantic mesh of fractured rocks, some as big as Erth's mountain ranges. Yet, it was a constantly changing environment. The art of flame-carving (a favorite pastime for creative dragon minds) had seen thousands of graig enhanced or reconfigured, some into structures as grand as the Kashic Archive, more often into decorative eyries, places for dragon families to settle.

It might have seemed impossible that anything could live on a world made up of broken stones. But even the smallest of labyrinths had their own indigenous microclimate, with an atmosphere the dragons could breathe or adapt to. Every labyrinth was capable of supporting a variety of life-forms. The bigger systems flowed with water, maintained small oceans, and grew Erth-like flora, though nowhere in Ki:mera was there an assembly of life as all-inclusive as that found on Erth. And not a single labyrinth supported the freethinking bipeds the dragons called Hom. Their discovery had been one of the real surprises of Godith's greater universe.

At the heart of it all was the giant star, Seren. The G'ravitational pull of the star, balanced against the weaker forces radiating from the moons of Crune and Cantorus, combined to keep the whole maze stable. Light flowing off the star permeated every bit of *intraspace* (the gaps between the graig), creating a fluctuating *ora*, or glow. The color of the ora was predominantly purple due to starlight reacting with crystals embedded in the graig. It would fluctuate to green sometimes, producing ribbons of both these colors when Crune and Cantorus were in certain alignments. And all around the planet—if planet it could be called—acting like a shield between Ki:mera, its moons, and the rest of the universe, was the mysterious Aurauma Fantalis, the intricate web of sparkling lights that dragons believed to be the home of Godith and the final resting place for their souls.

"Over there, I said. Are you deaf as well as clumsy?"

Goodle snapped to attention. "Sorry, Curator." Yet again, he bowed. Any more of this and he'd end up as bent as an aged matrial. "If I may, I'd like to return this stone to the Archive myself."

"Return it yourself?" Gorenfussental stretched a little more. "Don't be ridiculous. Do you think I'd let a blundering roamer anywhere near my Clusters and Arrays? I'd have stones floating everywhere! Just put it with the others and flap off." He flipped a claw in the direction of the widest bit of intraspace.

Goodle raked in his claws. This wasn't going well.

"You're still here," the Curator said dourly.

Goodle swallowed hard. Yes. He was. Still here. It was time to be brave and put his best scales forward. He'd been tasked with a great responsibility. A secret mission. A puzzle to solve. He must do his duty and see it through.

He sat up boldly and puffed his chest. "I have orders from De:allus Garodor. He wishes me to gather information from any stones linked to the one I'm carrying and—"

"Garodor?" The Curator's ear frills widened. "How would a mischief-maker like you know a dragon as respected as Garodor?" The crusty eye ridges creaked, shedding scale dust over Goodle's snout.

"I am Garodor's assistant. And I don't make mischief. I have traveled from the second colony on Erth, where the only De:allus present was Garodor. He chose me to help him because of my Aldien bloodline and, and . . ."

"Well?" The Curator tilted his head.

Goodle gulped. He'd gone a little too far with his boast. There was no *and*. Now he would have to make something up. "Because . . . I enjoy researching our past!"

That seemed to do the trick. Gorenfussental hummed approvingly. "Let me look at that." He flicked a claw, inviting Goodle to hand the stone over.

"It's just historical data," said Goodle, hoping not to give the stone up.

"Of course it's historical," Gorenfussental huffed. "Do you think I don't know my own Clusters? It would be red if it were a battle stone, green if it carried environmental records, yellow if . . . oh, just give it to me!" He leaned down and snatched it from Goodle's grasp. Until then, Goodle hadn't paid much attention to its color. When Grendisar had sealed himself back into the structure, he'd dimmed the orb's glow, leaving it with just a vague gray tint. It was dull compared to the ones in the stack.

"Trying to teach me my job," the Curator grumbled, spinning the stone fast in his nimble claws. He suddenly stopped it dead. "Just a *moment.*" He blinked his scholarly eyes. To one side of his head, a detailed cubic i:mage consisting of many racks of stones appeared. As he turned the i:mage and ran his eye along it, stones lit up like raindrops hitting the surface of a pond. In a heartbeat, he'd highlighted a gap.

"I thought so," he growled. "This stone was removed without my permission. Great Crune, it's been *tampered* with! The cryptographic codes have been altered to carry some sort of . . . *shadow.*"

Or vapor, thought Goodle, keeping very quiet.

"What's more, it's long overdue!"

Oh, good. That was all Goodle needed: a penalty for returning a memory stone late. "De:allus Garodor didn't say anything about that. Please may I return it myself? I promise I'll be careful."

"Certainly not."

Goodle ground his teeth. Now what should he do? He was reasonably certain that flaming a curator and storming the Archive would be considered a major crime. Being first assistant to De:allus Garodor wasn't quite as straightforward as it seemed.

Gorenfussental said, "This stone was originally encrypted by an Elder. It contains sensitive information. I've heard about that planet you say it came from. There are some peculiar rumors flying around the graig about that place. Things no blue should ever be involved with. What in the name of Godith was this stone doing *there*?"

"That's what I'm here to find out," said Goodle.

The Curator would not be moved. "This theft will have to be reported to the Higher."

"No!" Goodle stamped a foot.

"No?" growled the giant.

"You HAVE to let me through! I'm on a mission of the highest priority!"

"And I've got a tail made of moondust! Now fly, you young reprobate. Before I clip your wings and kick you to the far side of Cantorus."

"I can open it," said Goodle.

"You? Open *this*?" A long snort traveled down the tall dragon's snout.

"I can prove it," Goodle said. He was desperate now. And desperate times called for desperate measures. The Curator had called him a reprobate, so a reprobate he would have to be.

He squeezed his eyes shut. I:maging had never been one of his strengths, but he did it now, perfectly—stage one at least.

"What's this?" said Gorenfussental, looking at the numbers floating before him.

"De:allus Garo—" No. Goodle thought again. "De:allus Grendisar's secret code."

"GRENDISAR? That hoary degenerate! Now I've heard it all. Be gone, before I summon the Veng!"

Goodle closed his eyes again and sent the code into the memory stone's lock. It broke open, still in the Curator's grasp.

And out came the vapor.

"Bother," it muttered, looking up at the Archive entrance. "Bit rusty with the old coordinates, I see."

Gorenfussental dropped the pieces of stone and staggered back with his mouth wide open.

"Problem?" Grendisar said to Goodle.

Goodle nodded. "Don't hurt him—please?"

Grendisar rose up to five times his size. He was about to go through all the motions of roaring, clawing, and shadow-eating when Gorenfussental fainted in a crumpled heap.

"Well, that was easy," Grendisar said, swishing back to his normal size. "I must confess, it's rather fun being a vapor." He clapped his misty claws together. "So, Goodle of Aldien. Here we stand, on the threshold of uncovering a great mystery!"

"Umm," said Goodle. He couldn't help but gulp.

"Excellent. Excellent," Grendisar said brightly. "Right, then. Shall we go in?"

33

Before Goodle could raise a note of caution, Grendisar had flowed between the Archive's giant pillars (carved in the likeness of Gorenfussental the First) and disappeared from view. Goodle looked down at the current Curator, praying he would never be forced to i:mage the state he'd left the old dragon in. Gorenfussental was flat on his back with his feet in the air. A most undignified pose for a dragon of his status. Quietly begging the Curator's forgiveness, Goodle checked around for signs he hadn't been spotted, then gathered up the pieces of the memory stone and went after Grendisar as fast as he could fly.

This wasn't the first time he'd visited the Archive. As early as their third turn, young dragons were shown around it by their pers. It was a breathtaking experience. The Archive was somehow bigger *inside* than it appeared from the outer, and almost as complex as Ki:mera and its graig. Labyrinths within labyrinths within yet more labyrinths. An impossible depth of intraspace. No one, not even the wisest curators, could gauge the full extent of it. A few wingbeats in, and most juveniles were lost.

In every labyrinth, memory stones floated in perfectly arranged Clusters of carefully graded colors. On their inaugural visit, young dragons were encouraged to select any stone that appealed to them. They were then shown how to open the stone and how to use i:maging techniques to find additional stones that might be linked to their original choice. This was a risky procedure, for if the i:maging proved too wayward, it could lead a young dragon so deep into the Archive it might never find its way out. Per Gantiss liked to tell a tale about an unfortunate dragon called Gorme, who was lost among the Clusters for years. Gorme was eventually discovered wandering a remote labyrinth spouting words of dragontongue that *rhymed.* (The whole wyng had winced when they'd heard that.) For this reason, the pers would encourage the dragons to examine no more than three related stones on their first trip, which usually confined them safely to the same labyrinth.

Every dragon, no matter how lowly, was allotted an access code. The code determined where in the Archive a dragon could roam and how many stones they could borrow at one time. Failing to return a stone on time incurred an automatic ban, which only the Curator could reverse. It was a sad fact that many fighting dragons visited the Kashic Archive once, broke the returns rule, accepted their ban, and never went back.

Goodle had always returned his stones on time.

But until this business with Elder Givnay, he had never heard of a stone going *missing* before. He was puzzled about that, and with very good reason. On his first trip, he had learned an important fact about the Archive: Whenever a stone was removed from its Cluster, the Archive noted it. The *Archive*, not the Curator. Goodle had found this hard to comprehend. The explanation, when it came, had frightened him a little. He remembered being perched in the spectacular Labyrinth Auditaurum, hearing per Gantiss bellowing in a weighty but somewhat lackluster voice, *The Kashic Archive is more than just . . . a data store. It is a living . . . kompendium of thoughts, moods, and . . . other dreary matter* (his voice had tailed off a little there). *To navigate successfully, one must engage with it on a* conceptual *plane, not a logical one.*

Goodle was ruminating hard on this as he hurried after Grendisar, still carrying the memory stone Elder Givnay had removed illegally. It didn't take a giant leap of intellect to deduce that Givnay had used his mental prowess to somehow put the Archive into disArray. Many dragons had feared the Elder because of his ability to commingle with their minds and effectively take control of them. What if Givnay had commingled with the mind of the *Archive* and found a way to confuse or deactivate a Cluster? That would explain how he'd smuggled the stone out undetected. But the contents of the stone—all of Grendisar's work, in effect—would have been little more than background reading. And while the stone cited Erth as the probable location for Graven's shattered heart, there was nothing in the data to say where on the planet his blood would be found.

But help was at hand.

While Goodle had been brooding on this niggling conundrum, the Archive had been working with him. It had noted the i:mages of Erth in his mind and adjusted its mystifying intraspace to draw him into a crucial labyrinth. Grendisar was there already, drawing stones to him at a dizzying rate, spilling their i:mages all over the labyrinth. Goodle landed on a central viewing pedestal, staggered by the wealth of pictures in the air. The whole history of Grendisar's trips to Erth was swirling around like leaves in a gale.

"Look at this, young blue." Grendisar froze an i:mage of a canyon Goodle had never seen before. "Came across it on my first trip to Erth. Marvelous example of volcanic unease in the deepest layers of the planet. Oh, and here's one of—"

"De:allus!" Goodle stopped him there. He wasn't here to see pictures of Grendisar's favorite *landmarks.* They were supposed to be solving the Graven riddle. "Have you found any clues about the fhosforent?"

"No," the vapor said with a hum, shuffling a few of the i:mages around. Here in the Archive, his ghostly form was very much at home. He could sift the i:mages almost as fast as he could pop out of sight.

A poor i:mage of the old Prime, Greffan, flashed by, prompting Goodle to ask, "Is there a record of Greffan's reports?"

"Um?"

"Greffan. The Prime who led the Wearle before mine."

Right away, a stone zipped out of the Cluster and hovered in Goodle's eyeline. It was gray, like the one he was still holding, and probably encrypted in the same manner. He let go of the stone between his claws. It quickly floated back to its rightful position. The new one clicked open and displayed its contents.

"A fine range of mountains," Grendisar said.

"This was our domayne," Goodle muttered as pictures of Skytouch and its ice-bound lake panned out before him. Over the top of the i:mages came a gruff narration, presumably recorded by Prime Greffan.

I am pleased to report that phasing into a coastal area of the planet named Erth has been a success. The domayne I present for you here is an excellent habitat for dragons to colonize. The ground is unspoiled and well served by fresh water. Food is abundant. Air quality good. Threats can only be described as minimal. We have been forced to repel some irritating challenges from the semi-intelligent species known as the Hom, but we have them under control and could eradicate them at will, if directed. As requested, some i:mages of the mineral deposits, taken from the zone we were instructed to inspect.

A number of pictures popped up of the quarry near Vargos, where the old per, Grogan, had lost his life. One of the i:mages showed a thin seam of fhosforent, glowing pink. It made Goodle shudder to see it.

The mineral supply in this region is plentiful. The pink ore highlighted, which the mappers have named fhosforent, *has made remarkable enhancements to our flame. The ore is fragile and swiftly degrades. We do not have the full resources to mine it. Samples will be brought to Ki:mera if they can be stabilized.*

With wider regard to the classified work of De:allus Grendisar, I find no evidence of the fallen son of Godith. There is an interesting auma about this world, but I cannot bring myself to believe that Graven's heart lies hidden here. I suggest that further researches be abandoned.

"A travesty!" cried the vapor.

Indeed, thought Goodle. He'd hoped for more from Greffan's report. Some small clue he could work with. An unsolved riddle was worse than an itch in the ear canal. And having come this far, he did not want to let De:allus Garodor down.

He ran through the data again and suddenly had a new burst of inspiration. It was all to do with the throwaway part of Prime Greffan's report. *Instructed*, Greffan had said. Instructed by whom? The Elders? The Higher? Who had wanted to know about the mineral supply?

Goodle gasped and almost fell off his pedestal as a new stone appeared at the end of his snout. It was small, this one, and hard to see. He tried twice to unlock it. Both times, the stone refused to open. (One more false try and it would disappear.) "Grendisar, what's happening?" he said, watching the stone rotate. It threw out an eerie wisp of light that strobed the space between Goodle's eyes. Was it a stone or just a ball of light? It was hard to tell.

Grendisar floated over. "Oh, my fuzzy scales. Where did *that* come from?"

"I can't open it," said Goodle.

"Nor I," said the vapor. "That is not a memory stone, Goodle of Aldien."

Goodle reeled back. The light came with him, holding its place.

Grendisar sighed in amazement. "All my days, I never saw such a wonder."

"De:allus, stop babbling. Tell me what it is."

"That is a heart star, my friend. The essence of a dragon long dead—and marooned. The Archive must have been protecting it. I would bet my dusty isoscele that none of the curators knew about this. But who is it? And why are they here?"

"I don't know," squeaked Goodle. And right at that moment, he really didn't care. A high-pitched tone somewhere deep within the Archive had made him start. The memory stones had all begun to flash. One by one, they closed up and flew back to their Clusters.

Goodle looked sharply left and right, alarmed that the star was staying with him. "What's that noise? What's happening?"

Grendisar wafted a claw. "The alarm, I expect."

"What?!"

"The Curator must have woken and summoned the Veng."

VENG! Goodle put out his wings. "We've got to fly!"

"I'm afraid there is little point, my friend. The heart star has you in its thrall. It will not release you until it has what it needs."

"What does it want?"

"A good question," Grendisar hummed.

"Oh, you're hopeless!" Goodle wailed at him. "I wish I'd stayed on Crune."

"Of course!" Grendisar exploded briefly into particles. "You have the answer plainly! Crune is the clue. How could I not see it? Well done, Goodle of Aldien. I must commend your logic before I die."

"Die?"

"Alas, it is time," De:allus Grendisar said. "The Veng have never liked vapors. They will take much joy in turning me to smoke. Fear not, I will feel no pain. I will lead them in a dance, you can be sure of it."

"Can't you—can't we—*please* get away?" Goodle had his wings at full stretch now. But Grendisar was right about the star. Somehow it was holding the blue to the pedestal.

"Not I," said the vapor, resigned to his fate. "I have drifted far too long. But at last I see my work has purpose—though I was but an instrument all along. Your destiny is all that matters now."

"What destiny?" squeaked Goodle. At any moment, he was going to be arrested or flamed. The alarms were getting louder. He could smell the Veng coming. They were closing fast, from every direction.

Grendisar gave a sigh of content. "This is the work of firebirds, my friend."

"What?" Goodle's voice chords almost snapped. Firebirds? The so-called monitors of time and space? They were an even bigger myth than Graven!

But Grendisar plainly believed in them. "Only they could weave such a ruse with the Archive to bring you and me to this meeting with him."

"Who?" cried Goodle. Why didn't this vapor ever speak plainly? "Meeting with who?"

"Stay where you are or you die!" roared a voice.

Veng! They were in the labyrinth!

Grendisar flashed his tail, unafraid. "If I am correct, the weight of the universe will soon lie upon your wings, young blue. 'Tis a lofty responsibility you bear."

"Grendisar, tell me the dragon's NAME."

But a bright flame had already hit the vapor, lighting him up in a flare of orange. In a faraway voice, he wailed his final words, *"Bother! I hovered too long, as always. Fly with mercy, Goodle of Aldien. Forgive, forgive, forgive . . ."*

Forgive what? thought Goodle, staring at the place where the star ought to be.

But the heart star was no longer there.

It had flashed into his mind and was melding with his auma.

With it came the first light of understanding.

"YOU?" he said, oblivious to the catch of flames licking around him.

I hope you don't mind, said a Presence in his head. *The Archive thinks we're perfectly matched. I won't harm you. Violence was never in my nature. And don't worry about the Veng. We'll be gone in a blink.*

"But you can't be him. He's . . ."

G'restyn, yes, the Presence said proudly. *Younger brother of Graven. Second son of Godith. Lord of Crune. Do you like that title? I made it up myself. G'restyn: Lord of Crune. Has a nice ring to it, don't you think . . . ?*

Part Five

The Aurauma Fantalis

34

Garodor opened his eyes. All around him, like the shell of a giant egg, were the curved stone walls of the Alcazar Labyrinth, the only place in the entire body of Ki:mera that might be called a prison. Thankfully, there was no other dragon present. Scribblings and scorch marks made by previous occupants were carved on every rock, but all the marks were old. The prison had been empty for some time, it seemed.

Garodor settled on a piece of graig toward the center of the intraspace. He folded down his wings and breathed deeply through his spiracles, rolling back the lids on his eyes as he did. The dazzling light from their finely jeweled surfaces barely dented the purple ambience. But this wide open, his eyes could see all around his body, ready to spot any signs of attack.

He raised himself to full alertness, and spoke.

"If you want my advice, you'll show yourself, boy. I put a time delay into the phasing pattern, which means our arrival won't be detected immediately. But soon the intraspace will start to reconfigure, and that will send a signal out across the graig. Your invisibility won't help you then. This labyrinth was commissioned by the Higher. It has direct links to the Aurauma Fantalis. As such, it has a degree of consciousness. The Alcazar can synchronize with every shift its occupants make. It can hear a sound as quiet as your heartbeat and measure the heat from the flick of an eye. Once it detects a shift, it will be able to predict your movements and know exactly where you are. And don't be fooled by the gaps in the walls. They are bound by a prismic field that can't be shattered, flamed, or phased across. The only way you'll get to the other side is by shining a light weave over the locks. For that, you will need a De:allus eye. Time is ticking down for you, Ren. It won't be long before the Veng arrive. Then the Sensaurs will come, and not even a reborn son of Godith could resist the combined force of their strange minds. I suggest you talk to me. Now."

Three beats passed.

Garodor tightened his claws.

Could he have been wrong about the fire star?

No.

His primary heart banged against his chest as a shimmer of light wriggled out of the intraspace and Ren Whitehair faded into view. He was on a piece of graig right in front of Garodor, astride the white horse that had once belonged to Ren's father, Ned. They called the beast Wind. She was a curious creature, said to command mysterious powers. She had once been possessed by the spirit of a goyle and, like Ren, was touched by the auma of Graven. The twisted horn that grew from her forehead was not showing at present. Likewise, no wings were sprouting from her shoulders.

Ren himself looked no different from the scrawny Hom child Garodor had first met in Prime Grynt's eyrie. His hair was still the color of faded corn, his face pale, his eyes alert. But the childlike air of injustice that had once governed his boyish features had now been replaced by a sullen weariness more in common with that of a hard-bitten warrior. Darkness had sharpened the points of his eyes. Phasing him into this labyrinth was a risk. No cave nor pit nor high mountain ledge had held the boy captive for long. And while Ren might struggle to break free from this confinement, there was nothing to stop him turning on his captor with whatever powers he or his mount possessed. Garodor knew he must be wary.

The boy reached forward and stroked Wind's mane. From his mouth came a faint breath of praise. "You've been clever, De:allus. I guessed you would detect our presence in the fire star, but I didn't think there would be time enough to rearrange your endpoint. I underestimated you. Bringing us here . . . there was courage in that."

Perfect dragontongue, eloquently spoken in that thick Hom accent. Such progress in such a short space of time. Garodor glanced at the hand that Gariffred had bitten. The star-shaped wound was still at its center.

"You know where you are?"

Ren looked all about him. "I'm where the dragon high command has always wanted me: imprisoned. I thought we were on the same side, you and I?"

"Tell me your purpose and we might be."

Ren smiled faintly. "Where is Goodle?"

"Far away, I hope."

"In the Archive?"

"I doubt it. Is that where you hoped I would lead you?"

"Wind will take me wherever I ask her to. And no Veng will halt my progress, I assure you."

"That sounds like a threat."

Again, the boy looked vaguely about him. "I told you in the forest when Grynt tried to flame me, any dragon who stands against me will suffer. I let Grynt live because I didn't want a host of dragons coming here, roaring that they'd witnessed the wrath of Graven. His spirit rages inside me. It cannot be burned again. It has been weakened by generations of dying crows, but the spark is alive, nurtured now by the auma of Gariffred, tempered by his mother, Grystina."

"She's still commingled with you? Grystina?"

Wind snorted quietly, prompting Ren to cradle her ear. "She has been with me since the day I learned that dragons and Hom could be of one mind. I value her Astrian wisdom, especially in the face of Grynt's stupidity."

Garodor lidded his eyes a little. In those few moments, a harsh tone had cracked the swell of Ren's voice. A sign, perhaps, that he was not entirely in control of Graven. Dark scales were rising along the boy's arms. More troubling were the changes taking place in Wind. Black stripes had appeared down her neck and flanks. Her wings and horn had swiftly materialized, as if she—or the force that controlled her and Ren—was tired of this dialogue and was eager to force an escape.

Aware that time was ebbing away, Garodor blurted, "Listen to me, Ren. If you were shadowing my meeting with Grynt, you'll know the reason I returned to Ki:mera. Whoever sent the Wearle to those fhosforent seams never meant for the Hom to be involved. That dragon—if a dragon it was—is to blame for everything that has happened on Erth and should be brought to justice."

A slight growl left Ren's lips. "I will bring justice to bear, De:allus. And any who stand against me will suffer."

"No," said Garodor, shaking his head. "You are in terrible danger. Show yourself as a black dragon and Ki:mera will rise up as one and destroy you, no matter how much power you think you might have."

Ren touched Wind's head and the dark lines faded. She calmly folded her wings. "Then speak your terms: What would you have me do?"

"Go back to Erth. Seek Grymric's help. Make your ties again with Gabrial. Forge an alliance between our two species. Let *me* find out who's behind all this and what can be done to set the spirit of Graven to rest."

Ren pulled on Wind's mane and glanced at the spaces in the labyrinth wall. "It may be too late for that. The Veng are coming. Wind feels their presence. You would be wise to break us out of here. Unless you would be witness to more dragon deaths."

"Ren, don't do this," Garodor begged, watching the darkness grow in him again. "You might take the first wave, but many more will follow. If Grystina is with you, she knows I speak truly."

He is right, she advised, sweeping into Ren's mind. *We cannot fight them all.*

Wind whinnied all the same, as if she might try. For a moment, her beautiful head transformed itself into a dragon's skull. It was black and driven by thoughts of violence. But Ren spoke strongly to her, commanding a different transformation.

In the short time it took the Veng to stack up around the labyrinth, Ren and Wind had combined their auma and turned into the shape of a youthful green dragon. Garodor was still recovering from the shock when a Veng commander spoke through one of the hearing vents, demanding to know what was happening.

Garodor calmed his breathing and said, "I am Garodor, First Warden of the Academy Scientii and Regulator of the De:allus Class. By order of the Elder, Grynt, this roamer and I have returned from an exploration of the colony known as Erth. I made the mistake of letting him control the fire star coordinates, and look where he's brought us. I kept him here to teach him a lesson. I'm sorry to have disturbed your routine, Commander."

A dark growl filtered through the labyrinth walls. "You. Roamer. Identify yourself. I don't remember seeing your face before."

The green dragon raised his head. "I am . . . Gren," he said.

"What line are you from?"

There was a pause.

"LINE?" barked the Veng.

"Carlassian," said the dragon.

The Veng commander snorted. "As I thought: an idiot. Your name is noted. Don't let me hear it again. Next time, De:allus, choose your assistants more wisely. I suggest you post this one to a lonely graig as far away from me as possible." It barked a harsh command and the Veng were gone as quickly as they'd arrived.

Garodor allowed himself time to stop shaking. When his wings were steady, he looked slowly at the dragon in front of him. "If I set you free and swear no treachery, will you give me your trust and let me help you?"

The green dragon nodded.

Garodor took another long breath. Then, sending out a spectrum of colors from his eyes, he strobed the nearest opening. It shimmered down its center and two lines of light moved out to the sides. "Stay in that form and follow me," he said. And he swiftly flew out of the labyrinth, with his young green "assistant" close behind.

35

Garodor led them to an isolated darn, well away from any fixed dragon communities. He landed on the dark side of the slow-spinning rock, out of the glow from Ki:mera's center.

"We'll be safe here," he said, shuttering his wings, "but we cannot stay long. I made the mistake of telling that Veng commander we had come from Erth, a place rated a high security risk. If he checks and finds there was no 'Gren' listed on those missions, there's going to be trouble."

Ren brought his isoscele around in front of him, twisting it in the way a man might check the quality of a sword. "Have no fear, De:allus. I'll be ready."

Garodor's underscales prickled uncomfortably. Once again, flashes of black had appeared in the green all over Ren's body, flowing like dark water over his wings. It was hard to shake off the terrifying thought that at any moment Graven would break through and take control—a fear reinforced by Ren's next statement.

"Why have you brought us here, to this rock? We should go to the Archive and finish this."

"Finish what, Ren? What is your purpose here? I've already told you, Ki:mera will resist you in force if it has to. Finish what?"

"My complete transformation, the perfect union between Hom and dragon. I *am* the alliance you spoke of just now. When I unlock the Archive's secrets, I will be the most powerful being in the universe."

"And tell me, which mother will you sit beside then: Mell or Godith?"

"*Raargh!* You mock me?"

"No," said Garodor, leaning well back as he heard the dragon's fire sacs fill. To his horror, two hornlike stigs had curled out of the back of Gren's head. They were ugly and twisted and strung with fine barbs, the clearest indication yet that Ren was on the verge of transfiguring into something close to a goyle. "I merely say to you, this is a false quest. I'm trying to help you—Graven also. Entry to the Archive will not be easy. The labyrinth you were in just now is nothing compared to the power of that place. Even with Grystina's help, you'd struggle to break down its tiered encryptions. Any life-form that isn't pure dragon will set off the Archive's internal alerts. If it thinks it's being invaded or attacked, it will rearrange its core dimensions and—"

Ren, let me speak with him, Grystina said suddenly.

Ren roared again and tossed his dragon head from side to side. *I TIRE of words! Be gone from me. Let my destiny unfold. Let Graven rise!*

No, you are Ren. And you will always be Ren. A boy with dragon auma inside you. When we go to the Archive, you will master the darkness. I will not let Graven's angry heart shatter yours. He can be healed. And so can you.

I do not want HEALING; I want revenge!

For Graven?

Aye, Ren replied. *For the Kaal also. It was She, Godith, who caused these wars by sowing Graven's heart among an army of crows, She who turned the Wearle into goyles, She who drew my kin into battle. I will face Her boldly and She will answer to us BOTH.*

Very well, Grystina said urgently, fearful of losing her grip. The fury in Ren was mounting at a rate beyond her control. *But I must speak with Garodor first.*

Why?

I have a confession to make. When you have heard it, I will leave you—for good.

Speak to him? How?

Transform again.

Into what?

Into me. See the fear of you in Garodor's eyes. My form will be easier for him to bear.

A ray of light passed through a hole in the darn, making Gren's horns stand out even more. *Is this a trick?*

No, Ren. Do as I ask. Change into me.

Gren looked to his left. The far edge of the darn was lit bright silver. A sign that it was turning into the light. *You have until the light fully comes.*

Agreed.

And so, to Garodor's utter astonishment, Gren altered his body shape again and appeared to the De:allus as Grystina. The De:allus had met her several times before and could verify the i:mage was no fake. Mid-green, she was, with a noble face, flecked with decorative flashes of white. She had always possessed magnificent eyes, as stunningly beautiful as Gossana's were brutal. "Matrial . . ." he gasped.

"De:allus, listen well. We do not have long. Earlier, in the Alcazar Labyrinth, you spoke about bringing justice to those who had caused the goyle mutations. I must now confess my part in it. I have the answer to the question you seek. It was Givnay who sent the first Wearle to Erth—but it was me who showed him how to search for fhosforent."

"*You?* How?"

"A casual exchange of words, nothing more. We met by chance on the Day of Moons. He was debating Graven's existence with another of your class, De:allus Grinwald. Givnay challenged him about the properties of blood. I suggested, in jest, that Graven's blood, if spilled, might have changed color. You may recall that Seren turned pink at the eclipse. That color will haunt me always. I'm certain my words were a fateful spur for Givnay's obsessive quest to locate Graven. I know he'd been studying maps of Erth."

Garodor pored over these words for a moment. What Grystina had said seemed too absurd to have any real credence. Yet how many great discoveries had turned purely on a moment of chance? "Why didn't you speak of this before you came to Erth?"

"I should have, but I had no proof. The Higher would have ridiculed me."

"So you took matters under your own wing?"

She nodded. "When Greffan's Wearle did not return and I heard the reports about fhosforent, I began to grow suspicious. When I learned that a second Wearle was heading for Erth and that Givnay would be part of it, I suspected his intent was not entirely spiritual. So I followed him. I applied for the second Erth mission, saying I was in a laying cycle and wanted to have my wearlings born on the planet so they might claim the new world as their own. Givnay was furious. As queen-elect, I ranked above him. I asked him to oversee the mining of fhosforent and bring samples to me as soon as Gariffred and Gayl were birthed. While I was in the mountain, Givnay saw what was happening to dragons who ingested too much of the ore. He quickly realized what it must be and what the blood might do for him. By then, I had become a liability. When he saw the chance to be rid of me, his grievances, old and new, came to the fore. If Ren had not been in the mountain that day, none of this would have ever been known."

"And now it has brought us to this," said Ren. In an instant, he'd abandoned dragon form in favor of his natural self and Wind. "Time to leave, De:allus—but we will not go to the Archive."

There was a threat embedded deep in those words. What's more, Ren's eyes had suddenly turned black. "Why?" asked Garodor. "I don't understand."

"I think you do," the boy said darkly. "While Grystina was speaking, I read her thoughts—and her treacherous intent . . ."

Ren—?

SILENCE! He crushed her voice.

He let Wind rear. From the center of her head came the twisted horn. "Grystina cut you off before you could finish your description of the Archive. You were intending to say that if the Archive detects a form it does not recognize, it will rearrange its core dimensions to snare the invader in its fractal matrices. A dragon could disappear in there and never be discovered, isn't that right? Grystina was planning to lure me to its labyrinths and subdue me there. But I have suppressed her deceit. And now only you can stand in my way."

"Hmm, not quite," said a voice.

Against his better judgment, Garodor whipped around.

Perched on the highest point of the darn, casually peering down at them, was a blue dragon.

Garodor almost capsized in shock. "Goodle? How—?"

"That is not Goodle," Ren said angrily, forcing the words through gritted teeth.

The blue dragon tilted its head in acknowledgment. "You've changed, brother."

Brother? The blood almost froze in Garodor's veins.

Ren broke into a wry smile. "Then perhaps you would rather see my true form, G'restyn."

"Ren, NO!"

But Garodor's cry was wasted. Ren's resistance had finally run out. With a roar that broke the darn in half, he and Wind were transformed once more.

Into the black dragon of legend.

Graven.

36

In that moment, it must have seemed to Garodor that everything he'd ever lived and worked for was sure to be destroyed—by a creature, quite literally, of mythical proportions. Graven's regeneration was both startling and terrifying in equal measure. Yet this was no red-eyed monster standing proud against the purple intraspace. Graven looked magnificent, as perfect a dragon as Garodor had ever seen. The De:allus felt weak in the presence of a beast so huge and imperious. He found himself wanting to bow.

Yet there would be no conflict. G'restyn quickly saw to that. He closed his eyes in deep concentration and Graven simply froze on the spot, his jaws open and ready to flame, his strapping wings just beginning to lift.

Garodor was stunned. "Wh-what have you done to him? Is he dead?"

"Oh, no," said G'restyn, blowing a smoke ring. "I've put him in a phasing loop for his own safety. It will be easier to talk without my brother blowing scorn upon us. He always was difficult; the legends don't lie."

Garodor looked warily at the energy field shimmering around the black dragon. Loops were usually the result of a lack of focus on behalf of the dragon who was trying to phase.

They normally broke down quite quickly, "popping" the individual into a random area of space. "Is it stable?"

"Utterly," G'restyn reassured him. "Though it won't last long if those Veng attack."

In the distance, beyond the piece of broken rock supporting Graven, a large wyng of Veng could be seen. As always, they were in battle formation.

Garodor's hearts began to beat out of time. "I knew it. I knew they'd look for us."

"Actually, we're not the target," said G'restyn. "My sensory links to the Archive suggest there's been a spatial disturbance on one of the temporal fringes. They're probably going to investigate that."

"Disturbance? Has someone else followed me from Erth?"

"I doubt it. But the Archive doesn't tell me *everything*. We should avoid any ruckus all the same. Come, De:allus, I have much to show you."

Before Garodor could raise another question, the darn they were on began to spin so fast that the Veng had soon quickened to a dizzying blur. The next thing Garodor knew, he was perched on a mountaintop not unlike Skytouch. Graven, still trapped in his phasing loop, was on another peak nearby. And on a third, just across an empty patch of sky that seemed too small in proportion to the peaks, sat G'restyn. There was nothing but static cloud below and a canopy of glittering stars above, despite the fact they were sitting in the light.

Garodor dragged his claws against the rocks. They grated with the right degree of friction, but had no real sense of solidity underfoot. "This is a construct," he muttered.

"Indeed," said G'restyn. "I've moved us into the Aurauma Fantalis and created a pleasing environment, I hope. Now, I must tell you—"

"About Goodle," Garodor cut in. He stared pointedly at the blue. "You'll tell me first about Goodle. If I remember the legends correctly, the second son of Godith was flamed on Crune. So who or what are you, 'G'restyn'?"

"I am what you see," he said plainly. "My fire tear was preserved in the Archive. I always knew I might be released one day, though I had to wait an interminably long time for a dragon of the correct disposition to come through. You would have thought that countless generations of dragons would have produced one compatible with me a lot sooner—though I suppose you could argue that I wasn't really *needed* until now. I'm deeply grateful to Goodle. We are well matched. This is a pleasant union, I assure you. I am whole in body again, and Goodle feels his life has purpose. My time in the Archive was endlessly fascinating, but I'd forgotten how rewarding simple things can be: the wind beneath a pair of wings, for instance."

"There is no wind."

"Would you like some?"

"No. I want to know what's going on, G'restyn. Why have

you been 'released'? You said you weren't needed until now. Needed for what?"

G'restyn shuffled his feet and looked poignantly at his brother. "Ki:mera is in crisis. Only we, the sons of Godith, can save it."

Garodor's yellow eyes came to a point. "What are you talking about? What crisis? Are we threatened by invasion? Disease? War?"

G'restyn shook his head. "Our G'ravity is fading."

"What?"

G'restyn sat up straight, somehow managing to look more Goodle-like than Goodle ever had. "The evidence comes from the Archive. It regularly measures the pulses from Seren. They are weakening. Cracks are appearing in the graig. Small pieces are flying off and causing collisions with other graig. The orbits of Crune and Cantorus have changed. They're drifting, De:allus. Their poles have moved. Ki:mera is steadily breaking apart."

Garodor's eyelids wrinkled—a painful mode of expression for a dragon with eyes as prominent as his. "The orbits of the moons have never been stable. And faults appear in the graig all the time. Restructuring the labyrinths with constant flamework is bound to weaken any domayne. But it's never going to break the whole network apart. Millions of dragons will live and die before a star like Seren burns out."

G'restyn twizzled his ear stigs and hummed. "Ordinarily, I would agree. But this is Ki:mera. It's completely unlike any other star system. What is Seren to dragons outside your class?"

Garodor sighed before replying. "The heart of Godith." Even now, after all Garodor had seen and experienced, when a conversation dipped into the realms of fantasy, his responses became correspondingly terse.

"And if the Archive is right and the pulses are waning?"

"Are you trying to tell me Godith is *dying*?"

"Not *dying*. Just . . . discontent."

"About what?!"

"Him." G'restyn nodded at his brother. "Now his blood has been found, there will be no peace until his auma is secured. In the meantime, Ki:mera continues to deteriorate."

Garodor twitched. Here at last was a meaningful statement. If an Elder like Givnay could be tempted into darkness, other dragons might be led astray too. "So what are you planning to do? If your brother gets free of this phasing loop, he'll kill us both and destroy Seren for fun."

"Not while I hold this."

In his claws, G'restyn materialized what looked like a memory stone. He clicked it open to reveal a glittering fire tear.

Garodor's jaws opened and closed. "Is that . . . ?"

"My brother's tear. Yes. It too was kept hidden in the Archive. This is the most precious jewel in the universe, De:allus. This will heal the darkness inside him."

"And then?"

"We must stand before Seren—and Ki:mera will be saved."

"Stand before Seren? Where?"

"On Halo Point."

Garodor blinked in shock. Halo Point was the closest piece of graig to Seren, well inside the thermal zone where dragons, for their safety, were not allowed to fly. According to the best De:allus calculations, no dragon could survive the Point for more than four wingbeats. And should they be fool enough to test the heat of Seren, the intensity of light would blind them in an instant. "You'll die there, G'restyn. You both will."

The blue dragon shrugged. "That is our destiny. We will be one with our Mother again. Ki:mera will be stabilized and the New Age that the Archive predicts will begin."

"And Ren? What happens to the boy and his horse?"

G'restyn sheathed and unsheathed his claws. "Yes, well, that's the puzzling part. According to the Archive, the boy still has a role to play on Erth."

"How? Ren's as much a part of Graven as your brother's heart."

G'restyn nodded in agreement. "It is a strange conundrum, I agree. One worthy of Goodle's input. What I'm about to show you might shed more light on it."

G'restyn blew a fine stream of air from his nostrils and the cloud base quickly dispersed. In the space between the peaks, a panoramic landscape of Erth appeared. To Garodor's amazement, they were peering at a view of the mountain range the Wearle had colonized.

"This is not a construct," G'restyn said. "The Aurauma is allowing us to see events as they actually happen."

Garodor swallowed a plug of smoke. They were watching Erth's *timeline* unfold? How was that even possible? He looked again and saw movement on the sheltered side of Vargos. Dragons were gathering with some urgency there. They appeared to be flocking to Grendel's eyrie. Was this the coup Prime Grynt had always feared?

G'restyn waved a claw and zoomed the i:mage. "Grystina's female—the wearmyss, Gayl—has been abducted by the matrial, Gossana."

"What?" Garodor reeled in shock. "Why would Gossana do that?"

"The matrial has been tainted by an enemy who call themselves the Gibbus. The Wearle is gathering to go in search of the myss."

"What do these creatures want?"

"Power, De:allus."

"The fhosforent?"

"Perhaps. More likely Gayl's auma, taken through her blood. Records suggest that early tribes of Gibbus have clashed with dragons at some point, probably in the time of De:allus Grendisar. More disturbingly, one of their food sources is crows . . ."

"Then they too must be carrying Graven's auma."

"In fragments, yes. Enough to turn them hostile. They are growing in strength and appear to have some unusual abilities. As part of their plot to seize Gayl, they have taken some Hom captive."

G'restyn swished his tail and the scene changed again.

"That's the Hom settlement," Garodor muttered, looking down on a cluster of burned-out shelters.

G'restyn nodded. He blinked and the i:mage homed in on the captives. "There has been fierce conflict and more will follow. Yet the Archive predicts that one of these prisoners will rid the Erth of the last grains of fhosforent."

Garodor looked at the faces—and saw one that made his hearts beat double. "That's Ren's mother. I remember her well. She fought bravely for the boy when we went to the settlement once to take him captive. She attacked a Veng commander. Is it her? Will she be the one who removes the fhosforent?"

"For the boy's sake, I pray not."

"Why?"

G'restyn inhaled a wisp of smoke. "It's written in the Archive that whoever removes Erth's fhosforent will die . . ."

37

On hearing these fateful words, Garodor turned toward the black dragon, almost willing Graven to fly. "Release him, G'restyn."

"Release him?"

"Yes. Bring your brother out of the phasing loop and return his fire tear. If Ren's mother is in danger, the boy must be given a chance to save her."

G'restyn lifted his face to the stars. He made no sound, but his blue eyes flickered at extraordinary speed as his mind commingled with the Aurauma. "That cannot happen. If any one of us were to intervene on Erth, it would cause a major disruption to the timeline." As though by way of compensation, he added, "The Archive has more to show you."

Before Garodor could interrupt, G'restyn was swishing the cloud base again. A very different scene now appeared before them.

A goyle was flying through a bright blue sky, above an open stretch of water. It had no injuries Garodor could see, but it was tossing its head from side to side and thrashing its tail like a thing demented.

"I don't understand," Garodor said, watching anxiously. "I thought the goyles were all destroy—?" He looked up, wary of what he was saying. The one "true" goyle was still suspended in a phasing loop beside him. More worryingly,

Graven had seen the i:mage and his eyes were darkening, as if he was trying to reach out to it.

"This is a recording from a memory stone," said G'restyn, in answer to Garodor's question. "The dragon affected is Garon."

"Garon? Garon the blue? Gabrial's father?"

"Yes."

A long gulp ran down De:allus Garodor's throat. Few dragons other than Veng had suffered the goyle mutation. Garon was one of the unlucky ones, it seemed. "Why is he flying so awkwardly?"

"He is struggling to resist the change. He has escaped the war that destroyed the first Wearle and has flown beyond the mountains—to distance himself from that domayne so he cannot harm any other dragon. He's invoking every spark of his auma in an effort to i:mage his way out of the mutation. Watch. You're about to see something extraordinary."

Suddenly, the sky around Garon flashed and turned a peculiar shade of orange. At the same time, he lost control of his wings and began to plummet, over a body of water filled with many islands.

"What happened? Where is he?"

G'restyn tapped a foot. "His anguish has caused him to i:mage a small rip in the framework of space. He's entered a parallel world."

"What?"

"Look. He's crashed."

Garon had hit a wall at the entrance to a cave, snapping the suspension arches of his right wing. An excruciating injury, even for a goyle. Garodor winced as he watched the creature crawl inside the cave and out of sight.

G'restyn said, "This is where the girl, Pine Onetooth, will find him. You can see her here with the wearling, Gariffred, and a roamer called Gus. They were drawn to the rip while they were fleeing the Wearle."

"Fleeing?"

"The details do not matter. Note the creatures that come to greet them."

Garodor blinked in astonishment. He opened up the joints in his neck to get a better look. "What are they?"

"Wyvern. A gentle-mannered class of dragon. One of many related species sewn throughout the vastness of my Mother's universe."

Garodor shook his head in wonder. Parallel worlds. New species of dragons. Even for a De:allus this was hard to take in. "Why are you showing me this?"

"The Archive wishes you to see it. You will live to verify the tale, De:allus."

"G'restyn, I'm a scientist, not a storyteller."

"That's why it must be you. No other dragon would be believed. You have been chosen to speak of these events when the moment comes, when Ki:mera must know."

"Chosen? By whom?"

G'restyn wiggled his snout. "If I tell you, they'll expect me to erase it from your memories."

Garodor leaned forward. "They? Someone planned all this?"

G'restyn took a breath. "Firebirds," he whispered.

"FIREBIRDS?!"

Now Garodor had heard it all. Firebirds were an amusing topic the Academy had discarded centuries ago. The age-old belief that a species of dragon-like birds who lived in a cloaked dimension of the Archive could travel the universe monitoring time, space, and the force of G'ravity was utterly preposterous. And yet here he was, the greatest scientific mind of his age, sitting in a construct in the Aurauma Fantalis, talking to one of the sons of Godith while the other was trapped in a phasing loop . . .

All the same, he shook firebirds from his mind. And almost angrily, he said, "If what you're showing me is genuine, I can't just sit back and watch it happen. Gariffred is in terrible danger. A dragon so young could not survive a goyle attack. I must act. Where is the drake now?"

G'restyn commingled with the Aurauma again. "Gus is seeking the source of the rip so they might pass through it and return to the mountains. The drake is alive. He will rejoin the Wearle soon."

Garodor breathed out. Well, there was some relief in that. "And the goyle? What became of Garon?"

Here, the news was not so assured.

"Undetermined."

"What's that supposed to mean?"

"The goyle's timeline is excluded from my vision."

"You can't see it? Why?"

G'restyn merely shrugged.

A cold spike ran down Garodor's spine. "Are we part of it?"

G'restyn fanged his lip. "I don't know. But . . ."

"But what? Come on, G'restyn! You're supposed to be one of the most powerful beings in the universe. Think!"

"That disturbance on the temporal fringes . . . The Archive has traced its origins. It runs all the way back to the island world . . ."

"No," said Garodor, looking anxiously at Graven. "No, no, no. We have to leave, G'restyn. Right away. The goyle in those i:mages—it's coming for your brother."

The De:allus was right. In that moment, a sound like the crack of thunder shook the Aurauma. Garodor spread his wings, but was blown toward Graven as the sky cracked again. He flashed his tail for balance, only to feel his isoscele connect with the phasing loop—and puncture it.

The release of energy blew him—and G'restyn—far aside and sent ripples all through the Aurauma Fantalis. G'restyn's construct immediately popped. Clouds and mountains faded away and quickly morphed back to a web of stars.

But something new had appeared among the stars, a dragon that was almost a clone of Graven. Huge, blue, and ready for conflict.

Gabrial's father, Garon.

38

Free at last, Graven spread his wings. All around him, as far as the eye could see, appeared wave after wave of virtual fire. Ren, it seemed, had been completely overcome, Grystina's influence finally quashed. Here, in the sway of the Aurauma Fantalis, the evil black dragon of legend was all.

He saw Garon and roared, "Bow to me!"

Yet Garon, his own wings spread and beating, faced him fully, showing no fear.

"Why would a dragon bow to itself? Look closely, Graven. Touch my mind. I have your blood running through my veins. We share the same auma, you and I."

The black dragon lengthened his fangs. "I am Lord of the Stars and all they look upon!"

"And I am sent by Seren to claim you. I was healed by Her light. And so will you be. No more dragons or Hom shall be harmed in your name. Let the boy go and give up the false heart that beats inside him. Come to me, in peace."

Dark smoke poured from Graven's nostrils. "If it's peace you seek, you shall have it—in death."

And he launched against Garon, his huge tail flashing through the starlight, dragging rivers of flame in its wake. His body grew to six times its size, jaws a chasm of endless night. His fangs were like mountain peaks tipped with blood, his great hooked claws as sharp and frigid as ancient ice. He snapped his jaws around Garon and swallowed the blue dragon whole. For Garodor, who would indeed live to tell the tale, it was the single most terrifying sight he'd ever witnessed. Like G'restyn, he assumed that Garon was dead. But Garon was smarter than any of them had supposed. At the point the jaws clamped down, he opened his mind and phased into the frame of Graven's body. He had done what vapors were always feared for: become a wraith inside a host.

The effect on Graven was almost as horrifying as it was humbling. He shook and shook, and the world shook with him. For several bone-jarring moments, it appeared he would tear the Aurauma apart. But as his size returned to normal, two incredible things happened. His body blurred and broke apart, freeing Ren and Wind in the process. They careered into space, dazed but unharmed. What was left merged into dragon form again—but with one important difference. The scales could not settle to a single color. They were blue, part purple, then blue again. And in places, just for a moment or two, the brilliant wings glowed with the sheen of Graven's birth color: gold.

G'restyn shook off the mild concussion he'd suffered in the blast and flew to his brother's side, materializing a piece of graig for them to land on. Graven was weakened, seriously so. He fell against his brother's shoulder, panting. Any sign of wickedness had left him.

"I must leave, quickly," G'restyn said to Garodor. "Take the boy home. Erth needs him. My destiny lies on Halo Point."

"G'restyn, wait. What of Garon? What should I tell his son, Gabrial?"

"That his father tamed the mighty Graven and gave his life in the service of his Wearle. *Galan aug scieth*, De:allus. Tell our story true."

And with a wave that could have come from Goodle's paw, G'restyn and Graven disappeared into the darkness.

Part six

The Wild Lands

39

"What was that?"

A distant, anguished cry wound its way into Prime Grynt's eyrie.

Commander Garrison turned his head. "It sounded like a call to battle."

He stepped away from Grynt's side and made his way toward the cave mouth. Snow was still falling over the mountains. Wild flurries blowing across the eyrie were stacking up in layers along the entrance. In such conditions, voices traveled poorly. But a cry as stark as that rarely had an uncertain base.

It came again, the cry, fierce enough to sweep the snowflakes aside.

"That's Grendel," breathed Garrison. He flushed out his wings.

"What?"

"Grendel. She must be in trouble. I must go to her."

"STAY YOUR WINGS!" roared Grynt. "You're going nowhere without my permission. Did you set the patrols I ordered?"

"Yes, of course, but in these conditions, hunting for an enemy will not be easy."

"So most of the Wearle is out by the scorch line?"

"Not all. I posted some at—"

"I want them recalled."

"Why?"

"Don't you see? This is it. It's started. The coup. They're coming for me—Gabrial, Grendel, and their band of rebels. Call your wyng. Every dragon you can trust. I want them here in force. There must be no . . . Are you *listening* to me?"

A roamer called Gannet flashed past the eyrie, answering Grendel's call with one of his own.

"You hear that?" said Garrison. He turned to face Grynt. "That was a dragon pledging its allegiance to its future queen. If you've any sense, you'll do the same."

"What? How DARE you talk to me like that! I'll have your head for your insolence!"

The dark purple lines around Garrison's eyes contracted into an arrow shape. "No, Prime Grynt, you won't. One move against me and I'll turn the Wearle against you myself. Open your eyes. There is no coup. There's never been a need for one with a queen-elect in our midst. You rightly assumed command when Galarhade died and the Wearle was in turmoil, but it was never going to be permanent. You know as well as I that if Grystina had lived you would have been bowing to her by now."

"Grendel is a surrogate! She has no claim to power!"

"That's not how the roamers see it. And my claws are closer to the ground than yours. The Wearle would die for

Grendel if they had to. She's not in want of your eyrie. All she wants—and deserves—is your respect. From the tone of those cries, something is wrong. I *will* call my wyng, but I'm going to Vargos where I'm needed. I advise you to do the same. I remind you, the Wearle is under threat. The creatures that attacked Gossana are dangerous—the servants of Graven, for all we know. A show of unity will hold the colony together. If you want to be the leader you aspire to be, put away your fears of rebellion and join me at Grendel's eyrie."

With that, Commander Garrison nodded once, then turned and launched himself into the sky.

40

First there were whoops of triumph. Then some rippling grunts of doubt. Then what sounded like notes of panic, followed by high-pitched shrieks of anger.

"What's happening?" said the treegirl Leif. Her fine, bracken hair was quivering again, sending out hazy plumes of dust, a sign that her heartwood needed water. It seemed like another age had passed since their brave but foolhardy stand against the Gibbus. She and Mell had been beaten for that and thrown into a shelter that stank of urine. No food or drink had been given. But at least no bodies had been brought back from the river. Mell was confident the other women and children had escaped.

"A skaler flew over," she said in reply, looking up through a hole in the thatch. "My eyes took sight of it, just. I swear it was carrying a young one."

Leif closed her eyes, trying to stop her sap welling up in the corners. Too great a loss of moisture now could be the end of her. "Then we're doomed. I pray our end is swift."

"No, something is wrong," Mell murmured. "The Gibbus are angry. Mebbe we are not done yet."

She shuffled her way to the door and looked out. The Gibbus were in a furious mood, scattering the snow as they ran about the clearing. The one with graying tufts on its face was screaming at another that was sitting on the ground. The skaler skull was lying at the creature's feet, a ring of small fires burning around it. Colored stones had been placed in the bony eye sockets. The sitting one was bending over the skull, making gathering movements with its rangy arms. As Mell looked on, another Gibbus loped up. It spoke a harsh message to the gray and pointed in the rough direction of the river. In a terrible burst of fury, the gray one stamped on the skaler skull, breaking it at the second attempt. It picked up one of the colored stones. With a terrifying swipe, it cracked the stone against the head of the Gibbus on the ground. The creature fell back in a heap. Mell doubted it would ever wave its arms again.

"Leif! Be strong! They're coming!"

The gray Gibbus hurled the stone away and turned its mean eyes toward the shelter. Mell shuffled as fast as she could toward Leif, but the Gibbus were faster. Two of them stormed through the door. One grabbed Mell's arm and dragged her outside. The other did the same with Leif.

An angry conversation now took place between the gray Gibbus and another that was almost a whole head taller. Mell guessed from their mood that the skaler she'd seen was supposed to have landed in the settlement, guided somehow by the skull-waver. The fact that it had gone too far was forcing the Gibbus to alter their plans. The tall one drew a finger across its throat. It left Mell in no doubt about what it was demanding.

She looked toward the mountains and started to say, “Ned, my husband. Ren, my boy. I love you bo—”

Then the blow came and she said no more.

The last she remembered as the stars began to settle was being hoisted on to the shoulder of a beast and carried away. After that, there was only darkness and cold, and the fading sensation of snowflakes falling against one side of her swollen face.

41

Garrison flew toward Grendel's eyrie, calling orders to the dragons circling Mount Vargos. *Stay in the sky! Wait for my command!* Four within range had heard the cry and flocked to Grendel. More would follow. Farther down the mountain, two more roamers were standing over what looked like the body of another. Streaks of blood along the mountainside told their own tale: The dead dragon had fallen from the eyrie. It could only be the guard that Garrison himself had posted there.

With his primary heart thumping double, he landed in the eyrie and closed his wings. The first dragon he saw was the healer, Grymric. The old male was stretched out on his side, his eyes closed, his breathing labored. The mapper, Garret, was attending to him. There was no sign of Gossana. But Gabrial was here, taking instruction from Grendel. The blood had risen in Grendel's face. Every line that defined her distinctive features was heightened in glowing pulses of green.

Garrison caught his breath. "What's happened?"

Gabrial turned to him. "Gossana has gone wild. She attacked Grymric and killed the guard. She's taken Gayl."

"She will be found," Grendel said, her voice a growl. "So whatever you've come to tell me, Commander, I suggest you take straight back to Grynt. The dragons here have answered my call. Bow to me or war with me. That is the Law of the Wearle now."

Garrison bowed. "I've flown here against Grynt's orders. He is in no doubt where my loyalties lie. What steps have you taken? Do you know which way Gossana went? Or what made her commit such an act?"

Gabrial glanced at the stricken healer. "Grymric keeps muttering one word: *wyrm*."

Garrison reeled back, visibly shocked. "That must be why she was scratching her ear. If they've put a wyrm inside her, the creatures must be controlling her mind."

"The sooner we fly, the sooner we know," snapped Grendel, aware that vital time was passing.

"I've sent word to the sweepers," Gabrial said, "asking them to congregate around the Hom settlement. I'm about to take a wyng out there to investigate."

Garrison looked doubtful. "I suspect that might be a futile journey. The creatures will know we'd search the settlement first. My hunch is they've sent Gossana elsewhere. Garret."

The mapper turned his head. "Commander?"

"I need you here."

Garret touched his isoscele to Grymric's side and went to join the others.

"How is he?" Grendel asked, trying to stay composed. Grymric had always been a favorite of hers.

"Mostly winded," Garret replied softly. "The shock has wounded him more than anything. How can I be of assistance?"

"We need targets," said Garrison. "You've mapped areas outside the domayne. I need to know where the beings who attacked Gossana might be running to." He described them for Garret, hoping the mapper could match them to a likely habitat.

After some brief thought, Garret said, "This would be my best prediction." He i:maged a map of a rocky wilderness, barely touched by green life or trees. "It lies far to the west of the mountains and spreads out over a vast plain. There are labyrinths under the rocky exterior—"

"Labyrinths?" Grendel raised her head.

"Nothing on the scale of Ki:mera," said Garret. "We tested three small areas, but a dragon of our size could not gain access; the surface openings are far too small."

"But the creatures could hide in there?"

"Yes. And take in a wearling."

Garrison ground his teeth. "What else can you tell us?"

Garret reconstructed the i:mage to show them a view from ground level. "The highest aggregations of basal rock only stand a tenth as high as Vargos. The land is also dry. There is little in the way of food or water."

"You recorded no Hom-like movement there?"

"None."

"That doesn't mean the beings weren't present," said Gabrial.

Garrison nodded, remembering the beasts' ability to hide. "I agree. It's a good place to start. We can use heat scans or scent if the creatures go to ground. But as Garret says, it is a long flight. If we commit too large a wyng and we're wrong, we weaken our chances closer to home."

"There is a way to be sure," said Garret. "Though it may be a fading hope by now. Gayl will be frightened. She's likely to have left her . . . scent in the sky."

"You can track it?" said Grendel, pushing forward.

Garret shook his head. "My olfactic glands are not up to such a task. Only dragons of the Zyolian line would have a sense of smell sharp enough to follow a trail that faint. As far as I know, there's only one Zyolian in the Wearle."

"Who?" said Gabrial.

"Me," said a gruff voice near to the cave mouth.

The new arrival rattled his wings and stepped forward. "Well, are you just going to stand and stare or shall we form a wyng and find this wearling?"

"Prime," said Garrison and Gabrial together.

Grendel raised her head and stared proudly at Grynt. "The Prime will fly at my side," she said. "Garret, find a competent roamer to take care of Grymric, then follow us." She stared again at Grynt and nodded. "Let's go."

42

"Wait!" Grynt cried, stalling the rush to fly. "If we're to battle these creatures, we need to talk tactics. Grendel?"

She nodded her consent.

Grynt gave a curt bow. "Gabrial, get in the air and organize those roamers circling the mountain. When we fly, we go in a broad line together, low to the ground, ten wingspans apart. Grendel and I will be at the center. Garret will fly above us to give him the broadest view of the land. Any scents or sightings, send a call. Do not attack without my order. Is that clear?"

Gabrial glanced at Grendel. "Gossana is not to be harmed," she said.

"Understood," said Gabrial. He left quickly, barely moving the air.

"Commander Garrison."

"Prime."

Grynt nodded at Garret's i:mage of the wilderness. "Record this and give it to the roamers on the mountainside, then send them to your border patrols and have them fly . . . ?"

"West," said Garret.

"Due west. They'll find us quickly enough. Educate the

messengers about this foe. Me too, as soon as we're in the air. Go."

Garrison gave a stout nod. He recorded the i:mage and departed at speed.

Grynt then turned to the mapper, Garret. "Give me a moment with Grendel."

"Yes, Prime."

"And, Garret, find some aid for Grymric. I want him closely guarded. Go quickly. Be ready to fly as soon as we leave the eyrie."

"I will," said the mapper. And he too was gone.

When they were alone, Grynt said to Grendel, "This is not the time for speeches, I realize that. I merely wish you to know you have my support. Show me where the wearmyss lies at night."

Grendel took him at haste to Gayl's sleeping chamber. As he bent his snout so he might inhale and learn Gayl's scent, Grendel said, "Grynt, there's something you need to know. When the Hom that Grymric was treating died, he shed a fire tear."

Grynt brought his head up.

"Gayl swallowed it," she said. "Nothing happened, as far as I'm aware. I just want you to know that it's not only dragon auma you'll be fighting to save."

Grynt blew a line of smoke. "Is the boy involved?"

Grendel shook her head. "We don't know where Ren is. That's the truth. All the evidence suggests these creatures are working alone. Grymric thinks they've put a wyrm in Gossana's mind."

Grynt breathed out silently. "Very well. I have what I need. Let's fly." And with the cave floor pounding to the beat of his steps, he moved toward the cave mouth and launched himself into the snow-filled sky.

43

When Mell woke, she was on the ground, her face smudged into a layer of snow. Her cheek ached fiercely on that side, hands and feet both rigid with cold. She had to flex her fingers a number of times to allay the dread that the Gibbus had maimed her. She blinked and saw Leif on the ground nearby. The treegirl wasn't moving.

"Leif."

The word was barely off Mell's lips when one of the Gibbus hauled her to her knees and forced her to look straight ahead.

On the ground a little way in front of Leif was the skaler Mell had seen fly over the settlement. The beast was motionless, probably dead, surrounded by a crowd of shrieking Gibbus. On a shout from the Gibbus holding Mell, the bodies parted a little. Now Mell saw the reason for their taunts. A young skaler was trapped beneath the big one's body. It was alive and baying for help.

Not since the Kaal had been driven from the mountains had Mell ever thought she'd feel pity for a skaler, but her heart went out to this little one now. Perhaps, in time, it would be her foe. But all she could think of at present was its anguish.

Through a blur of pain, she watched the Gibbus arrange themselves along the big skaler's body. With a collective shriek they pushed hard enough to roll it back a little and free the pupp. One of its wings was broken. The tribe screeched again and flapped their arms, mocking it. The skaler roared back but made no fire. It snapped at one Gibbus and almost took a paw. The gray leader barked a command. The pupp was quickly restrained, then bound in a cradle of sticks and twine.

Two Gibbus picked up the cradle, and a group of them began to lope away at speed. One of the stragglers picked up the sickle Mell had used to such deadly effect. Her heart pumped, as she feared they would turn it against her. How much did a young skaler eat at one meal? A hand? A foot? Either cut was easy for a blade like that. But the target was not Mell. She twisted her face away as she saw the blade swing toward the dead skaler's eye. At that point, one of the Gibbus slung her over its shoulder and carried her away, sparing her any more gruesomeness. She saw Leif picked up and heard the girl cough. *Thank you*, Mell whispered to the Fathers. They were both alive.

For now.

44

The line of dragons was quickly formed. Spearheaded by Grynt and Grendel, they made their way at speed toward the western reaches of the scorch line. There the storm began to ebb and they were given better sight of the land. Every green thing was pasted white. It was the most beautiful vision of Erth Grendel had ever seen.

"Anything?" she cried.

Grynt's voice burst through the last of the blizzard. "No! I may need to go on ahead! I'm picking up the wearling's scent on you! It's confusing me! Who's that?"

Another dragon was approaching from a forward angle.

"It's Gruder!" Gabrial called, shaking snow off his snout. He sent the sweeper a cry of recognition.

Gruder swept over them and quickly doubled back, dropping into the space between Gabrial and Grendel. *Are you searching for Gossana?*

The words flowed into Gabrial's mind. It was easier to commingle with others in flight, rather than fight against the noise of wind pressure.

Yes, she has Gayl. Have you seen them?

No. But a short while ago I picked up a female scent near the scorch line, farther along toward the sea. I thought nothing of it until I got word from Garrison's patrols that something was wrong and Gossana was involved. I was coming to report it. If I'm right, you need to bank ten points south.

"South!" Gabrial screamed to every dragon within earshot. He quickly changed course and was pleased to see the whole line slot into place.

"Has he sighted them?!" called Grynt. He eyeballed Gruder.

"No! But he had a trace on Gossana!"

Grynt called to Garret. "Mapper! Report!"

Garret was in place above Grynt and Grendel, the only dragon flying higher than the rest. *The Wild Lands are vast*, he replied, spreading his thoughts among the whole wyng, *but this course will take us away from them. My advice is to split up—half to follow the trail Gruder detected, half to fly for the Wild Lands.*

I agree, said Garrison, joining in. *Gossana could have dropped Gayl into the creatures' clutches by now. They could be using the matrial to draw us away from the wearling.*

He's right, said Gabrial. *I'll take Gruder and two roamers and we'll—*

Wait, said Grynt. *Stay on this course.*

He surged forward suddenly. Gabrial broke the line and accelerated up to him. *You've found the trail?*

A faint trail, yes. I can't be sure if it's Gayl or the matrial. Until we know for sure, stay with the wyng.

With a powerful beat, Grynt swept another three points south.

On they flew, farther and farther away from the Wild Lands, but closer and closer to the scent. Until, in time, they came across an elongated hump in the windswept crust of white below.

The shape of an adult dragon.

Gossana.

She was lying on a patch of open ground, away from trees or other hiding places, close to a stream that was cutting a hazy black line through the land. A long gouge in the snow behind her suggested she had come down and skidded some way.

While Garrison gave the general order to circle, Gabrial and Grynt swept over the body.

The first pass told Gabrial what he needed to know.

Gossana wasn't moving and Gayl wasn't there.

They *should* have split up.

"Don't land!" he heard Garrison call. "Flame around her first! The creatures can hide in the ground!"

"Do it," said Grynt, sweeping past.

So Gabrial burned a circle around the matrial, quenching the snow and laying dead anything that might be hiding.

No creatures leapt up screaming in pain.

And still Gossana didn't move.

Grynt waited for the ground to cool, then landed quietly beside her.

She was dead. He knew it before he could bring himself to look at her famously vindictive eyes. The sockets were empty, bloodied but clean. Her killers had taken those harsh red jewels and left her staring at permanent darkness.

Gabrial landed beside the Prime, Grendel next to him.

For a moment, none of these dragons spoke. In time it was Grynt, fire flickering in his throat, who whispered, "Godith, take her auma. Shield it in your heart of hearts." He lifted his isoscele and touched it point to point with Gossana's. It was the greatest show of kindness to the matrial Gabrial had ever seen.

Grendel said, "I don't want her burned here."

Grynt gave a solemn nod. Raising his voice to the sky he bellowed, "Pick her up. Take her back to the mountains."

Two roamers glided down to lift her.

Gabrial shuddered as he watched the frame rise—a shudder that soon became a terrifying chill when he realized something was wrong about the lift. It was taking too much effort to pick Gossana up. The matrial was large, but the roamers Garrison had assigned to her were strong. They should have been handling her corpse with ease. It was heavier, clearly, than it ought to be, as if she had gorged herself before she'd died—or something weighty had been put inside her.

Then he saw it: a gash in the belly that had been resealed with some kind of gel.

"Put her down!" he yelled.

"What?" said Grendel.

"She's been cut!" the blue shouted. "Something's wrong! Put her down!"

He had intended to add the word *slowly*, but by then the roamers had opened their claws and dropped Gossana from a small tree height.

She hit the ground with a solid thump, landing not quite belly side down. The impact opened the gash and discharged a spurt of goo from the abdomen. For one moment, Gabrial couldn't look. He feared the creatures had slain the wearmyss and cruelly sealed her inside Gossana. But it wasn't Gayl that punched her way out of the hole. It was two large Gibbus.

Gabrial was still in shock when the first one came for him. It was three strides away when it was hit with a twisting column of flame. Grendel had taken it out. She turned to flame the other, but Grynt was already there. For the first time, Gabrial was able to witness how fearful a dragon Grynt could be. The Prime had his tail end around the creature's neck and was holding it off the ground. It wriggled like a hung fish, gagging for air.

"Where are the others?" Grynt said calmly. "Show me and I'll let you run."

The creature kicked its powerful legs.

"Show me," said Grynt. He tightened his grip.

The creature bared its teeth. Saliva ran over Grynt's isoscele. "I should take your eyes for hers," he said, "but that would be a poor exchange. You picked the wrong dragon to war with, creature." And he tightened his grip again, until bones cracked and muscles melted and there was nothing left to support the beast's head. The head fell to the ground and rolled down a shallow slope into the stream. With a cursory snarl, Grynt dropped the remains and cleaned his tail idly in the snow.

"Did you read it?" asked Gabrial.

Grynt looked sideways at the young dragon. "Of course I read it. The creature's mind was weak. It gave me everything I wanted to know. Its kind call themselves Gibbus. Garret was right about their location. They're taking Gayl to the Wild Lands along with two Hom. What you see here is an ill-hatched plot, put into place because Gossana flew off course. You did well to spot the cut in her belly. You've stopped them getting to the heart of the mountains."

Gabrial looked down at the matrial's body. "She must have been fighting the wyrm. Why else would she stray off course?"

"Because she realized what was happening and was trying to save Gayl's life," said Grendel, making it sound like a statement of fact.

Grynt kicked aside the corpse of the Gibbus he'd killed. "True or not, that's how she'll be remembered."

Gabrial glanced at the headless body. "You said you'd let it run."

Grynt snorted at the blue's naivety. "And have it sink its teeth into one of us? Bring the head; it might be useful. Burn the rest."

"Gossana too," said Grendel. "I've changed my mind. Set a fire all the world can see. Let the creatures know we're coming. Let there be *war*."

45

To Mell's surprise, the Gibbus, when they ran, moved like men. Their stout legs hit the ground with vigor, taking them at speed across the roughest of terrains.

So it was that they reached the Wild Lands in far less time than Mell had imagined. It was a barren place where grass grew thinly in cracks of stone and barely a snowflake lingered. Not a great deal was known about the Gibbus, but Mell had heard it said they lived below ground in caves no Kaal would want to occupy. Looking at the changing landscape around her, she knew she must be close to her journey's end.

She began to hear grunts of exertion and realized her carrier had started to climb. With an effort, she cast a glance to one side. The tribe was breaking formation, disappearing into the rocks through any gaps they could find. If Mell had given light to any hope of rescue, those thoughts were dashed when she saw how far the Wild Lands stretched. The rocks ran as far as the mountains grew high. She looked to the stony horizon and felt as if a wall had been built in her heart.

Without warning, her carrier came to a halt and dropped

her like a sack of old bones. The back of her head struck a lump of stone. Taking no note of her cry of pain, the Gibbus hauled her toward a hole. It bundled her inside and sent her tumbling down a shaft that took its fair share of skin and blood. She slithered to a halt at the bottom, and there was grabbed by more strong hands. They dragged her along a winding tunnel that stank all the way of heat and decay. After several changes of direction and a journey across a perilous bridge, she emerged into a gigantic chamber. No daylight pricked this place, but the Gibbus had inserted fire pouches all around the walls. They lit the whole cave with a warm orange glow, though that was little comfort to Mell or her wounds.

Her entrance was greeted by a roar of scorn. The Gibbus who had dragged her this far now lifted her high above its head, as if she were as light as a caarker feather. It turned so many circles that the walls of the chamber blurred and Mell hardly knew she was being thrown until her body crashed to the ground once more. Every bony part of her erupted in pain, yet she still gathered strength enough to look for Leif. The girl was on her knees a few paces away. Her brittle limbs were weeping sap, but she didn't look as badly treated as Mell.

They pulled Mell up until she too was kneeling and made her look at a fat Gibbus who sat atop an even fatter rock. It was old, this creature, with slow-moving eyes and even more gray on its pudgy face than the one that had led the attack on the settlement. That gray came forward and bowed to the fat one. Then it did something Mell could hardly believe. It put its hands to its head and produced a floating picture out of nowhere. Mell swallowed blood when she saw it. It was a vision of the guard she had killed in the shelter. The scene caused uproar within the chamber. Everywhere, Gibbus were calling for her head. The fat one wiggled a finger.

"No!" Mell screamed as two of them came for her.

They pulled her to her feet and dragged her closer to the gray. Keeping its cruel eyes firmly on her, it reached out sideways.

Another Gibbus put a knife in its hand.

To Mell's surprise, her bonds were cut. Hands and feet. Two slashes. Swift.

The gray barked a command. The guards let her go.

Mell looked up in confusion, rubbing her swollen wrists. Her red hair fell in sorry waves, almost cloaking the defeat in her face. "Loathsome creature, what do you want?"

It stabbed the knife into the ground and backed away.

A fight? Was that it? She was supposed to take the knife and defend herself?

She looked at the Gibbus and saw its eyes drift to a place behind her.

She turned slowly.

And there was the opponent they had matched her with.

The baby skaler.

46

"Spread out!" Grynt called to Commander Garrison as the Wearle came within sight of the Wild Lands. "Sweep the edges first, then bring the lines in slowly. Keep them high and silent. Report any movements on the ground to me."

"You heard the Prime!" Garrison barked at his patrols. "Spread out and start looking! Speak in thought until you're ordered to attack! No fire! No war cries! Go!"

This doesn't look good, said Grendel as she raced over the first few pillars of rock. *I see the holes Garret was talking about, but no way in for us. Do you still have Gayl's scent?*

She's in there, I'm sure of it, Grynt replied. *How deep, I can't tell. Garret, can you chart these rocks?*

I'm trying to, the mapper said, his gaze strobing back and forth across the terrain. His eyes flickered at remarkable speed as they bounced light waves over the coarse gray surface. *The topography of this sector supports what I said earlier. We're looking at a shallow subterranean network. Small caverns linked by bridges and tunnels.*

Any large spaces? Gabrial asked, swooshing under Garret's flightpath.

Difficult to tell. There's so much rubble. It's hard to construct an accurate i:mage.

What about there?

Grendel drew their gaze toward a skinny vein of water, one of only two within visible range. Blotches of greenery were spread around its shores. A dry shrub here, some weed cover there. Sad flowers, struggling to stretch their petals, cowered in the cold, flat air. To one side of the water, the rocks heaped up. Grendel could see no obvious openings, but she instinctively felt that something could hide there.

Garret had news to support that impulse. *There's a void underneath the highest stack.*

How deep? asked Gabrial, his eyes scanning every warp and shadow.

Double your wingspan and more.

Size? said Grynt.

Trying to calculate it now. It's big, served on every side by shafts and tunnels.

Gabrial dropped lower and circled the mound. *Anything we can dig through?*

Garret produced an i:mage for them. *Given time we could break through the upper shafts. But any movement of erth is sure to send them running. As you can see, they have plenty of escape routes—if they're in there, of course.*

They're in there, said Grendel. Even in thought, the dragons felt her snarl. *This void, is it big enough to take one of us?*

I don't advise phasing in, Garret cautioned. *Without knowing the inner contours of the void, your chances of transiting safely are minimal, especially as you'll be passing through densely packed strata. The probability of atomic displacement is—*

Thank you, Garret. I know the risks. Grendel came around in a circle. *I'll do whatever it takes to get Gayl out of there. I might end up half rock, half dragon, but it will scare those creatures out of their wits.*

I phase faster than you, Gabrial said, sweeping by. *If anyone is going in, it ought to be me.*

Enough, snapped Grynt, zooming past. *I'm not prepared to lose either of you. I agree we could do a lot of damage from inside, but there's no guarantee we can save the wearling. They could take her down a tunnel and we'd be no wiser.*

Then what do you suggest? By now, Gabrial was desperate to land and start pulling rocks apart.

Smoke, said Grynt. *We take up positions where the tunnels reach the surface and blow dark smoke inside. We ought to be able to create a cloud to fill that cavern. Garret, do you agree?*

Yes, said the mapper, tilting his head to continue scanning. *I'm getting no traces of heat from the tunnels, which suggests they haven't posted guards. But to give the smoke a chance to carry, we'd need to clear some of the access points. That's going to take time—and stealth. If we start throwing rocks around, the echoes will travel.*

Then we'll be careful, Grynt said. *We'll work from three sides and leave the creatures an escape route. If the smoke doesn't choke them, it will drive them out. When they come, we'll be waiting. The wearling won't like it, but she'll survive.*

What about the Hom they've taken prisoner? said Gabrial.

I can't help them, Grynt said bluntly. *Our priority—your priority—has to be the wearling. I'll give the order not to flame any Hom that escape, but I can do no more than that. Grendel?*

Agreed, she said, gliding around.

Gabrial?

The blue sighed heavily. *Agreed.*

Grynt banked and dropped another tier lower. *Show Garrison the i:mage and bring the roamers in. Let's give these creatures something to think about. Begin.*

47

Although she had never experienced the terrible drain of dehydration before, Leif had been warned of the symptoms many times. Cracking joints. Withering fingers. Hair strands drooping and falling out. Grinding splits in any part of the body, especially across the neck and shoulders.

A slow, slow closing-down.

Despite the thunder of voices around her, Leif was back in the Whispering Forest. She was running with the flutter-flies, chasing sunbeams through the trees. The bracken was dry and light underfoot. Frooms grew everywhere, ripe to pick. The scent of pollen was heady, but fresh.

Sprites were all around, in the trees and not. They hid as fast as a raindrop falls whenever Leif tried to look their way. She laughed, for she knew the games sprites liked to play. They were leading her somewhere.

Into the clearing.

Straight to the boy.

She skidded to a halt. The boy was sitting at the base of a tree, balancing a cone on the palm of his hand. It was dry and woody, perfectly formed. Its dark brown scales were fully open.

Ren Whitehair, said Leif. She pointed at him as a small child might.

I am, he replied. *Will you sit with me, Leif?*

She sat, cross-legged, and picked a wild froom. She hooked a finger under the cap and peeled it. *You are not of the forest, Ren Whitehair.*

I am not, he replied. *But I care for it as you do. I like its forms.*

The cone in his hand closed up for a moment. When it opened again, tiny stars were glistening in its woody nooks.

Those are strange seeds, Leif said, craning forward. *What manner of tree will grow from them?*

Until they are sown, I cannot say, Ren answered.

Leif licked a finger and touched the air. *There is no wind to spread the seeds.*

The scales of the cone opened wider still, making a pleasant popping sound. *The wind for these seeds blows from another world, Leif.*

Leif thought about this as she ate her froom. *I carry a cone for luck*, she said brightly. She pointed to her middle, where her robe made a pocket.

This is that cone, Ren said kindly. *I have borrowed it, Leif. It was parched and sore in need of water.*

Leif stopped peeling. She felt her pocket. Dry and unfilled. Her heartwood, she realized, felt the same. She clamped her arms suddenly and looked around her. She thought she felt a crack beginning in her shoulder. *Am I dying, Ren Whitehair?*

Changing, he said. He handed her the cone.

Leif dropped it gratefully into her pocket. She looked up. The sky appeared to be made of stone. No blue, no cloud, no birds, no tops. Her throat ran dry. Sap seeped from her joints. An angry wave of noise began to close in around her. The brutal chants of an army of Gibbus momentarily invaded her fragile delirium. *Will you light my way, Ren Whitehair?*

My mother will, he said, fading from her. *My mother will light the way for all, Leif.*

When the time is right.

48

The skaler was gangly, unsteady on its feet. Not much bigger than a rangy mutt. But it was hurt and in pain and could rip her wide open. Mell was sure of that.

The Gibbus screamed at her to pick up the knife. Mell was one bound from it; the skaler, three. She shook her head and looked at her foe. It was a beautiful thing, as dark as the juice of a purple thornberry, with wings a little lighter and a tail of matching shades. Until moments ago, when the Gibbus had cut it free of its cradle, the beast had been crying great sheets of distress. Wailing for its kin. Its guardians.

Its mother.

That last thought brought Mell down to her knees.

The Gibbus roared, enraged by her weakness. One capered around her, smacking its repugnant teeth in anger. It kicked a spray of dust into her swollen face. The dust burned in her cuts and dried her tongue. She fell forward, coughing, and placed her trembling hands on the erth. *Forgive me*, she whispered to the Fathers of her tribe. *Forgive me, but I will not fight this pupp.*

That was when a strange thing happened.

She heard a voice in her head, and it was coming from the pupp.

Mell, pick up the knife, it said.

Her face creased in confusion.

The knife, said the voice, *do as I ask*.

Gibbus voices screamed all around her.

Fires flickered in the stagnant walls.

The air began to feel oddly stale.

"Spirit, why do you taunt me?" Mell said. She wanted to cry. She did—a little.

You know me, said the voice. *I am one with this creature. She means you no ill. Pick up the knife.*

Mell rested her bleary gaze on the blade. "I know you?" she muttered.

Aye, said the voice.

The knife lay close, handle nearest. Its cutting edge glinted at every nick.

Do it, said the voice.

Mell's fingers crept forward.

HAAR! The cave erupted with noise. Everywhere, Gibbus hollered their approval.

You know me. You trust me, the voice continued. *Do not be afraid. Do as I ask and help will come.*

Mell swayed momentarily. "Who are you?" she whispered. Her hand closed around the twine that Waylen had used to bind the handle of the knife.

All around the cavern, Gibbus whooped and beat their chests hollow. At last. A fight! But while most of them argued about the victor, only one—the gray—turned its head and twitched its nostrils.

There was a change in the air.

A wisp of something that should not be present.

Smoke.

Mell brought the knife to her breast. The skaler tilted its head and graarked. In its eyes, a dim light shined. The light of dawn rising over the mountains.

I am not as I was, but you know me, said the voice. *My name was Rolan Woodknot. I rode with brave men against the skalers. But what you see here is no foe to the Kaal.*

"Rolan?"

Aye.

Mell smiled faintly. She saw her reflection in the flat of the blade. "I hear you, Rolan. What is it you would have me do?"

Look at the clasp. The sign marked there.

Mell turned the knife against the flat of her hand. "The sun, the moon, the stars," she said.

The Kaal had used the mark for centuries. Three wavy lines that did not meet. A symbol of fortune, gifted by the old ones, blessed by the Fathers.

A symbol mostly forgotten.

Carve it, Mell, and help will come.

"Carve it." Mell was almost delirious.

Make the sign in the erth, said Rolan.

Mell nodded weakly. Her hands clasped double around the knife.

49

She was halfway to scratching out the second line when the gray Gibbus grew suspicious.

It lumbered up and knocked her sideways.

The knife fell from her grasp.

The Gibbus looked down at what she had drawn and wiped it clean with one twist of its foot. It snatched up the blade, then kicked Mell away, rolling her on to her back. As she made eye contact, it raised the knife.

Two things stopped it ending her life. First, something dropped out of one of the shafts and rolled a short distance across the cavern floor. It was the head of the Gibbus Grynt had killed. A shocked silence gripped the chamber. The gray Gibbus turned to look. In that instant, Gayl rushed forward and bit straight through the creature's ankle. The gray screamed in agony and toppled over, blood gushing from the wound. The knife fell from its hand. Gayl was immediately at the gray's throat, sinking her bitter-sharp teeth into its neck.

For all this, the Gibbus fought back well. Its strong arms lashed like fury at the myss, catching the broken bones of her wing and ripping one section of the sails to shreds. A rough hand gripped the base of her tail and twisted it brutally. Gayl squealed in distress and surrendered her bite. Instantly, the other hand shot toward her head to close around her slender neck. Despite the dreadful wound to its leg, the Gibbus sat up, raising Gayl aloft. It squeezed her throat, slowly, remorselessly, causing her spiracle vents to crack. Then it squeezed again until her jaws spread wide. Gayl wriggled and started to weaken. Her wings drooped. Her pre-claws bunched. The gray Gibbus gurgled in triumph, ready to apply the fatal press.

That gurgle was the last sound it would ever make.

Using every grain of strength in her body, Mell heaved forward and plunged the knife deep between its shoulders, piercing its wicked heart. The Gibbus rocked as the life bled out of it. A veil came down on its glazed brown eyes. Mell swiftly withdrew the blade and hustled the cumbersome body aside to be as ready as she could be for the next assault.

But the Gibbus weren't coming for her anymore. Some kind of terror had gripped the whole tribe. They were heading for the tunnels, but reemerging from them as soon as they'd gone in. All around the cavern, they were spluttering and hacking, falling to their knees, their hands to their throats. Great plumes of smoke were rolling across the far side of the chamber, cloaking the Gibbus in a deadly cloud.

Skaler breath!

Mell felt the first wisps sting the corners of her eyes and knew she must act or die, choking.

Covering her face, she rushed to Leif's side. Quickly, she slashed the girl's ties. Leif was gasping, her once lively eyes now red with pain. She collapsed as Mell freed her. "Leave me," she whispered.

"I will not," Mell said. She raised Leif by the shoulders and shook her awake. "We have to run, Leif. *Run*. The skalers are attacking."

"Too weak . . ." Leif croaked. Her head fell forward.

She gasped once more and quickly passed out.

By now, the Gibbus were desperate to escape. Some had worked out that the side of the cavern where Mell was positioned was least affected by the smoke. As Mell shielded Leif against her chest, two Gibbus swept past and dived into a tunnel. She heard them scrabbling toward the surface and tasted a tang of clean air in their wake. There, she thought, was the route she must take.

Putting the knife into her belt loop, she struggled to her feet with Leif in her arms. The girl weighed no more than a nest of twigs and was easy enough to carry. But carrying was one thing, climbing another. Still, Mell reasoned, she had to try.

Mell, wait.

The voice again. In her rush to get away, Mell had forgotten the heroic pupp. She saw it now, half cast in shadow. It had crawled behind a rock to be out of the chaos.

More Gibbus swept by, stampeding for the openings. Mell pressed herself back into the darkness, coughing as the smoke worked into her lungs. *I must flee, Rolan, or the girl will die. I pray your new kin come for you.*

No, he begged as she started to move. *Hide if you can. I will draw the smoke from you. You may be caught in flames outside.*

A shriek came from deep within the tunnels. A knot of Gibbus tumbled back into the cavern. The last three to fall were all on fire.

Hide, Rolan urged her.

Mell shook her head. *Nay, I have no quarrel with skalers. This child is wounded. You know them, Rolan. Surely they will show her mercy?*

They will, but they may not see you in time. And if you cross the Gibbus, they will cut you down. Hide and make the sign. I promise you, help will come.

That was his last communication. The tall Gibbus Mell had seen at the settlement, the one that had wanted to finish her off, pushed through the rest and dragged the pupp out of hiding, clamping its throat to keep the jaws at bay. The skaler kicked but had no more fight.

What they planned to do with it, Mell could not imagine. But here, she thought, was a chance to flee. Yet the moment she turned to run, one of the ogres was blocking her path. It was bearded, this one, and ugly for it. Its lips peeled back off its broken teeth. Mell braced herself and slowly retreated, until her shoulders bumped the wall and she could go no farther.

The Gibbus sneered. Mell spat in its face. The beast immediately sprang forward. It tore Leif out of her arms, tossing the girl aside as if she were made of nought but air. Mell screamed and went at it, fists flinging. But the Gibbus was quick and its reach was long. It pinned her by the throat and put her back against the wall until her toes could barely touch the ground. It rumbled sourly, its breath as rank as fouled water. With the back of one finger, it stroked her hair. Mell turned her face from the touch and saw a solution at her side. In a flash, she'd pulled one of the lights off the wall and thrust it into the creature's face. It screamed and fell back, its beard alight. Quickly, Mell pulled the knife from its fastening at her waist. *Forgive me*, she whispered to Leif in her thoughts, *for here our journey must surely end*. And yelling for the honor of the Kaal and forest folk, she went in for what she thought would be her final kill.

But others were arriving by then, the tall Gibbus at their head. It clamped the wrist that held the knife with a grip as tight as three men might levy. It pulled the weapon out of Mell's hand as easily as plucking fruit from a tree. For one beat of her brave Kaal heart, she thought the beast would drive the blade through her, the way she had killed its companion, the gray. Instead, it would do her a small favor. With her free hand, she tried to gouge its eyes. But it caught her again and turned the blade against those fingers, drawing the edge across her skin until her blood ran freely and she wept with pain. Then it struck her with enough force to leave her dazed. Dazed, but not entirely adrift. For as they picked her up again, she pressed her hand against the wall and drew, in blood, the sign that Rolan had wanted.

Come swift, she muttered in the blur of her mind.

Before she too, like Leif, passed out.

50

Gabrial! What's wrong?

As the wyng drew back to rekindle their fire sacs and the second wave of dragons moved into position, Commander Garrison sped over the blue, surprised at his apparent unwillingness to fight. Several Gibbus had come to the surface, where they had met a fiery end. Yet Gabrial, who was part of the first line ordered to attack, had barely warmed his nostrils. He'd been scouring the landscape for any signs of Gayl. *This isn't right, Garrison. There ought to be more of them.* Gabrial had expected to see a huge exodus of Gibbus, not a few half-crazed stragglers. *We can't take the mound apart unless the creatures flee.*

Garrison banked sideways, scanning the rocks. *The smoke may have poisoned the rest.*

Or we can't see them. Or they've gone deeper. Either prospect made Gabrial's hearts beat faster. *Didn't you say they had some hiding trick? What if they're cloaking Gayl from our sight?*

It appears they don't want to. Look.

Two creatures had suddenly emerged from the mound, dragging Gayl between them. One was brandishing a knife.

Now Gabrial's battle stigs rose.

A warning cry went out from Grendel, quickly echoed by another from Grynt. The Prime had seen the wearling and ordered an immediate cessation of fire. But the sighting had gone to Gabrial's head. He swooped down, screaming loudly. The beasts responded by yelling hysterically and retreating toward the hole they'd come out of. Only at the final moment, thanks to a forceful shout from Garrison, did the blue dragon come to his senses. He tilted his wings and soared overhead.

Grendel was livid. The gold beads along her face were glowing so brightly they could have been on fire. "Do that again and I'll cut you down," she skriked, no longer bothering to keep the silence.

"They've hurt her," snarled Gabrial, his wings clapping as he pitched around her. "It looks like she's been bled."

"They'll hurt her worse if you go in again," snapped Grynt. He glided past, calling out to Garrison. "What's your assessment? What do they want?"

"Safe passage," the commander said. "We let them go; they give us Gayl."

"Can we trust them?"

"I doubt it. But I don't see what option we have. Another challenge like that and they'll finish her, for sure. I suggest we pull back and see what they do. There's no way we're going to negotiate with them."

"Do it," said Grendel, circling overhead.

"Grendel—?" Gabrial started.

"She's frail. I'm not going to risk her, Gabrial. Garrison, give the order."

Grynt nodded at the commander. With one sharp cry, the roamers moved to a higher loop. "You, too," said Grendel, snorting air under Gabrial to make him lift.

"This is wrong," he said as he climbed beside her. "It's a trick. I know it. These creatures aren't fools. Remember what they did to Gossana."

"They're coming out again," barked Grynt. "Watch where they go, but do not engage."

Gabrial looked down and saw Gibbus emerging all over the mound, from openings the dragons hadn't flamed. There were more of them now, but still not enough to allay his suspicions. To Garrison, he said, "What if they're just delaying us long enough to let most of them get away unseen? How do we know they won't turn on Gayl when they're all aboveground?"

"We don't," said Garrison. "That's why we're watching."

"This is madness," said Gabrial. "There must be something we can do?"

Gabrial.

The blue gave a sudden start. The voice in his head had come from high above, and not from one of the wyng. He twisted his supple neck left and right. To his amazement, he saw Gus flashing through the cloud layers with Pine Onetooth riding his back.

Garrison had seen the big roamer as well. "In the name of Godith, where did *he* come from?"

The roamer broke through the clouds again. Gabrial saw Pine leaning over a wing, pointing toward the top of the mound as if she wanted Gus to land. At the same time, he heard a clamor of voices. Chief among them was Grendel's.

"GARIFFRED!"

Gabrial immediately switched his gaze downward. To his horror, he saw the drake on the ground. He was approaching the two Gibbus holding Gayl.

Ignoring the fury of voices at his back, Gabrial dived again. From some way off, he heard the Gibbus bark a punitive warning at the drake. One of them pressed the knife against Gayl. Gabrial bared his fangs. His only hope of saving her was to phase before the knife cut deep. But just as he was i:maging his phasing point, he saw Gariffred barrel his chest. All the ears in the air heard the faint click of jaws. Gabrial glanced at the Gibbus and noted they were showing no sign of fear. *Another small, insignificant dragon*, they were thinking.

How wrong they were.

For Gariffred had found his spark. He took one breath and lit it with a flame that flowed over the Gibbus and Gayl as well, engulfing all three in the same inferno. Gabrial's spirits lurched and then soared. Suddenly, he realized Gayl would survive and the Gibbus would burn. By the ancient laws of Godith, set down after Graven had accidentally killed his brother, no dragon was able to flame its own kin. Gariffred was the only dragon who could save his sister by such means. And he'd done it. In style.

Long before the igniting burst died, Gabrial had his claws around Gayl and was lifting her away. "Fly!" he screamed. He looked back to see Gariffred opening his wings. Relief flooded Gabrial's hearts. But the joy was short-lived. The drake wasn't rising high enough. Something was preventing him taking off fully.

A Gibbus hand had closed around his leg.

51

Now Gabrial knew that his fears about the creatures were not misplaced. There *were* unseen Gibbus on the ground, ready to ambush any dragons that landed.

Gariffred flapped and pecked and savagely clawed. His pin-sharp fangs took a chunk of Gibbus flesh and nearly slashed through an eye as well. He beat his wings so hard that the creature was dragged along a short way, causing both of them to slide down a shallow incline. Foolishly, the Gibbus refused to let go. At the bottom of the slide, with the weight in its favor, it had a fleeting moment of glory. It sank its teeth into Gariffred's leg and wounded him cruelly behind one knee. The drake howled and blew a spike of fire, but couldn't bend his neck to an angle sharp enough to light his aggressor. But by then it didn't matter. A snort from behind made the Gibbus turn its head. It had the momentary luxury of staring into the glittering eyes of a ferocious female dragon, then saw nothing but fading clouds as its head sailed over the Wild Lands, taken from its shoulders by Grendel's isoscele.

The ground around Grendel erupted with bodies. As Gariffred flapped clear, Gibbus shimmered out of hiding and swarmed over Grendel in the same way they'd attacked Gossana. In size, Grendel was half a wing smaller than

Gossana. But the future queen had youth on her side and fire in every grain of her body. She took off with five assailants on her back. They clawed and bit and did all they could to bring her down, but their mission was always doomed to fail. They were already giddy with the rush of air, when Grendel soared and performed a roll, hurling all five aside like sparks. Three of them didn't even reach the ground. Garrison picked one off in midair, snapping it to mulch in his giant jaws. Two more were burned to cinders and given over to the wind's amusement. Another went down like a shooting star in the body of water beside the mound. The fifth ended life as a blemish on the rocks.

In that sense, it was a one-sided contest. The dragons swooped and phased and flamed freely, killing any Gibbus fool enough to reveal themselves. But Gabrial was still concerned about what might be happening within the mound. If there were Hom captives, he felt he had a duty to rescue them. At the moment, he could do little about it, for he was still carrying Gayl and thinking about a safe place to set down. Although unharmed by her brother's fire, the myss was suffering some mild heat blindness; little light shined from her youthful eyes. Her cuts were sealing—like all dragons, she had the extraordinary power to rapidly self-heal minor wounds—but her wings were wrecked and she was weak from the loss of blood. Gabrial seriously feared for her survival. In any other circumstance, he would have flown her straight to Grymric. She needed herbs and counsel and rest. But the healer himself was hurt and far away.

What to do?

That was when he thought about Pine and how she had mended Gus on the cliffs. He immediately began to look for the roamer. In two flicks, Gabrial had him. Gus was lowest in the sky, dangerously close to the top of the mound. Garrison flashed overhead demanding to know what Gus was doing. Gus had his claws spread ready for a landing, but was actually hovering just off the ground. Gabrial's hearts thumped as he saw Pine ease herself along Gus's spine and get ready to jump.

"What's she doing?" he yelled as Garrison came past.

But the answer was clear as soon as Pine dropped.

She clung fast to the rocks as Gus lifted away, her hair and robe flying in a frenzy around her. Then she climbed into a narrow opening.

And disappeared into the Gibbus stronghold.

52

I pray that on the day I die

The wind will come and raise me high

And all the birds will sing my name

For I will be a drop of rain

That falls upon the mountainside

To water any flower I find . . .

Mell thought she must be dreaming. As the Gibbus veered away from the main cavern and started climbing toward an adjacent chamber, an old Kaal lullaby drifted through the haze.

To water any flower I find . . .

The tall Gibbus whipped around and barked at the others to halt. It dipped its shoulder and let Mell fall. Mell landed with a heavy crunch, her lungs too sore to force a cry. She blinked and gave her eyes time to settle. Through the lower wisps of smoke, she saw feet approaching. A bare-legged girl, in a Kaal robe.

Pine? Mell mouthed. "No, child. *Run.* Run, you must run."

For once, no one kicked Mell or struck her down. They seemed too mesmerized by Pine's soft voice to do anything other than stand and stare. Like Mell, they must have been asking themselves how a dot of a girl could be here among them, singing in the heat of so much smoke. But singing she was.

A drop of rain. A drop of rain.

I will find the erth again . . .

She passed through the fug like the wisp she was and came to stand in front of the Gibbus. She pulled a flower stalk through her fingers.

"My name is Pine Onetooth. I am Kaal—and more. I come to offer this flower for your prisoners. How say you, Gibbus?"

She held the flower out.

A daisy, it was. Its center yellow. Its petals white.

The creature spoke not a jot of Kaal, and clearly felt no need to learn. Issuing a rasp that had spittle strings running off its grimy teeth, it stepped forward and clamped Pine's hand in its own, closing its brawny fingers tight. It meant to crush her bones, her flower. But Pine was showing no signs of distress. She continued to look it fast in the eye.

She held up the hand that Gayl had once bitten, the one that bore the three-lined scar.

Mell, watching on in dizzy disbelief, recognized the shape and began to feel a sense of hope.

Pine spoke again. "See, Gibbus. I am touched by dragons. I carry some of their powers also." She twiddled her fingers. The daisy now showed in her scarred hand.

Several Gibbus grunted in confusion.

"This flower holds many fates in its petals. Choose well and you leave in peace. Choose foul and you and your companions die."

This the Gibbus did understand. For Pine had miraculously changed her voice and spoken in the native tongue of the Wild Lands. A shocked murmur ran among the horde. They snapped at Pine and called her "gwadrach," roughly meaning "witch."

Pine turned the flower by its stalk.

The tall Gibbus sharpened its gaze.

It picked the flower from her hand and looked it over, still not letting Pine loose.

Then it did a foolish thing.

It put the daisy into its mouth, chewed it to a pulp, and spat it away.

"So be it," Pine said.

She opened her hand again. The wall behind the Gibbus gave a splintering groan. Instantly, three large cracks appeared, mirroring the pattern of Pine's scars. Through the gaps came the only erth element the Gibbus truly feared.

Water.

It began as a spray, but swiftly turned to a gush as the stone continued to heave and split. More cracks appeared all around the cavern. The Gibbus panicked and quickly broke ranks, leaping for the highest ledges they could find. One of them let Leif fall to the ground. Even as Mell scrabbled over to her, the treegirl was beginning to float, so fast was the cavern filling.

The Gibbus holding on to Pine roared in fury and tried to attack. But the moment it fixed its eyes on hers, Pine mesmerized it the way a dragon would. And as it fell to its knees, she said, "Surrender to the light, and your kind will live."

She pulled her hand clear.

"Pine!"

Mell was on her feet with Leif in her arms. Water was welling around her knees.

"Pine, this girl clings faint to life. She cannot swim. I beg you, help her."

"I must go, Mell. I have done what I came to."

Mell shook her head in disbelief. "Girl, you have magicks plain to see. Will you not free us from this hole lest the water take us?"

Pine gestured at the terrified Gibbus. "They are your solution now."

"Wait!" Mell splashed forward, the hem of her robe floating freely. She shook her head again. "The Gibbus are my enemy, true. But I am not so short on pity that I would see them burn if they show themselves to skalers or swallow a lake if they don't."

But all Pine would say was "They are the way."

On these words, she closed her eyes and phased out of sight.

Mell gave an agonized cry. Despair! Despair! Swim for a tunnel. That was all she had left. Get Leif to an opening before it filled. Climb. Follow the drag of cold air. Pray the skalers would show her mercy.

But as she looked for a tunnel, the tall Gibbus waded in front of her.

"Stand away," Mell pleaded. "I beg you, let us go."

The Gibbus barked a command, though it was not aimed at her. Another large creature dropped into the water.

"No," Mell whispered, and backed away. In doing so, she slipped and let go of Leif. To her horror, the second Gibbus reached forward and pulled Leif from her.

"NO!" Mell screamed.

But it had Leif now and there was nothing Mell could do.

"WHY?" she yelled at them, dashing the water. "WHAT DOES IT MATTER NOW?"

The tall Gibbus twitched its nostrils. Then it reached out and pulled Mell from the water, cradling her in its sturdy arms.

"What? What's happening?"

The Gibbus waded powerfully toward a tunnel and gave another snap command.

The next thing Mell knew she was being carried up a winding path toward the surface. She looked behind her and saw a long line of Gibbus following. One of them was carrying Leif.

When they reached the top, the creature holding Mell ordered a stone to be moved to make an opening it could pass through with Mell in its arms.

Outside, it dropped to its knees and laid Mell out.

A huge green skaler immediately bore down.

Mell heard its jaws click and closed her eyes.

But another sound came from the sky. A sharp squeal, like a command.

The ground rocked as the green skaler streamed over. Dust and fury followed in its wake. But no breath of fire issued from its jaws.

Out came the Gibbus, kneeling as they did. The one holding Leif set her down gently.

Now Mell saw their intent. She lowered her head and gave praise to the Fathers.

The war was done.

The Gibbus were raising their arms in surrender.

53

It was the easiest fight the Wearle had ever won. From above, they had heard the mound cracking and seen water from the lake nearby draining in. They were astonished to see it, and have their enemy yield. Yet there was one more twist to come.

As the wyng regrouped and thought about landing, a fire star shimmered on top of the mound and a boy astride a winged white horse appeared.

Ren!

The only dragon to truly react was Gariffred. He gave a *graark!* of joy but obeyed his mother's orders to stay in the air.

Ren glanced up at the circling dragons. Casually, he stroked Wind's mane.

"Now," he whispered.

From Wind's magical, twisting horn came three intense rays of purple light. As Ren turned her, the lights strobed over the Wild Lands, revealing a multitude of Gibbus still hiding. Grynt, when he saw the enemy exposed, was eager to launch a blistering attack. But Grendel quickly countermanded the order. There was a reason Ren had lit up the Gibbus. She wanted to know what it was.

The creatures squirmed like newborn pupps, unable to run from the light. Gabrial thought for a moment they were going to shrivel or, worse, implode. He turned in the air, trying to shield Gayl from any more grisliness. But what came to pass was a thing of great beauty, not a terrible act of retribution.

Out of each creature's mouth came what appeared to be a small black star. As the stars rose into the air, Gabrial was astonished to see that they were not stars at all but tiny crows. He remembered how Graven's heart was supposedly hidden among those birds. He held his breath, half expecting to see Ren burn the whole flock. Instead, the birdlings formed a twisting, three-lined shape in the air, then turned to white flakes and dispersed on the breeze.

The rays of light faded. On the ground, the Gibbus shook themselves alert and seemed perplexed by the shadows sweeping over them. When they saw the dragons, the fear in their faces told its own story: Their aggression was tamed—they no longer posed a threat. Grendel gave the order to let them disband. Before long, they had scampered away from the mound, soon to be in holes far away from water.

Gariffred could wait no longer. He graarked again and settled on the mound as Ren dismounted.

"Galan aug scieth," Ren whispered to the drake.

Gariffred nuzzled his hand like a mutt.

"Ren? REN?" Mell was on her feet, stumbling across the rocks to be with him. She fell against his chest and threw her arms around him. "Is it you? Is it really you?"

"I am what you see, your son," he said.

He kissed her hair and she wept freely.

"You're hurt, Ma." Her wounds were plain to see.

Mell looked at her bleeding fingers. "Not as badly as some."

She took his hand and drew him to where Leif lay. The partial exposure to water had brought some color back to Leif's face, but her limbs were still cracking and shrinking. She was breathing fainter than a ghost. "This child of the forest saved many Kaal lives. Can you help her, Ren? She is sore in need of healing."

"She must return to the forest," said a voice. "The trees call her." Pine had appeared behind them. She was sitting cross-legged on a smooth gray rock, playing with a single daisy. "The little one too." She pointed down the hill.

Ren looked down to see Gabrial set Gayl in front of Grendel.

Grendel wailed in distress when she saw Gayl's injuries and pawed the wearling with her isoscele. Gayl's wings had collapsed along both arches. And because of the heavy blood loss she'd suffered, most of the purple had drained from them too. This was true of her neck as well, which was a ghastly shade of white and green. But the tail injuries were worse to see. Her fragile tail was broken at the point where it joined her back. Even if the myss recovered, she would never fly again.

"Prime Grynt!"

The Prime dragon forced himself to look up at Ren.

"Any war there was between us is ended. The darkness that fell upon dragons and men will soon give way to a brighter dawn. De:allus Garodor will return to Erth shortly with tales more astonishing than aught you see here. He has much to say about the sons of Godith and the healing light of Seren. Gabrial, my friend, I bless our bond but I cannot help Gayl. Take her to the forest along with this treegirl. They are part of the New Age that will shortly come to shine upon us all."

"Ren Whitehair. Pine One-Fang." Now the future queen, Grendel, spoke through her grief. "I pledge this Wearle to any just cause that will guarantee peace between our species." She looked along the line of dragons. "If any dragon disagrees with my ruling, they are free to leave and return to Ki:mera. Those that stay will colonize this world, but in harmony with *all* its kind. Will your mother spread this word among the tribes of Erth?"

"She will." Ren put a hand on his mother's arm.

"What do they say?" Mell asked, a little awestruck. She had heard nothing but grunts and growls.

Ren turned his mother to face the creatures she had so long loathed. "Here are my second kin, Ma. Love them now as you have always loved me. They will never do harm on you again. Speak well of them wherever you roam. That is all I ask of you."

Mell looked at Wind, admiring her beautifully feathered wings. "You talk as if you would leave me again."

Ren ran his hand down Gariffred's neck. "Go to your guardian," he whispered in dragontongue. "Your work is done. We will meet again soon."

Graaark!

The drake fluttered down to be with his sister.

"It's time," said Pine, standing up in one movement.

"Ren, wait. We are so little met," Mell begged. She looked hopefully at Pine. "Will I see you again—either of you?"

"Look to the stars this night," Ren said. "To those that shine newest and brightest. There you will find us both. *Galan aug scieth.* Remember these words. Speak them whenever you think of me."

And he kissed his mother fondly on the cheek.

And together with Pine, he climbed onto Wind's back and faded out of sight.

54

“The forest,” Gabrial said softly to Grendel. “We must do as Ren said. Quickly, I fear.” He looked worriedly at Gayl. The myss was fading.

“Matrial, I would like to assist.” Gus stepped forward, bowing to Grendel.

“Not you,” said Grynt, lashing his tail across Gus. “You’ve got a lot of explaining to do.”

“Enough,” said Grendel, almost snorting fire. “This is no time for petty arguments. Gabrial’s right. I trust Ren’s words. We will go to the forest. Gabrial, carry Gayl as gently as you can.” She glanced at Mell, who was kneeling beside Leif, trying to stir the girl awake. “Gus, let the Hom woman ride on your back.”

“She won’t be able to carry the treegirl,” said Garrison. “Not and hang on to Gus as well. The girl looks to weigh no more than a vapor. If any of us pick her up, we’ll crush her.”

“Not all of us,” Grendel said. “Gariffred!”

Graark?

“Take the child gently in your claws and follow. Gus, lead us to the clearing where Gallen came down. Grynt, I want the whole Wearle to attend.”

The Prime gave a solemn nod. He looked at Garrison. "Bring the others from the mountains. Go."

Snow was still falling in pretty twists when Gus put down in the Whispering Forest. The air was silent, the trees still. The Erth sun had done most of its work for the day. The few spare rays it was able to cast were lighting the clearing with a dark gold glow.

Mell was shocked by the extent of the destruction she saw. The first ring of trees were bent back and broken. Fragments of charred wood were poking through the snow, despite the heavy drifts left by the ice storm. The long frame of Gallen was pushing through also, ribs and tall scales draped and dripping. The sight of those skaler bones made Mell shiver. There, she suspected, lay the reason for this crime against the forest.

She slid off Gus's back, breathless and trembling, more from exhilaration than fear. Never, not even in her wildest dreams, had she ever believed she would ride a winged beast. She found the courage to pat his neck and tried not to wince at his awful breath. How had Ren ever put up with *that*?

All around, dragons began to land, though most of them stayed in the air, circling. The little one carrying Leif was among the first to come down. He fluttered awkwardly near to the ground, but dropped Leif kindly, causing no hurt.

The big blue skaler was next to arrive. He put their injured one down beside Leif.

Mell picked up the skirts of her robe and hurried over. Her intention was always to go to Leif first, yet something compelled her to kneel beside Gayl. She looked up at Grendel, begging her permission to be this close, then ran her hand softly over Gayl's head.

The wearmyss didn't respond.

Mell shook her red hair. "No," she whispered. Snowflakes danced on the warmth of her breath.

Gariffred stepped up. He blinked at Gayl and tried to rock her gently.

Gaaraarrk? he said.

It was the most plaintive sound Mell had ever heard.

A tear left her eye and dripped on to Gayl's neck.

The wearmyss stared at the sky. She was dead.

Prime Grynt said to Grendel, "I'm so sorry for your loss. May Godith bless her spirit. She was brave to the last."

Gabrial lowered his head in mourning. "She was gone when I lifted her," he confessed to Grendel quietly.

Grendel put her head back and wailed.

In the sky, the Wearle began to echo her grief.

Gabrial turned his face away, hardly knowing what he could do or say. He looped his tail around Grendel's back, but knew his touch would be little consolation. He was sure that Grendel had known deep down how serious Gayl's injuries were, but Ren's words by the mound had given her cause for hope. Where was this New Age the boy had spoken of? What good could come of losing Gayl so young?

One of the roamers gave a warning grunt. Gabrial looked up to see faces among the trees. Forest dwellers. That made him glance at Leif. The treegirl was still alive, but something odd was happening to her. The fingers of one hand were thinning out and creeping slowly over the snow, turning down wherever they found gaps in the bracken. The girl, it seemed, was putting down roots.

Mell had seen the change too and now went to Leif, being careful where she placed her feet. Gariffred likewise was picking up his claws and moving away from the spread of Leif's fingers, which were splitting all the time, claiming more and more ground. More filaments broke through the soles of Leif's boots. They began rooting too.

"Leif," Mell whispered. "Is there aught I can do?"

She doubted the girl could hear. For Leif's face was now wooded, her features shrinking into the grain. Yet she managed to extend what would have been a thumb and point to what remained of the pocket of her robe. Mell put her hand inside. She found a pinecone there.

Its scales were fully open. Stars were sparkling in all the places its seeds would sit. Although she could not say why,

Mell blew softly across the cone and the stars spread as dry seeds would in a breeze. Some fell on Gariffred. Some fell on Gabrial, Grendel, Gus. Some fell on Mell herself. But most of them settled on the wearmyss, Gayl.

From Gayl's eye came a glowing fire tear. It rolled down her cheek and dripped into the snow, lighting it in glistening shades of amber. And where the light from Gayl touched the roots of Leif, green shoots began to appear.

Mell gasped and stood up quickly. She turned a full circle. Shoots were everywhere. Small, but growing fast.

"Fly," she said. She flapped at Gariffred, who immediately took off. "Fly!" she cried at Grendel and the others. She ran for Gus's back and clambered on smartly. "Fly," she cried to him as well, slapping his neck to encourage him to lift.

They took to the air, every dragon present. They circled and watched a young forest grow in the place where fire had claimed the old trees. Thus, the New Age on Erth would commence, with the death of a dragon commingled to a man of the Kaal, and their eternal union to a child of the forest.

Mell closed her hand around the cone she'd been given and held it close to her beating heart. *"Galan aug scieth,"* she whispered to the universe. "Here the tale truly begins . . ."

Part seven
Legacy

55

The Dorothy Frutton Retirement Home

Erth timeline, present day

"Emily."

"Dr. Whitaker. Thank you for coming. Sorry to be bringing you out so late."

"Not at all, not at all. Besides, it's a lovely evening for a drive. Agatha, again?"

"I'm afraid so, yes."

"Remind me, which room?"

"She's in the lounge."

Dr. Whitaker raised an eyebrow.

"She refuses to go to bed."

"I see. And she's rambling again?"

"Worse than ever."

"About dragons, you said?"

Emily smiled. She gestured down the hall.

The small lounge was lit by nothing but moonlight, flowing in through the garden windows. Dr. Whitaker threw Emily a questioning glance. "She wanted the lights off," Emily whispered. "To see the stars better. Shall I . . . ?"

"No." Dr. Whitaker stayed her hand. "It's all right. I'll talk to her as we are."

He walked over to the windows and pulled up a chair.

In an armchair facing the garden sat a light-framed, elderly woman. She was wearing slippers and a dressing gown. Her slender face was creased by ninety years of life, but her eyes were still as keen as a hawk's. She was blessed with a strong head of hair.

"Miss White? Agatha? It's Dr. Whitaker. We met last week. Emily tells me you've been a bit restless."

"Hair."

"I'm sorry?"

"Whitehair. Not *White*." The old lady's voice grated like a rusty door hinge. "We've all been Whitehairs. Since the dawn of time."

The doctor put down his bag. He perched forward on the final third of his chair. "What's that you're holding?"

Agatha closed her hand around a small object tight to her breast.

"It's a pinecone," Emily informed the doctor. "She says it's been in her family forever."

Dr. Whitaker's thin mouth twitched at the corners. He followed Agatha's gaze outside. "I love clear nights like this," he said, brushing a little fluff off his knee. "I could see every star on the drive over here. Do you have a favorite star, Miss White . . . hair?"

The hawk eyes scanned the sky. "Cantorus," she answered.

"Cantorus? I don't think I know—"

"Coming into alignment with Crune." Miss White raised a finger. She pointed upward through the window. "That's where he went. There. To *Cantorus*."

"Who?" asked Emily.

Agatha's gaze slid into the middle distance somewhere between herself and the window. "Ren," she breathed. "And the girl went to Crune. That's where the New Age truly began, on the moons of Ki:mera, when the sons of Godith were turned into stars." She smiled, as though it was all coming back. "Aye. Ren and Pine. They were the first."

"The first what?" Dr. Whitaker asked.

The old lady swayed a little. Her gaze settled on the night sky again. "The first Hom to colonize the dragon world."

The doctor and Emily exchanged another glance.

Emily crouched by Miss White's chair. "Agatha, is Ren your son?"

The old lady snorted like an engine blowing steam. "I have his *auma*. Here, in my heart. Passed down on his mother's side."

"Auma?"

Miss White threw the doctor a scornful glance. "Dragon fire," she hissed at him. It seemed for one moment that she might even breathe some. Her hand closed tighter around the cone.

Emily offered a comforting hand. "Agatha, sweetheart. Just come to bed, huh? The doctor will give you something to help you sleep."

"Don't need *doctors*," Miss White snarled. "I have herbs. I can sleep all I want to. I must stay awake. Mustn't miss it."

Dr. Whitaker glanced at the garden. "What exactly are you waiting for, Agatha?"

"The eclipse of Seren," Agatha replied, fogging up a tiny area of glass. "I must beg Her forgiveness. I've failed to bear young. Or find a new keeper. Don't you see? I have no one to give this to." She opened her hand and let the pinecone balance there. Its scales twinkled where they caught the moonlight.

Dr. Whitaker clicked his tongue quietly. He interlaced his fingers and tapped his thumbs together. "Why is it important to pass that on?"

"So the Hom don't *forget*," Miss White said grittily, her pale green gaze now drawn to her hand. "It's all here. In the seeds. The legacy of the Wearle. It must be bestowed or they will all be forgotten."

Dr. Whitaker scratched his well-trimmed beard. "'They' being . . . ?"

"Dragons," Emily said quietly.

Agatha stared at the garden again. The wind was chasing leaves around the lawn. "She couldn't bear it," she said plaintively. "The queen. Grendel. Despite her pledge, she couldn't bear to live out her life on Erth. Not without the wearmyss at her side." The old eyes began to mist. "So they left. All of them. Never to return. And now, when I die, no Hom will remember."

A tear rolled down the old lady's cheek.

Emily touched her gently on the shoulder. "What can we do to make it better?"

"Believe," said Agatha, gripping her hand. "If you truly believe, you can take the cone, child."

Dr. Whitaker hummed to himself. His hand went down and unclicked his bag. "I'm going to give you something, Agatha. It's mild, I promise. But as Emily says, it will help you to sleep. We can talk about this again tomorrow."

Agatha hardened her gaze. She pressed three fingers against the window and drew an invisible sign there. "Fool. There's no such thing as 'tomorrow.'"

The doctor smiled to humor her. "Well, according to my calendar, there is. Water, Emily?"

Emily nodded. She reached over to a table and half filled a glass.

As she moved to hand the glass to the doctor, a sharp pink light shined over the garden, as if something had slit the air with a laser.

"It's happening," said Agatha.

She let go of the cone. But instead of tumbling to her lap or to the floor, it hovered in midair and began to spin.

Dr. Whitaker's mouth fell open. He dropped the pill he was holding in his fingers. The pill Agatha White would never take. At the same time, Emily dropped the glass. It hit the arm of a chair and tipped its contents. A small avalanche of water headed for the carpet. A carpet that would never be wet.

For Agatha was right. Far, far away, in the distant night sky, Cantorus and Crune had come into alignment and eclipsed Seren.

And time on Erth had mysteriously stopped . . .

EPILOGUE

(OR THE WAY THINGS WERE, OR MIGHT HAVE BEEN)

Floor 108 of the Great Librarium
Time period: Undefined

"Again? You stopped the Erth timeline? AGAIN?"

Azkiar's ear tufts looked like two rockets set for launch. Aurielle had rarely seen a firebird so flustered. His feathers were rustling to such an extent that the little creatures who sheltered among them were leaving in droves, along with the dust.

Aurielle lowered her cream-colored head. "I had to," she said.

"Why?" he asked sharply.

"The sector keeps fading, petering out."

"What?"

Aurielle leaned forward, mantling her wings. Her apricot ear tufts sat up straight. "Whichever way the daisies bend, the timeline only runs to one descendant of Ren's mother—and that descendant always fails to pass the memories on.

You know what that means. Graven and the Erth Wearle will be *forgotten*. Their words will fall out of the books."

Azkiar shortened his beak at the tip. It was moments like these when he yearned to be back on Floor 17 sorting out the timelines of toads and rabbits. "How many resets have you done?"

Aurielle bunched her claws. "Six."

"SIX?!" The dust exploded off him. "You do realize you're only allowed seven?"

She gave a timid nod.

Azkiar sat down in a huff. "Well, there's only one thing for it." He arched his eyes toward the ceiling.

Aurielle sighed. The Dome. Yes. She had hoped it wouldn't come to that. But after six resets there was no other option. They must visit the Dome on the top of the Librarium, and there seek help from the Higher.

"Will you come with me?" she begged.

"I suppose I'll have to," he grunted.

That made her chitter happily. Azkiar might be the grumpiest firebird in the Librarium, but he always helped.

She spread her wings and dashed outside, gathering speed again as she turned and flew upward. Her aim was to land by one of the windows that opened outward on the shell of the Dome, before quietly slipping inside. Azkiar did just that, closing the window behind him as tradition dictated. But Aurielle, because she was so concerned to find a solution to the Erth situation, flew through a window at speed and found herself deep within the matrix of stars the firebirds knew as the "Is."

Immediately, she felt a Presence all around her, and saw what she thought was a length of ribbon, twisting and curling in the glittering space. As it twizzled, it produced three uniform contrails, making the ancient symbol of the universe, the same sign Gayl had left on Pine's hand, the sign Mell had drawn in blood in the Wild Lands, the sign Agatha had made on the window of the Dorothy Frutton Retirement Home.

To Aurielle's amazement, the sign began to take form. And what a form! With barely a whisper of movement, a small dragon materialized in the Is. Aurielle was charmed and a little bit terrified, even though the dragon was no bigger than she. It had huge, kind eyes and glistening green scales. She formed the conclusion that it might be a male, though its auma was so far-reaching and radiant that it could have had many, many identities. She nearly crumpled inside when he smiled at her.

"Hello, Aurielle."

"Hello," she squeaked.

At that point, Azkiar appeared in the matrix.

"Ah, two of you," the dragon said gladly. He sat back, pressing his paws together. "How can I be of help?"

"It's all my fault," Aurielle blurted. This wasn't the opening she'd rehearsed on her flight, but the words just tumbled out of her beak and now she couldn't seem to stop them. "A page broke free from an old Erth volume. It was all about Graven, the firstborn son of Godith."

Azkiar snorted through one nostril. "He's a dragon. He knows who Graven is. Get on with it. And keep it *short*."

Aurielle bowed so low she almost toppled over. "When I studied the book the page had come from, I saw the terrible unrest on Erth, caused by the finding of Graven's auma. So, with Azkiar's permission"—Azkiar rolled his eyes—"I formed a plan, a very BIG plan, to settle the timeline and put things right. Would you like to see a summary?"

"I would," said the dragon. He beamed brightly.

So Aurielle produced a vast collage of i:mages, showing the web of dimensional links between all the major events on Erth and the fateful "occurrences" her plan had engendered. It was all there, from Ren in the mountain rescuing Gariffred, to Garon entering the world of the Wyvern. The last few i:mages showed what became of G'restyn and Graven when they stood before Seren on Halo Point. Both were transformed into bright new stars and sent out into the universe to be orbited by Crune and Cantorus respectively.

"Perfect." The dragon drummed his claws. "You've done well, Aurielle. It's a very good plan."

She lowered her head. "There were . . . casualties."

The dragon looked at her kindly. "There always are." He moved a paw and sent her a rainbow of healing. "They'll bc cared for. You know that."

Aurielle nodded.

"So what was the problem?"

Oh, yes. The problem. Aurielle ruffled her wings and shuffled her feet. She straightened her beak and twice attempted to calm her breathing.

But Azkiar had grown impatient by then and he said it all for her. "The plan keeps failing at a crucial point. The timeline diminishes after the same number of Erth iterations. The end result is that dragons fade from the Hom consciousness. Aurielle has performed six resets of the timeline and it's always the same. It trickles down to one believer when there ought to be millions. That's why we're here."

"I see," said the dragon. "Six, you say?"

Aurielle blushed profusely. "I don't know what I'm doing wrong."

The dragon hummed and tapped his paws together. "There must be a glitch."

Azkiar sucked in sharply. That was a word he didn't like to hear. Glitches in time were the worst embarrassment a firebird could suffer.

"Run it through again," the dragon said. "As fast as you like. Show me all the details, not just a summary."

So Aurielle closed her eyes and re-i:maged the complete timeline, everything from Grendisar's first Erth visits, to Ned Whitehair dying, the goyles, the Gibbus, the pinecone Mell had taken from Leif. It even showed Leif's auma spreading into the mountains and cleansing the last grains of fhosforent on Erth. Every little detail was there, all the way down Mell Whitehair's generations to Agatha in the retirement home.

When it was done, the dragon tapped his paws together again. Then he twiddled a claw and brought back one particular scene: the part where Mell had made the sign in blood on the cavern wall.

Aurielle flattened her ear tufts when she saw it. "Was I wrong to allow them to use the sign?"

"No," said the dragon. "The sign is everything. But watch what happens to it as the blood runs."

Aurielle gasped loudly. A trickle of blood from the topmost line had run down and joined with the central one! How could she have missed something that simple?

That crucial?!

Azkiar covered his eyes with one wing. He was thinking exactly the same thing.

"But I don't understand," Aurielle spluttered.

"Don't make this worse," Azkiar advised.

Aurielle frowned. Not an easy thing for a firebird to do.

"The lines of the symbol represent the history of men, dragons, and ice bears."

(For firebirds, this was a universal truth.)

"Thank goodness bears weren't involved," muttered Azkiar. Whenever bears were mixed up in something, there were always ramifications. (That was another word he didn't much care for.)

"But the lines that merged are the ones for men and dragons," said Aurielle.

"So?" Azkiar puffed his feathers.

"Well, wouldn't that make the belief patterns stronger?"

"It doesn't quite work that way," said the dragon. "When the lines run together, it *narrows* the field to the strand of the character who made the sign. So if Mell's family line should come to an end . . ."

Aurielle slumped her wings. "Then I really have failed."

The dragon's mouth curled up at the edges. "No, Aurielle. You haven't failed. You've done the right thing; you've come to me."

From somewhere under his arm, he magically produced a notepad. On the pad was a drawing of the symbol with its pesky trickle of blood in place. Out of nowhere, the dragon then produced a pencil stub. Aurielle noticed it had a neat tip. But the dragon chose not to write with it. Instead, he turned the pencil upside down. On the blunt end was a tiny eraser.

Azkiar and Aurielle both leaned forward and watched him gently rub out the line that was running from the top wave toward the middle. As he did, the stars around him reconfigured and a huge vision of Erth appeared. There was Mell in the Gibbus cavern, slung over the tall one's shoulder. She made the sign on the wall with the blood from her fingers. And though a little blood ran from all three lines, Aurielle knew they would never meet now. By the time the dragon had blown the rubbings off his pad, the timeline had run right through to Agatha, who was sleeping contentedly in her chair. Emily was putting a blanket around her. The pinecone tumbled out of Agatha's hand. Emily picked it up and carefully placed it in the dressing-gown pocket. Then she kissed Agatha gently on the head, stroked her wonderful hair, and said, *Sweet dreams. Say hello to your dragons from me. Hrrr!*

Aurielle wiggled her tail in delight.

Azkiar sighed. Tail wiggling! So embarrassing, especially in the presence of Infinite Creativity.

"That's it—she believes," Aurielle said.

"Not just Emily," the dragon added. "In this timeline, most Hom do—though they'll never be quite sure *why* they believe. Even those that don't will *want* to believe. It's all there, Aurielle, deep in their auma. The timeline is flowing beautifully now. Dragons will never be forgotten by the Hom. And those who seek the truth about Graven and G'restyn will find it—if they look hard enough. Now, there's one last thing we need to do. For the sake of the bookshelves on Floor 47, we need to let go of the failed volumes and install just one—with a new title."

He swept a paw across his pad and the symbol disappeared.

Then he turned the pencil over again. And this time he did touch the tip to the pad.

He looked at the firebirds—and waited.

"You want *us* to make up a title?" said Azkiar.

The dragon wrinkled his snout. A smoke ring left his nostrils. It floated through the Is, turned into a butterfly, and fluttered away. "One letter will suffice."

"One?" said Aurielle. There were very few books with single-letter titles.

"Hmm," said the dragon. "What's your *favorite* letter?"

Both firebirds replied together. "*A*."

Just as dragons revered the letter *G*, so firebirds loved the opening letter of the Librarium's alphabet. It was why their names began with it.

The dragon wrote the letter *A* on his pad.

Aurielle felt the stars stirring again.

The dragon blinked his oval eyes. "Now the Librarium decides," he said.

The firebirds stared into the matrix again. More letters were appearing there.

Aurielle counted four in all.

T

R

H

E

They danced around the pad for a moment or two, then decided to settle either side of the *A*.

"Done," said the dragon.

He turned the pad around and showed them the result.

And there was the title of the new book on Floor 47.

EARTH.

GLOSSARY

Aether—a strange, omnipresent force that permeates the island world of the Wyvern and maintains an atmosphere of peaceful coexistence.

Auma—the life force or spirit of a being, derived from an ancient word for "fire." When a dragon dies and sheds its fire tear, its auma is believed to return to the creator, Godith.

Aurauma Fantalis—a mysterious belt of stars around Ki:mera, thought to be the eyrie or "playground" of Godith. Each star is believed to be the spirit of a dragon, though there is no tangible evidence of this. Described by the De:allus as "an infinite matrix of space and time," most dragons, out of fear, never enter the Aurauma. Those who do rarely emerge sane.

Auricular flaps—small flaps of skin that protect a dragon's ears.

Caarker—Hom name for a crow.

Cantorus and Crune—the two moons of Ki:mera.

Cold flame—under certain atmospheric conditions, dragons are capable of producing a cool flame (pale blue in color) that does not ignite combustible materials.

Commingle—a "coming together," usually of minds. All dragons develop the ability to communicate telepathically, i.e., using thought alone. A deeper extension of telepathy is *commingling*, in which a dragon focuses its awareness to such an extent that it is able to meld with another dragon's consciousness and read or know *all* of that dragon's thoughts.

Darn—a free-floating piece of graig.

De:allus—a highly intellectual class of dragon whose lives are devoted to understanding the wonders of Godith's universe. De:allus are scientists or problem solvers, characterized by their bright yellow eyes. It is not known how their eye color developed, though it's often said (somewhat disparagingly) that their optical triggers have become impaired because the De:allus like to look too long at *small* things.

Domayne—any parcel of land claimed by a dragon; their home territory. The term can also describe a large region of land mapped out during colonization.

Drake—a young male dragon (sometimes also called a weardrake).

Elder—a senior dragon (usually, but not exclusively, male) whose role is to administer Ki:meran law. Up to three Elders would normally accompany a colonizing Wearle, to steer and advise them.

Erth—home planet of the Hom.

Eyrie—an ancient word of dragontongue meaning "high nest." Now more commonly used to describe a superior cave or settle, such as that of a queen or the Prime dragon.

Fathers, the—the spirits of Hom dead.

Fhosforent—pink crystalline mineral found in Erth's volcanic rock, said to be the blood of the fallen dragon, Graven. Ingesting large quantities of fhosforent is known to cause devastating mutational effects in dragons, though some still believe the ore can be used to a dragon's advantage.

Firebirds—a highly colorful species of bird, closely related to dragons but very much smaller than them, who live in a cloaked dimension of the Kashic Archive known as the Librarium. Their job is to watch for "rips" in the fabric of time and space and repair them as quickly as possible, even if this means manipulating the destiny of living beings.

Fire star—a portal in time and space, called a "star" because of the flash of light emitted when something passes through it.

Fire tear—a single tear cried by a dragon at its death, said to contain its auma in the form of a spark. In extreme circumstances, a dragon might die without shedding its tear. In this case, its primary heart will turn to stone, along with the rest of its body if it is not burned. To die and not be called to Godith is the worst fate that can befall a dragon.

Flutterfly—Hom name for a common butterfly. The flutterflies on the island world of the Wyvern are able to glow in the dark.

Frooms—the Treemen's word for mushrooms.

Galan aug scieth—a sacred phrase of dragontongue meaning "we are one." It is spoken as a greeting between dragons with a close bond, but can also have a more literal meaning, as in the permanent commingling between Ren and the Astrian dragon, Grystina.

Gibbus—a Hom-like variant who dwell in underground caverns in the Wild Lands, a barren area of natural rock. Described historically as "playful," they have been growing steadily more aggressive since moving from a fruit-based diet.

Glamor—a rarely used word which describes a dragon's ability to mesmerize others (usually prey) with a stare.

Goyle—a word used to describe anything ugly or grotesque, particularly the mutant form of a dragon (known to the Hom as a "darkeye").

Graig—a word from the old tongue simply meaning "rock." The component parts of the dragon world Ki:mera are constructed from millions of pieces of linked graig (see also ***darn***), which form the labyrinths and mazes the dragons inhabit.

Guardian—a male dragon who protects a matrial and her wearlings.

Gwadrach—a witch, in the Gibbus tongue.

Heart(s)—dragons have three hearts, closely linked. The largest or primary heart maintains bodily functions and is concerned with power and strength; the second, about three-fifths the size of the primary heart, controls love and emotional reactions; the third, which is small and just hidden by the second heart, gives a dragon its spirituality.

Higher, the—name for the collective minds of the most advanced beings on Ki:mera. These creatures (their exact number is uncertain) have evolved beyond their physical form to exist in a neural web. It is not known whether the Higher evolved purely from dragons or are a construct from the mind of Godith, but they guide dragons, spiritually, in everything they do.

Hom—an early form of the human race.

Hopper—Hom name for a rabbit.

I:mage—the ability to create external structures from mental images. There are two types of i:maging, *natural* and *physical.* A natural i:mage is a floating three-dimensional picture (a kind of hologram) that fades as soon as it outlives its usefulness. Physical i:maging is used to create more permanent structures or to alter the parameters of existing matter. (See also ***phasing***.)

Intraspace—quite literally the collective space between the pieces of graig that make up the structure of the dragon world, Ki:mera.

Isoscele—the triangular scale at the end of a dragon's tail. Primarily designed for balance during flight and as a navigational aid. Also a valuable tool in battle. Commonly used to point or gesture.

Kaal—a tribe of humans. The origin of the name is thought to derive from "cave" and refers to the Kaal's preferred choice of habitat: any mountainous region near water.

Kashic Archive—a vast, complex labyrinth on Ki:mera that holds the entire history of dragonkind in thousands of "memory stones."

Ki:mera—the homeworld of dragons, created for them by the breath of Godith. Literally meaning "place of fire and light."

Librarium—see ***firebirds***.

Mapper—a dragon who maps out territories. A good mapper can record the layout of a landmass from a variety of heights or directional approaches and reproduce it accurately, in the form of an i:mage, for other dragons to see.

Matrial—an honorific title for a female dragon who has had wearlings.

Memory stones—orbs of condensed energy, housed in the mysterious Kashic Archive, that contain information in the form of stored i:mages. Memory stones are to the Archive what books are to the Librarium.

Mutt—Hom name for a dog.

Myss (or wearmyss)—a young female dragon.

Nutterling—Hom name for a squirrel.

Olfactic glands—tiny organs at the back of a dragon's nostrils that give them their powerful sense of smell.

Optical trigger—the mechanism that controls a dragon's extraordinary ability to zoom its vision and record i:mages of any landscape. The class of dragon called "mappers" have the most advanced optical triggers known to dragonkind.

Ora—the ubiquitous soft purple glow that gives color to the "atmosphere" (or intraspace) between the millions of labyrinths on Ki:mera.

Per—an honorific title given to a dragon who mentors a younger dragon or one of lesser status.

Phasing—the ability to move through time, usually during flight. The technique is a sophisticated form of i:maging, in which the dragon must be able to "see" itself ahead of time and then "dissolve" into the dark energy of the universe as if it were no heavier than a breath of wind.

Prime—an Elder who is also the supreme leader of a dragon colony.

Pupp—Hom name for a young mutt, but can be used for any young creature.

Redfur—Hom name for a fox.

Roamer—a young dragon who is experienced enough (in the opinion of a per) to be allowed to "roam" where he or she pleases, within reason. At least half of a colonizing Wearle will be made up of roamers.

Sawfin—fine scales in a ruffed shape behind a female dragon's ears.

Scorch line—a line charred around the boundary of the dragons' domayne, which the Hom are not allowed to cross.

Sensaur—a rare breed of dragon, thought to be able to see or sense spirits.

Seren—the star at the center of Ki:mera's network of graig. A debate has raged for centuries about whether Seren is Godith in physical form.

Sier pents—term meaning "green fish," used in a derogatory way to describe the Veng.

Skaler—Hom name for a dragon.

Skrike—a squeal or sharp cry.

Snorter—Hom name for a pig.

Spiracles—breathing holes in a dragon's body, most notably along the sides of the throat.

Sprites—Erth spirits revered by the Treemen. Sprites govern wind, rain, sunshine, and many other natural things.

Stigs—the horny extensions on a dragon's head (and to some extent their wings) that contribute to their ferocious appearance. Most stigs are inert and purely decorative, but some, like the primary stigs, are sensitive organs that can be used as antennae to detect signals or surroundings or changes of air pressure.

Sweeper—a dragon who patrols the scorch line, checking for incursions or threats.

Symbol of the Universe—an image recognized throughout the universe as a sign of spiritual illumination and creativity, most closely linked to the dominant species of humans, dragons, and bears.

Tada—a word for "father," from the old dragontongue.

Transference—the ability to transfer huge amounts of information by mental power alone.

Treemen (or Tree People)—a Hom-like tribe who inhabit the Whispering Forest. They are so well adapted to their environment that they often grow moss and other flora on their backs.

Vapor—a floating dragon spirit, a "ghost."

Veng—a particularly fearsome class of fighting dragon, commonly employed as security for a new colony.

Wearle—a large community of dragons. A Wearle would number more than a wyng, but anything more than a hundred dragons would be considered a fixed colony. There were twenty-four dragons in the first Wearle to visit Erth, sixty in the second.

Wearling—a young dragon of either gender.

Whinney—Hom name for a horse.

Whispering Forest—home of the Treemen.

Wild Lands—a vast, and mostly barren, rocky area to the west of the mountains occupied by the Kaal. Home to the wild creatures known as the Gibbus.

Wyng—a small group of dragons with a common purpose (e.g., a search wyng).

Wyrm—a deadly parasite similar to a slug. When inserted into a creature's body (usually via the ear) the wyrm will attach itself to the host's neural network and disrupt brain function.

Wyvern—a gentle class of dragon who inhabit a world of many islands that appears to run in a timeline parallel with Erth's. They have none of the colonizing instincts of their bigger cousins and are happy just getting on with their lives.

Acknowledgments

This will almost certainly be my last major foray into dragon culture. I couldn't have written such a poignant story without the help of some great creative minds. Notably they would be my UK editor, Sarah Leonard, and her US equivalent, Lisa Ann Sandell. I'd also like to put in a mention for my old friend Sue Cook, who copyedited the UK text and was so generous with her comments about it. And last but not least there is Jay d'Lacey, who kept me believing in the project through numerous drafts and some dark winter months. My dragons and firebirds love you all for helping to bring them to life on the page. One last time, from Erth to Ki:mera—*hrrr!*

About the Author

Chris d'Lacey is the author of several highly acclaimed books, including the *New York Times* bestselling Last Dragon Chronicles series (*The Fire Within; Icefire; Fire Star; The Fire Eternal; Dark Fire; Fire World; The Fire Ascending;* as well as *Rain & Fire*, which he co-wrote with Jay d'Lacey), the UNICORNE Files trilogy (*A Dark Inheritance*, *Alexander's Army*, and *A Crown of Dragons*), and The Erth Dragons series (*The Wearle*, *Dark Wyng*, and *The New Age*). Chris lives in Devon, England, with his wife, Jay, where they are at work on his next book.